Small Town Lies

a novel by

Charlie Hudson

American Quilter's Society

PO Box 3290
Paducah, KY 42002-3290
americanquilter.com

Located in Paducah, Kentucky, the American Quilter's Society (AQS) is dedicated to promoting the accomplishments of today's quilters. Through its publications and events, AQS strives to honor today's quiltmakers and their work and to inspire future creativity and innovation in quiltmaking.

EXECUTIVE BOOK EDITOR: ELAINE H. BRELSFORD
COPY EDITOR: CHRYSTAL ABHALTER
GRAPHIC DESIGN: LYNDA SMITH
COVER DESIGN: MICHAEL BUCKINGHAM

This book is a work of fiction. The people, places, and events described in it are either imaginary or fictitiously presented. Any resemblance they bear to reality is entirely coincidental.

American Quilter's Society
P.O. Box 3290 • Paducah, KY 42002-3290
Fax 270-898-1173 • e-mail: orders@AQSquilt.com

Additional copies of this book may be ordered from the American Quilter's Society, PO Box 3290, Paducah, KY 42002-3290, or online at www.AmericanQuilter.com.

Text © 2013, Author, Charlie Hudson
Artwork © 2013, American Quilter's Society
Library of Congress Cataloging-in-Publication Data

Hudson, Charlie, 1953-
Small town lies / by Charlie Hudson.
    pages cm
    Summary: "Welcome to Wallington, Georgia, home of widow Helen, and her daughter and son-in-law. A small town full of lies. When a local journalist turns up dead, what's the reaction of Helen and her small-town friends? Life around the quilting frame just isn't going to be the same for Helen, her friends, and their (formerly) quiet way of life"--Provided by publisher.
    ISBN 978-1-60460-065-0
    1. Widows--Fiction. 2. Journalists--Crimes against--Fiction. 3. City and town life--Fiction. 4. Georgia--Fiction. 5. Domestic fiction. I. Title.
    PS3558.U28945S63 2013
    813'.54--dc23
                        2013004511

Acknowledgments

What a wonderful project this has been for me. I am grateful to American Quilter's Society for beginning this.

A very special thank you goes to the ladies of the Tuesday evening quilting group in Homestead: Pauline Bradbury, Sue Broome, Dolly Carson, Charlotte DeOgburn, Linda Fayant, Phyllis Frank, Janie Gorman, Ann Martin, and Betty Jo Smay were incredibly generous of their time and sharing their love of quilting.

As always, my wonderful husband, Hugh, provided me the support I needed whenever I was "stuck" on a plot point.

CHAPTER ONE

W ell, it's not as if we can narrow suspects based on motive."
Dave Mabry shifted his bulk from one foot to the other.

Justin Kendall stood by the patrol car with Dave, his focus more on Sheriff McFarlane and the substitute medical examiner or what he could see of them through the large window of the studio above the garage. "Mr. Thatcher had enemies? I didn't think the *Wallington Gazette* roused that much emotion."

Sheriff McFarlane was shaking his head, his arm sweeping across the room—the overturned chair, folders scattered, a pewter gooseneck lamp fallen to the floor, and a dead body with bruising to a face not yet rigid in death. The still form sprawled face down on a rug that looked to be Persian—antique, most likely, based on the softened colors in the pattern and the rest of the furnishings. The massive oak desk was for sure antique. There was a large quilt hung on the wall like a tapestry, and even not knowing more about quilts than he did, it looked to be a complicated piece and sort of artsy.

Justin, having been first on the scene, had not turned the

1

body. He'd only checked for a pulse and stepped away carefully; he wasn't senior enough to begin the investigation. He'd observed everything closely, though, until the sheriff and Dave arrived, soon followed by the ME from the next county over. Dr. Cotton was away for a few days and Justin didn't know the old man who had creakily climbed from his car, nodded to them vaguely, and was now staring down at the floor as the sheriff talked.

No sign of robbery and not much blood. The way Justin figured it, the assailant must have slammed the victim's head onto the edge of the desk or struck him with an object. Did he know he'd killed Mr. Thatcher? Or had he simply left him unconscious, not bothering to check the real damage? Second-degree murder or manslaughter seemed to fit Wallington more than premeditated murder.

Dave's broad face showed a slight sour expression as if he'd bitten into a dill pickle. "Shoot, boy, how long you been in town? Eight months, isn't it?" He thumped ash onto the driveway, the two police cruisers on the grassy lawn. "You don't know about Gabriel Thatcher?"

"Guess not." Justin's surprise at finding Mr. Thatcher hadn't been unfamiliarity with death, not after six years on the Baltimore force. It was that crime in Wallington had so far been confined to traffic violations, property thefts, bar fights, minor drug possession charges, and sadly, inevitable domestic altercations.

The only reason he'd stopped at the classic gray-sided, white trimmed bungalow was because the garage door was wide open and Mr. Thatcher's new Sirrus bicycle and Honda Goldwing motorcycle were alongside the red 1976 Corvette Stingray that Justin always admired. There had been a rash of bicycle thefts that they were sure was a group of mouthy adolescents. They should pin them down pretty soon, but if Mr. Thatcher was absorbed in something either in the house or in his studio, the expensive Sirrus could be gone within seconds.

When there was no response at the door and no movement to

indicate that Mr. Thatcher had noticed someone on the premises, Justin had clamored up the stairs to the studio. Seeing the door ajar, he called out loudly twice before easing it fully open with his foot, hand automatically on his holstered pistol.

The unmoving body was prone, a gash on the back of the head, but not as bloody as it could have been; the left arm and hand extended off the rug and onto the hardwood floor. He assumed unconsciousness due to a fall until he saw the bruising along the side of Mr. Thatcher's jaw.

An unbelieving Sheila answered when he called dispatch. "Gabriel Thatcher's place? Are you sure about that?"

He'd stopped before snapping an answer; he knew better than to get on Sheila Tipton's bad side with a sarcastic response. He repeated the address slowly, knowing word would spread rapidly among those monitoring the police band.

"Let's put it this way," Dave said with a grin, bringing Justin back to the subject of suspects. "Gabe's been involved with lots of women in town—well, more like the state when you get right down to it—over the years and that's caused plenty of trouble. Been a bullet, that would make the list longer, but not many women around here are likely to get that kind of punching in." He sucked the cigarette to its end, glancing at the sky that was lighter now. He blew a stream of smoke away from Justin, a consideration even he, like most of the older members of the small force, chafed under the discussion of making public buildings smoke-free.

"I suppose I could go around to Herb's place and ask what he's heard." Herb's was a popular bar and grill where much of the town's gossip was exchanged.

"We haven't been in the house yet; and aren't we going to canvass the neighbors?" Justin had already been disappointed with no tire tracks or noteworthy footprints to show the county crime scene technicians that were en route, according to Sheila. The railing to the staircase could be a good source of fingerprints. Justin had seen only a single coffee mug near the sink and one whiskey glass rolled away from the desk, a tiny puddle in an irregular shape on the oak floor. The bottle of Knob Creek bourbon on the counter was one-third full, the Bombay Sapphire gin half full.

Dave straightened, ground the cigarette out on the sole of his shoe, and inclined his head toward the staircase as Sheriff McFarlane and the visiting ME descended. The emergency response vehicle pulled into the driveway with the forensics technician behind him in a black sedan. Everyone piled out at almost the same time.

Bob, you and Doreen are going to have to let Hank get photos first," the sheriff said, shaking hands all around. "It's not complicated. Get the shots you need, Hank, and dust for prints after they take the body." He continued to the clustered group, "Dave, you go on and see if any neighbors are at home. Justin, you come in the house with me and see if it looks like anything happened in there. Pretty sure it didn't, but let's take a look."

Justin didn't register the surprise he felt. As the junior man, shouldn't he be sent to do the canvass and let Dave stay with the sheriff? Everyone nodded with understanding and set about their tasks as the ME stepped over to speak to Bob and Doreen, the emergency medical technicians. Hank took the stairs two at a time, not touching the railing.

Dave moved close to the sheriff and gestured with a fresh cigarette that he hadn't lit yet. Justin couldn't make out what they were saying, but the conversation lasted less than two minutes.

"We're swapping," Dave said, walking up to Justin and pointing to the patrol car. "You'll either ride back with the sheriff or someone will come get you. I'm going to see Herb after I'm done with the neighbors."

Sheriff McFarlane was striding up the walkway between the detached garage and the house, so Justin nodded to Dave and hurried after their boss. As in many of the area's houses, most people used the back entrance—in this case a combination mudroom, laundry, and pantry. An alcove immediately to the right of the door held a large black garbage can, but yesterday had been trash pickup day. The linoleum floor was a slate pattern with a dark gray entry doormat and a washer and dryer to the left of the door. There was a wooden coat rack against the left wall—the bench type with space beneath for shoes, a tall back with three wrought iron hooks, and a shelf on top. One pair of tan leather boots and a pair of running shoes were in place; a red hooded rain jacket was on the first hook, a black umbrella on the third hook, and several spray cans were on the shelf, but Justin didn't stop to identify them as he crossed into the kitchen.

"I don't expect we'll find anything, but Hank prefers not to be disturbed. He'll be done pretty quickly, so we might as well check in here." Sheriff McFarlane had removed his hat; his short brown hair, salted with white, made him appear older than Justin knew him to be. The sense of age was heightened with skin leathered by outdoor hobbies of canoeing and fishing. He was an inch taller than Justin, barely missing six feet, and either deliberately kept his weight a little under 200 pounds or that, too, was a product of his physical activities. Justin had initially thought him to be lacking in drive until he realized that his easygoing style masked a close eye for detail. He seemed to know everything that happened in the office and anything important around town.

Justin stood in the middle of the room that was updated without having an ultra-modern look: a galley section for stove, refrigerator, dishwasher, and double porcelain sink with almond-colored appliances rather than the popular stainless steel of current remodels. The countertops were good quality butcher block.

The microwave was an over-the-stove model and a bank of lower cabinets with a breakfast bar and three dark blue painted metal high-back stools opened onto the dining area. A round table that could seat four was positioned between a window on the end wall and a bay window looking onto the front yard and road. The floor was wide-planked pine and the braided oval rug was blues and greens. There were no dirty dishes in sight; a telephone stand with a mobile phone against the far wall had a drawer, a telephone directory in the open area underneath, and a dark green leather address book next to the telephone. A lack of faint cooking odors probably meant the freezer and pantry held mostly microwaveable items, not unexpected for a bachelor unless he was into cooking shows.

"See if there's a redial function on the phone, and I'll look in the den after I check his bedroom," the sheriff instructed as he walked through the opening that might have once been a door closing the kitchen off from the rest of the house.

Justin slipped on a pair of surgical gloves that he carried despite jibes from Dave and found six stored numbers in the telephone, all but one being local. The address book was actually only phone numbers with initials and held no enlightening scribbled notes. There were quite a few, a mix of local and other area codes.

Sheriff McFarlane glided back into the kitchen, shaking his head, his brown eyes neutral. "Nothing that we need in there. Hank's probably done by now and then I'll tell you what comes next." His voice had an uncharacteristic tightness that Justin didn't remember having heard before. What was going on?

"Town will be buzzing over this," the older man said evenly as they retraced their steps. "Get stickers and tape from the car, but no sense spreading it all over—just the doors of the house, garage, and studio. We'll lock up when we finish. Should be spare keys to the doors hung on a hook in the mudroom. That's where most people keep them. Make sure a patrol car comes by every couple of hours. Gabe doesn't have any family in town to contact, so we'll have to find out who the closest relative is."

"Yes sir," Justin said in reflex even though he rarely called the sheriff "sir." However, it seemed appropriate with the more somber circumstances.

By the time Justin completed his task at the house, the covered body was being loaded and the sheriff motioned for Justin to wait as the emergency vehicle cleared out of sight and they were alone.

Sheriff McFarlane exhaled deeply, hooked his hands into his belt and rocked slightly onto his heels, then back to stand solidly, an almost bemused look on his face. "I doubt Sheila kept this quiet for ten minutes. You know the last murder we had was pushing twenty years ago. I'm not counting bar fights getting out of hand. We get one of those every year or so. Situation being what it is, I'll probably have you work this as primary."

"Sir? What situation? Not that I mind," Justin said quickly, trying to regain a little cool instead of sounding reluctant. "I don't get it."

The movement of the sheriff's mouth was not quite a smile. "Dave tell you that Gabe Thatcher has had some kind of involvement with about every woman in the whole county and I'm not even talking about the women who come in from who knows where to see him? Problem being is that me and most everyone else in the office has been ready to beat on Gabe ourselves at one time or the other, and you're about the only one doesn't have bad history with him. Well, neither does Cyrus, but he's still on light duty from that operation. I don't doubt this is related to Gabe and some woman, but I need someone looking at it who'll be objective."

Wow! Justin wasn't sure what to say. "Well, yes sir, I…"

The sheriff held up a hand. "Listen, we may kid you about being a big city boy, but the truth is that I've been impressed with you. You pay attention and you're fitting in just fine. Not every man would be willing to leave a promising future because his wife wants to get back to a place where stealing bicycles is the major crime spree." His jaw tightened a bit before Justin could react.

"I'll tell you more later, but right now I need you to go over the studio again and I'll send Lenny or someone to pick you up. You'll want to find Gabe's cell phone and I'll get someone started on his telephone records. If his e-mail is password protected, we'll have to get an expert in from the county. I didn't notice his cell phone on him or the desk, but it's probably around. You bring it and the laptop in and I'll see if Dave's got an earful from Herb about who's got it out for Gabe at the moment. You okay with this?"

"Yes sir," Justin said, his mind churning ahead.

"Go on then, and let's see if we can wrap this up in a day or two." The sheriff moved to his car, shaking his head slowly.

Justin didn't wait for him to pull onto the two-lane road to begin a more studied stroll around the garage looking for anything he might have initially missed. Nothing upstairs was going to move, but the breeze that had picked up could scatter something like a gum wrapper. The expanse of grass ran to the road to the left, to the house to the right, and in the back before it ran into a stretch of shrubs and trees that separated the Thatcher and Fairfield properties. Thick, neatly trimmed boxwood shrubs formed a U around the garage and there was no sign of broken branches or other disturbance—it wasn't as if someone had crouched hidden in them. The grass bordered on needing mowing, although the garage was devoid of any type of lawn mower. Based on what little he did know of Gabriel Thatcher, who wrote multiple columns for the bi-weekly *Wallington Gazette* and occasional articles for some of the larger surrounding newspapers and regional magazines, he would have left hard labor to the landscaping service annotated in his address book.

Outside seemed clean enough. If there had been something, it wasn't to be found. Justin, still wearing the gloves, walked up the stairs slowly this time, studying each step. He wanted to center himself, enter the studio with a fresh pair of eyes. Ah, there,— at least one thing he'd missed. The door to the studio opened outward and while he had been alerted to the fact that it was slightly ajar, he hadn't noticed the flecks of white paint on the edge beneath the knob or the fresh scrape on the white painted railing. The door had probably been yanked open and flung against the railing, not an inadvertent careless bump. This might speak to anger from the beginning, not an escalating argument.

Justin played it in his mind, imagining whoever pounding up the stairs. Had he, figure he for now, tried the house first? Everyone knew about the studio above the garage. Justin stepped inside, stopping on the heavy-duty brown doormat. The signs were not of a prolonged struggle. Considering the angle of the chair at the desk and the glass on the floor, Mr. Thatcher was probably at his computer, shoved back, and rose at the intrusion. Then what? Stepped around to try and reason with the man? That would make sense, but wait. Justin closed his eyes, thinking back to the body. He hadn't seen it turned face-up and didn't know if the shirt had been torn. He saw it now, though; there had not appeared to be defensive wounds on the hands. He was certain of it. Had the first blow been a sucker punch? A reeling punch by a significantly bigger man? The wounds had been made with fists. He knew what a pistol whipping or baseball bat beating looked like. A few blows to the face and maybe body, then a blow that sent him tumbling against the edge of the desk. There was no readily visible blood on the desk, but there had been hairs that the technician obviously bagged. Since the gash on the back of Thatcher's head had not bled profusely, the odds were that the wound had produced a subdural hematoma rather than instantaneous death.

Justin checked the portable telephone to verify that it was an extension of the house phone and didn't see a cell phone on his initial survey. The laptop was password protected, and while it was no doubt something simple, it would be best to let an expert have a go at it. Where was the cell phone? Justin stood at the corner of the desk and stared at the deep red upholstered sofa and matching chair that created a sitting area. He crossed, knelt, and lifted the short piece of fabric around the base of the sofa. He withdrew the black cell phone that appeared to have been smashed like with a heel stomping it, then kicked away. So much for getting numbers immediately. He bagged it and continued his cautious, observant movements until he made his way into the bathroom. The mostly white room wasn't large and there was a corner fiberglass shower stall. It was the type of stall that came in a kit with a molded soap dish. The medicine cabinet held an unopened toothbrush, atravelers' size tube of Colgate, and a bottle of Advil. The dark blue wicker wastebasket was nearly empty with a few tissues and the white plastic top to a medicine bottle. He pulled it out gently and lifted the basket to verify that it was only the top, no bottle. That was strange, but he wasn't sure if it meant anything and made a quick note in his book so he wouldn't forget it.

His radio crackled for attention. "Hey, you 'bout done? Sheriff told me to pick you up if you're ready. I'm leaving the Hawkins' place right now." It was Lenny, the fourth deputy on day patrol. The Hawkins' farm was close by and their goats had probably wandered into the neighbor's garden again in the on-going feud between the properties.

"Yeah, I'm wrapping up." Justin wanted to get the telephone and computer back to the station. He would call the sheriff to let him know they needed county support and maybe if they weren't too busy, they could send a technician first thing in the morning.

The sheriff had been correct about word spreading rapidly and Lenny pressed him for details. "Ain't no way Gabe was killed over anything but a woman," he pronounced with a mixture of what sounded like satisfaction and awe. At twenty-five, Lenny was the youngest police officer. His status as both a former Army military policeman and having been born and raised in Wallington meant he was senior to Justin despite being younger. On the other hand, he had yet to display any indication that he wanted to do more than be on patrol. That wasn't to say he lacked ambition. It was more as if he felt genuinely comfortable in his present situation. He was a head shorter than Justin, not as hefty as Dave or as muscled as either Justin or the sheriff. He'd retained the military-style haircut for his black hair and his eyebrows were short and thick, almost as if they'd been partially shaved or burned off. Lenny was the most talkative of the deputies, and other than Sheila he was Justin's main source of information about people in town. Well, his wife, Tricia, and mother-in-law, Helen, were his most trusted sources, although they didn't offer as much spontaneous commentary.

Dave had come and gone at the station and after the ritual of shift change, Sheriff McFarlane drew Justin into the office, closing the door behind him. He propped on the corner of his uncluttered wooden desk and motioned Justin to take the wooden chair in front of the desk, its seat and arms worn smooth from years of use. It was a utilitarian office with two windows opening onto the street, and a pair of heavy dark blue curtains that could be drawn for privacy. They were open, as the sheriff usually kept them, and the weakened afternoon sun slanted in.

"We got a computer forensics lady coming in from County at nine o'clock tomorrow and the telephone report ought to be done about then too. Preliminary cause of death is fatal blow to the head, but the autopsy won't be done for a couple of days or more.

Doc Cotton is due to be gone another four days and they got a backlog at the morgue, believe it or not." He wagged his head in slow motion. "Anyway, Herb told Dave as how Gabe's got two different women that he's been seen with lately: Isabelle Jenkins and Lisa Dearborn. Isabelle's been legally separated from Roger for a while, but the divorce isn't final yet and Roger's got a mean streak in him when he's drinking. Big enough guy, too. Lisa's husband is on the road a lot, and she's not known for sitting around the house all the time he's traveling, if you get my drift. Fact is, I called and he left three days ago for a week's trip. Not to say he couldn't sneak back into town, but I don't see that as likely."

"You want me to go see if Roger Jenkins has an alibi?" Justin vaguely recalled the man. Mechanic? Air conditioning repairman? Plumber? Something like that.

The sheriff nodded and passed a slip of paper with the address. "Only other thing that might be nothing at all is Abby Lister told Dave she saw Paul Newton's pickup tearing past her place this afternoon going way too fast, as far as she was concerned. Could have been around the time of death. Not much to go on, but he's not at work or home. On the other hand, he's still single and his ex-wife is already remarried, so I don't know what he'd have in for Gabe. You want a backup with you at Roger's?"

Justin stood and glanced at the paper. "Might not hurt. I'll have dispatch send the patrol. I should be able to meet up with him if I leave now."

"Call if you're bringing Roger in. Otherwise, take the night off and we'll start again in the morning."

"Yes sir," Justin said, thinking that if Gabe were killed over a woman, that certainly tracked with the usual top motives. He was in the patrol car getting ready to leave for Jenkins's address when Lenny called on the radio.

"I'm at Jenkins' house, but he's not around," Lenny said. "He works at Gabler's, if you want to swing by there. There's usually someone at the office 'til about five thirty."

"Will do, thanks," Justin said, turning left. Gabler Air, Plumbing, and Heating was two blocks away, and when he pulled into the small parking lot there was a black Ford F-150 with a Gabler's sign painted on the truck and an older silver Chrysler minivan.

Gabler's was a red brick building with two wide white metal garage doors that opened onto the parking lot. They were closed and he went into the office. It was a rectangular room with a black vinyl couch and a wooden coffee table against the left wall. An empty coffeepot, a short stack of paper cups, and a square blue plastic basket containing sugar and creamer packets were on the table. A blue Formica-topped two-tier counter was to the right and a door in the center of the wall facing the front door was closed, no sign to tell what it led to. A woman about Sheriff McFarlane's age was sitting in a gray fabric office chair, four gray three-drawer metal filing cabinets lining the wall behind her. Neat stacks of file folders and a telephone were to the woman's left, a computer and printer to her right.

The woman looked up as Justin entered, a smile making her narrow face seem less severe. Tortoiseshell reading glasses were perched on her sharp nose and her gray-streaked brown hair was pulled into a bun. Justin wondered if she weighed much more than 100 pounds. "Deputy Kendall, what can I do for you?" She stood and reached out her thin hand, no polish on the short nails. "You're looking for Roger, I imagine?"

"Uh yes, I am," he said, mildly startled. Maybe everyone did know everyone else's business.

"Well, he had a job out at the Suttons earlier this afternoon, then Karen called about half hour ago—they had a faucet gushing at the church and that whole setup is old as the hills. He got the water shut off, but has to go all the way to Ferguson's to get the right part. He won't be back for a while and said he'd take tomorrow off instead of clocking overtime, so unless you want to wait two, maybe three hours to talk to him, you can find him at home in the morning."

Justin hesitated, wishing he knew where the Suttons lived. Was that close to Mr. Thatcher's? If Jenkins had a guilty conscience, would he be working a late job? Unlike Paul Newton, no one had reported Jenkins being around Thatcher's place, and the sheriff had already indicated this could wait until morning. Since Justin was due at his mother-in-law's house for dinner, it didn't seem worth cancelling that to wait for Jenkins.

"He's supposed to call me at the house when he gets the job finished. How about I let him know you'll be at his place tomorrow? You an early morning person?" She pulled the glasses off, holding them in one hand. "Course, Roger's liable to be hung over, so I'm not sure that being there real early will do you much good."

"Thank you, Mrs. Gabler," Justin said, assuming he was correct in identifying her as such. "Yes, you can tell him that I intend to come out around eight thirty." He handed her a card. "He can call the station if he wants to see me tonight and they'll get a message to me."

She looked skeptical at that possibility. "I'll do that, and you tell the sheriff I said hello."

"I will, and it was a pleasure meeting you," he said, backing out of the door. He called into dispatch and asked that the night patrol drive by Jenkins's address just in case he unexpectedly disappeared in the night.

Justin also asked about Newton and was told that the sheriff was checking Newton's whereabouts himself. He wasn't entirely sure what that was about, but he did want to run by the house, change out of his uniform, and grab a bottle of wine to take to Helen's.

CHAPTER TWO

Helen Crowder sat at the custom-built drop-leaf pine table in what had been an oversized formal living room. Apparently, by design, there was no foyer, with entry from the deep front porch directly into the living room; the fireplace was set into the right hand wall rather than the longer one opposite the front door. A short hall to the right of the fireplace led to two bedrooms and a bath. The dining room was to the left through a rectangular archway and a smaller arch on the left led into the kitchen.

After Tricia, her youngest, left for college, she kept the corner closest to the fireplace with two Queen Anne chairs upholstered in muted floral chintz, an antique pine end table between the chairs, and converted the rest of the room into an ideal setting for quilting. The planks of the hickory floors had been refinished and an area rug from old Mrs. Powell's estate sale defined the seating arrangement from the main quilting area. She'd replaced the gold floor-length damask draperies with sage green Roman shades topped padded valances of a forest and sage green striped material. That allowed more light to come through the triple windows.

The table she'd had built was six feet long and three feet wide with a one-foot long hinged dropleaf on either end. The table was positioned to the right of the sofa and comfortably sat two on each side with the end leaves dropped down. On those occasions when needed, one or both of the sections were lifted to extend the length to up to eight feet. Continuing around to the right of the table were two hoop stands placed in an arc with a chair in front of each, then three more chairs curved around toward the sofa. The armless, handcrafted antique pine chairs were sturdily built, had padded quilted cushions, and were designed for comfort, something that Helen often found lacking in newer furniture.

The fireplace had been retrofitted with a gas insert with ceramic logs that gave the appearance of glowing embers when lit, although she had maintained the original heavy mantle that had been made from a reclaimed barn beam. Three staggered shelves made from other reclaimed barn timbers were attached to the wall on the far side and held old oil lanterns of different sizes. They were decorative and came in handy when the power went out.

A custom-built unit made from pecan wood took up much of the length of the back wall. There was a table insert for the Singer sewing machine that she had grown up with, and the insert connected two cabinets; each had three wide drawers at the bottom and two open shelves on top. The drawers held fabrics and patterns while the shelves showcased one of the best collections of quilting books and magazines in town, well, really in the entire county and maybe the region. The large unit was set out from the wall to allow space behind it to store the folding wooden adjustable quilting frame that could be set up in the room. It was actually a holdover from before Helen had the table built, and one of these days she was going to contribute it to someone who had real need of it. Another clever addition that Helen enjoyed was a matching long cabinet mounted to the right of the wall unit that concealed a foldout ironing board and had an interior shelf to hold the iron. It was neatly stowed, easy to get to, and completely out of sight the rest of the time. Completing the room was a large armoire also made from pecan wood; it stood against the left wall, shelves and drawers inside filled with quilting supplies.

Helen had hesitated when she first came up with the idea of doing away with the formal room. Mitch, God rest his soul, had pointed out that the room was used far more for quilting than for anything else and she might as well optimize it. As soon as the project was completed, she was thrilled, as were the rest of the women in the quilting circle. Art for the cream-colored walls was, of course, quilts or parts of quilts made by Helen, her mother, grandmother, and even one from Great-Grandmother Pierce. Three quilted picture frames that Tricia had made as a fiftieth birthday present for her were spaced along the mantle. The frames, a forest green, a medium blue, and a cranberry, were stitched with metallic gold thread, the corners meticulously mitered. Each held a wedding photo: Helen and Mitch; Ethan and Sharon; and Tricia and Justin, replacing the original photo of Tricia in her graduation robe.

Helen wanted to finish stitching the last square for the bottom right section of the quilt before Justin arrived. The ladies would be coming the next night for their weekly meeting and, with everyone's attention on Gabe Thatcher's murder, who knew how much quilting would actually get done? She put that thought out of her mind, completed her finishing stitches, neatly clipped the thread, and then dashed into the bedroom to run a brush through her hair.

She liked the new cut that Edna talked her into: short feathery bangs and a little bit of layering rather than the swept back longer style she'd worn for the last twenty-plus years. They didn't change the color, though, a slightly lighter chestnut than the richer shade she'd passed on genetically to Tricia, along with sable brown eyes and thick lashes that rarely needed mascara. She had never worn much make-up, but was always diligent with cleansing, moisturizing, and protecting her skin from the sun. It was paying off with fewer wrinkles than many women approaching their sixtieth birthday. She couldn't take too much credit, though, for the fact that she was only two dress sizes larger than when she graduated from high school. She did walk regularly, but she'd been blessed with an active metabolism so she didn't have to struggle with her weight, as did so many of her friends. The back door opened and she heard Justin call out.

Justin, at five foot ten, was more than a head taller than Helen and she went up on her tiptoes to greet him with a quick peck to his cheek. He stepped into the farmhouse-style kitchen and breathed in deeply, a silent acknowledgment of the aroma of chicken and homemade dumplings. Two other pots filled with cream-style corn and green beans simmered on the stove. He held out both hands with white and red wines, having not asked what was on the menu. He was a good-looking man with a solid build, not what she would call classically handsome, but more on the rugged side. Basketball had been his sport in high school and he and Tricia had bikes they rode regularly. He kept his light brown hair short, as did the other men in the department. He was quick with a smile, revealing a minor overbite with teeth that must have been in braces when he was younger. The scar on his chin was allegedly left over from a childhood accident and not a result of being on patrol in Baltimore.

She had already put wine glasses, the corkscrew, and a chilled cobalt blue ceramic wine holder on the tiered kitchen island. Helen pointed a finger at him in the way a schoolteacher does.

"You can open the white and pour before you start talking and don't bother to tell me you can't say anything. Everybody knows Gabe was killed over a woman—it's just a matter of who, or whom, I should say. It never should have come to this, but then very few people understood the truth about Gabe." She turned to the pots on the stove. Tricia was away with girlfriends, a kind of retreat to help one of them celebrate or commiserate about a divorce. Helen had been a little unclear as to the actual intent, but she assumed it involved spa treatments and martinis.

"You know, I haven't heard anyone suggest any other motive, but it sounds as if you know something extra," he said carefully, pouring the wine as instructed.

Helen gave the pots a quick stir, turned off the gas, and looked at him over her shoulder. "It's what makes sense. We don't get home invasions here or random killings. Of course, you should be looking for someone he's been involved with for a year or less. The others always get sorted out, like with Norm. That's what I mean about knowing the truth about Gabe."

"Sheriff McFarlane is who you're talking about?" Justin took a sip of wine.

Helen turned her head briefly as she picked up a plate from the counter next to the stove. "Put that basket of rolls on the table, please, and move the wine, too. I'm serving right from the pots. Yes, I mean Norm. You could say that Gabe broke up their marriage, if you want to be strictly accurate about it, but the truth is that Cindy was all wrong for Norm; and if you want my opinion, Gabe did him a favor. That's what's always been so puzzling about Gabe. His romancing practically every woman around has usually had good effects, whether that was the intent or not."

She carried both plates, his piled high, and hers more moderately filled. A small platter of sliced tomatoes and cucumbers was on the oval pine pedestal table that had been handed down through Mitch's family. "Was his head caved in or was there really not much blood?"

Justin looked as if he was about to choke at that one and she waved her hand for him to sit. "I didn't think it was that bad. I do understand Norm wanting you to investigate, though. Dave wouldn't be the best choice considering that he flattened Gabe two, maybe three years ago. They tell you that?" She suspected that the sound of authenticity in her voice surprised him, but he might as well understand that she was indeed one of the only people in town who knew the dimension of Gabe Thatcher that he'd kept hidden.

"Uh no, I didn't hear that exactly."

She smiled invitingly. "Would you like me to explain about Gabe and then I'll tell you who I would be looking at, and I don't mean Roger Jenkins?"

Justin's surprise must have shown because Helen giggled despite the seriousness of the situation. "Goodness, don't look so startled. Our family has been in this town for five generations, one shy of being founding members. This is a backwater place and I say that with proud affection. I've made no secret that I think it's wonderful that you were willing to move here so Tricia could be close by again, but you've got to realize that we just don't have murders. Warren Dearborn did chase Danny Lister around the town square threatening him with a hatchet fifteen years ago." Helen shook her head at the memory. "Didn't catch him, mind you. The last murder we had was when Roscoe Willis killed his own brother, but that's long passed, and was as tragic a story as you can ask for."

Justin paused with a forkful of beans. "I have to admit that I've been getting bits and pieces about Mr. Thatcher all day, but not what you would call a total picture."

Helen signaled for him to keep eating while she talked. Tricia was a better than average cook, but she wasn't in Helen's league and they all knew it. Helen intended to send leftovers home with Justin, too.

"The Thatchers originally came from somewhere in New York. Gabe's grandparents, I mean. I think it had something to do with looking for a warmer climate, although I don't think that anyone knew the whole story, not that it mattered. Anyway, Gabe's grandfather had the first real pharmacy in town. Stanley, their only son, wasn't particularly interested in running the business and got in with one of the drug companies. He was a stereotypical traveling salesman and everybody except Virginia, his wife, knew that he had an eye for the ladies when he was on the road; it just goes to show that the old saying 'the apple doesn't fall far from the tree' has merit. I don't necessarily mean that Stanley did anything more than flirting, but he wasn't a stay-at-home sort, either." Helen finished her wine and pushed her glass forward for a refill.

"That's part of why Virginia joined the quilting circle. Now that wasn't mine; we were both in another one that rotated among houses. After a couple of the older ladies passed on, I started this one, but that's another story for sure. The point is, the circle was a nice outlet for her, and she loved quilting as much as anyone. Gabe, their only child, was a downright pretty baby even if he was a boy, and with Stanley gone much as he was, Virginia doted on the child. He was, in a word, spoiled rotten even though I'm not talking in the nasty kind of way."

Justin wrinkled his forehead. "Not a bully, you mean?"

Helen waved her hand dismissively. "Not in the least. Charm was Gabe's signature, just like it was his daddy's. I mean, from the time the child could speak a sentence, he knew exactly the kind of thing women and girls wanted to hear. He was strong enough too to be a decent athlete, baseball actually, and while not a star, it kept him in the popular circle. Virginia and Stanley weren't wealthy, but they were well off and she made sure that Gabe had stylish clothes, the new bicycle, that sort of thing. He was smart, too, although hardly what one would call a genius. Had a way with words from fairly early on. He was the high school yearbook editor and at the beginning of his senior year, Stanley died of a heart attack when he was outside raking leaves on a pretty fall afternoon. Not a sound from him after he collapsed. Poor Virginia nearly fainted from shock herself. I'm not speaking ill of her, but with Stanley gone like that, she poured every ounce of love she had into Gabe. He was flawless and brilliant in her eyes and of course, she thought he would be stifled in this town. Even though she hated for him to be away, she was bound and determined that he should go to an Ivy League college."

Justin buttered another hot roll, his face attentive.

"Stanley had left insurance and he made a decent living, so the house was all paid for and it's not as if Virginia ever had to work a day in her life, but I don't mean that unkindly. Gabe recognized that he wasn't going to qualify for Ivy League, but she found some liberal arts college near Boston to get him into and acted as if that was the same thing as Harvard. Now is where this all starts to tie together," she said. "Oh, I have lemon pound cake for dessert. Leave all this and move to the counter while I put coffee on."

They repositioned and Helen continued, moving easily about the kitchen. "We don't know exactly what happened, but Gabe was gone for oh, I guess six years, maybe a little longer. He majored in English with a journalism minor or vice versa. Wrote some acceptable poetry and had a few short stories published although not in major magazines. He was doing okay and naturally, as far as Virginia was concerned, he was on his way to a Pulitzer Prize. He came back for holidays and visits and he had gotten someone's attention. He was hired to a major publishing house as an editor's assistant and that's where his romancing ways got the best of him." Helen shook her head with a half smile.

"He was doing his usual juggling of multiple women and became involved with one of the board members' daughters, of all things, and we're not talking about proposing marriage to her if you understand. It didn't take her long to find out that she was not the only one he was seeing. The upshot was that Gabe Thatcher was sent packing and basically blacklisted from any major house and newspaper he might want to work for."

Helen pushed the on button of the coffeepot and lifted the top from a rose motif ceramic cake stand. She looked over her shoulder again. "Virginia had developed some kind of heart ailment about then and Gabe rushed to her side, or tucked his tail between his legs and ran home, depending on which way you want to look at it. God rest Virginia's soul, she became more or less an invalid and she barely lasted a year. In the meantime, Denise Grigsby, who had been close friends with Virginia's mother, took over the *Wallington Gazette* after her husband died and she had a soft spot for Gabe. She's the one who put him on the staff."

Helen motioned for him to come get the cake while she carried full coffee mugs. "All right, now I've got the stage set for your murder." She paused, tilted her head slightly and her tone mellowed. "You see, Gabe saw himself as this romantic figure who loved women so much that he could never bring himself to commit to just one. All things considered, he might have had a point, but it did make for a convenient excuse. And Gabe certainly knew how to attract women. In addition to his poetry and his time away, he traveled. I personally don't feel deprived in not

23

having seen Paris, although it would indeed sound romantic to a woman who's never been further than the state capital or maybe all the way to Orlando to Disney."

She took a tiny nibble of cake, wiped her mouth and sighed, a sound of affection and exasperation. "It was my sister that fell for him for a while. I won't get into the details of what she passed on to me, but she was like all the other women who, I swear, would lose their senses over the man with one of his smiles. It wasn't any time after her divorce, and that was Gabe's specialty—women right after a breakup or who were feeling vulnerable for some reason and needed an ego boost." She sighed dramatically this time and placed a hand over her heart. 'This has been wonderful, but you know, my dear, you deserve a man who can give you a full life and I simply have too much of the wanderer in me. It wouldn't be fair.'"

Justin stared at her, spearing the last bite of pound cake. "Are you serious?"

"I kid you not. Like a line right out of some sappy old movie, but let me tell you, it worked."

"You said something about Sheriff McFarlane's wife."

Helen pushed her plate with a small chunk of cake toward Justin. "Yes I did, and that requires a bit of an explanation of why men would be angry with Gabe for a spell."

"I'm listening," Justin said, not hesitating to eat the remains of Helen's slice of cake.

"Well, what it comes down to is that many marriages go through rough patches, maybe even a trial separation. Some smooth out and some don't, or it can be like the Thompsons who have been divorced and remarried three times. Anyway, men around here have a habit of still feeling pretty possessive after a divorce, and that's important to understand." Helen shifted on the stool and smiled wryly.

"That wasn't the case with Norm, so I'll go ahead and tell you about his situation. The real truth of the matter is that he and Cindy were not suited for each other for reasons that I won't go into. She started having girls' night out on a pretty regular basis and they tended to hang out at the Wallington Inn, one of Gabe's favorite places. It isn't that anything serious was going on between them, but there was a lot of flirting as there always was with Gabe. Still, it did cause some arguments between Norm and Cindy, as you can imagine. What the whole business led to was exposing the flaw in their marriage that most of us already knew was there. When Norm is being honest, he'll say Gabe actually did him a favor by bringing it all to a head."

"This is almost making sense. And Dave punching Mr. Thatcher out?"

Helen shrugged. "That was at Herb's. One of Dave's favorite cousins was all ga-ga about Gabe, thinking she was the one that could settle him down. The girl got silly about it, made a little bit of a fool of herself talking all over town and then Dave saw Gabe with one of his lady friends who'd flown in for a visit. Dave had one too many beers in him and things got a little out of control. It was over in the snap of a finger and the cousin went by the wayside like every other woman who falls for Gabe. She married Buster Dunford not long after that, had three kids, and is doing well. Like I said, Gabe loves them, using the word loosely, leaves them, and it becomes this sweet memory they cherish forever."

Justin took Helen's mug, refilled both their coffees, and sat down again. "And the deal with men after divorces? How does that tie in?"

Helen arched her eyebrows. "I suppose it could be this way in other parts of the country too, but around here, most couples that divorce do remarry other spouses, but it's pretty raw in those first several months. As I said earlier, that's also when women can feel terribly vulnerable and Gabe would be right there to bring comfort. Now, mind you, it wasn't as if he had any intention of it being anything other than temporary; but it did serve as a transition, I guess you could call it. Gabe being available so soon tended to raise the ire of the recently divorced husband, however, because the husband might think there was a chance at reconciliation or was just not ready to see his wife with another man. She might not still be his wife according to the law, but there seems to be an unwillingness to admit that it's actually over. I'm not saying it's a logical reaction, but it is a very real one."

Justin nodded his head thoughtfully. "I can see that. I'd like to ask you if you think Mr. Thatcher was the kind of guy who would fight back if someone came after him."

Helen raised her eyebrows. "Gabe kept himself in good shape, but the truth is that he knew good and well he deserved a punch in the nose on a pretty regular basis. So I'd say, he might take a blow or two like what happened with Dave, but he'd try and stop it there. Why do you ask?"

"Just checking. You said you had your own idea of who to look at."

Helen tilted her head again. "I'll let you off the hook about not giving me more details because you've been patient with the meandering story. There are really three possibilities as I see it. Melissa Newton, Paul Newton's baby sister, works part time at The Sandwich Stop. Gabe eats there regularly. She's sweet as she can be, and for months we've been talking about what she might want to major in when she goes to college. I was in, oh, I guess it was Monday since school was off for some reason, and I passed Gabe coming out. I sat down at the counter and Melissa had this look on her face that I've seen before—that dreamy trance that women get around Gabe. She starts in about how thoughtful he is, well traveled, etc., and then makes a comment about how exciting it must be to be a writer and maybe she shouldn't be rushing off to college. Maybe she ought to stay around, get some more life experience until she really knows what she wants to do. She graduates next month and actually has at least a partial scholarship awarded. I told her that she was going to love college and she could always take general studies the first semester. I admit she's much younger than Gabe usually goes for and there might not be anything going on, but I'll put a twenty dollar bill down that if Paul knows about this, he's the guy you should be looking for. He doesn't have a mean bone in his body, and I hate to say it because I think the world of his mother and all three kids. The problem is that he's the oldest and has had to pretty much be the man of the family since he was a teenager. He's not about to take kindly to Gabe Thatcher sniffing around Melissa."

Justin nodded once. "You know I respect your opinion, Helen. Who are the other two?"

She lifted her finger. "I don't think Roger cares enough about Isabelle to go after Gabe, but then again, I don't know him all that well. I heard a reliable rumor the other day that Abigail Turner, wife of Joe Turner of Auto World, was seen having drinks with Gabe. Then there's Fred Hillman who owns the furniture store downtown. He's got a horrid streak in him, not withstanding the fact that he's a deacon and wraps himself in a claim of Christianity that's no more than an excuse to be judgmental. He's mouthed off plenty of times that Gabriel is a stain on this town's reputation, and quite frankly, Gabe has written a couple of pieces about hypocrisy that everyone knows are aimed at Fred—last one was maybe a month ago. Fred's not about to go up against Gabe with more than words, but his son, Tommy, has always been a no-kidding bully. I'm not saying that he did go over to confront Gabe, but I wouldn't put it past him either."

Justin sighed the contented sound of a man with a full stomach and drained the last of his coffee. "I appreciate the information, I do," he said and swung his feet to the floor. "Let me give you a hand with these dishes."

That was one of the many things Helen admired about her son-in-law. She leaned over and patted his cheek. "It's sweet of you to offer, but I'm fine. Let me get some leftovers put together for you, and you can be on your way. You're going to have a very busy day tomorrow."A thought suddenly struck her and she snapped her fingers. "Heavens, I forgot to ask. Did you find a contact number for Fletcher Brown? To the best of my knowledge, he's the only relative Gabe had."

"There may have been one and the sheriff had a call in to the *Gazette* to see who might have been on Mr. Thatcher's contact form," Justin said.

Helen transferred a meal's worth of leftovers into a clear plastic container with compartments and a snap-on lid. "Well, it might not have been officially noted as an emergency contact, although Denise probably knows. Fletcher, like Gabe, was an only child. Victoria, Virginia's older sister, lived over in Tifton and Fletcher came with her sometimes when she visited. She and her husband were killed in an automobile accident when I believe Fletcher was in college. He and Gabe weren't close like some cousins are, but he did come to Virginia's funeral."

"I'll leave a voice mail for the sheriff at the office in case he doesn't have that," Justin said, exchanged a hug for the container, and gently closed the back door on his way out.

CHAPTER THREE

Helen loaded the dishes into the dishwasher, did the pans by hand, poured the last bit of coffee down the drain, and rinsed the pot to be ready for the morning. The kitchen was the first room she and Mitch remodeled after Ethan was a newly graduated Georgia Tech mechanical engineer and Tricia was in her junior year at Augusta State. The main structural change was to replace the door to the dining room with an open arch mirroring the one leading into the living room. Getting rid of that door provided a greater sense of openness and allowed a circular flow from living room to dining room to kitchen. New cabinets in a milk-washed maple gave an antique look when paired with the brushed nickel hardware she'd found for a great price online. The manufactured stone counters in a milky color with blue-green flecks, the porcelain farmer's sink, and the tiered kitchen prep island she had always wanted fit into the existing space. An off-white ceramic tile backsplash now went all the way from counter to cabinet. Mosaic tiles with green, blue, and yellow were scattered artistically to add pops of color without being overwhelmingly busy. While she loved decorating with quilts, that wasn't what she wanted for the kitchen walls.

She had initially been reluctant to follow the trend of stainless steel appliances, but it had been the right choice and it was only fair to let Mitch have the final say about one or two items. They'd looked at so many flooring options she thought they might never make a selection. Porcelain tile that mimicked slate blended perfectly and that was something she could always change out later if she chose to do so. She hadn't really understood why the paint color had been called "Beach Glass," although it had a balance between green and blue that was the look she was going for.

She turned the burner on under the cobalt blue enamel-coated whistling teakettle and began to wipe down the counters. Herbal tea was her nighttime beverage and, if she remembered correctly, *The Ghost and Mrs. Muir* was scheduled to start at nine o'clock. She loved old movies, although she didn't watch them exclusively. She'd seen this one so often that she could watch the movie, drink her tea, and let her mind wander in and out of the excitement of the day.

She took one of the bright yellow mugs embossed with a spray of daisies and opened the wooden tea box that Mitch had found for her as they were in the final stages of the remodel. It was hand crafted of pine, but treated with an antique white crackle effect and had six interior sections, deep enough for both tea balls to fit. Tea balls were like teapots; she did have two lovely ones she used at times for company, but when it was just her, she didn't bother. Unless someone was a purist, tea bags really were easier. She decided on orange zest, and added a packet of sweetener as the kettle sent out the first noise that would escalate to a piercing sound if she left it on the burner. Once she had the tea steeped to the strength she liked, she took the mug and switched off the kitchen light, leaving on the light over the sink.

The den was off the kitchen through another rectangular opening. In what she and Mitch had discussed as somewhat odd, this room had the only door that led to the backyard, but perhaps it was because people used their front porches more in the 1950s when the house was built. Expansive decks and patios did not come along until later and truthfully, the yard, enclosed with honeysuckle-draped gray metal hurricane fencing, had been primarily for the children's swing set, makeshift forts, and the storage shed that held lawnmower and assorted tools.

The den, more often called the family room, was the place to hang out, watch television, and to have the manly recliner. Ethan, more rambunctious than Tricia, had mainly kept his tumbling and dashing in the yard. The evidence of children had been scattered dolls and toys that Tricia was good about picking up at the end of her play, then adolescent interests of music, books, and horses for a brief while. Mitch's recliner, a dark brown nubby fabric that went with nothing else in the room, was the single piece of furniture that he had personally picked out and she didn't begrudge him the choice.

Helen set the mug on the end table next to her chair and glanced around the room as she often did. This had been the first redecorating project after the shock of Mitch's death, an urge that had overcome her one day not long after the second anniversary of that terrible day culminating such a short and intense battle with pancreatic cancer. The unrelenting rapidity of the disease and the inescapable reality of the years they would not have together had made those few weeks both precious and heartbreaking. How did you concentrate what should have been another three or four decades of companionship into mere days?

It had taken her months to bring herself to give away his clothes, to sort through other items. Each time she tried ended with only a little progress. Yet the small amounts added up and during one meeting with the quilting circle, Phyllis mentioned that Esther Landers was selling her house and moving to Marietta to live near her oldest daughter. She was going into one of those active retirement communities, was taking practically none of her furniture, and was looking to sell the rest at bargain prices. Helen had been in Esther's house more times than she could count and always admired the handmade pieces that weren't quite old enough to be antiques. She'd gone the next day to see Esther and after making the deal, she'd stopped in at the hardware store to look at paint.

The end result was as much library as den, four bookshelves placed side by side against one wall. The entertainment center with one of the new thin profile televisions in it was the only piece of furniture that didn't come from Esther's. She had found it as a kit, easy to put together, and she'd stained it to blend in. It too had ample shelves for books and was adequately deep so the electronic boxes that ran the television were recessed to where you could hardly see them. There was a couch to the right of it with a square end table on the far side featuring a classic stained glass Tiffany lamp that had belonged to Mitch's grandmother. The table on the right hand side of the couch was slightly shorter, but Helen preferred a tall floor lamp to cast a better downward light. It was fashioned after an old gaslight streetlight in a bronze finish. The furniture was all oak with variations in speaking to it being solid wood instead of veneer. The lines were clean in what was similar to a mission style. Upholstery for the couch was a pinstripe of navy and pale blue and Helen's chair was a comfortable stuffed armchair in a coordinated medium blue fabric with a matching rectangular footstool. A rocking chair fit perfectly to the left of Helen's chair. The single window in the room was on the left wall and had a navy blue roman shade and padded valance rather than curtains.

Slate blue was the right choice for the walls since the quilts hung as art all contained at least some blue. Helen allowed her gaze to linger on these, many of them crafted during the years that the quilting circle had been together. She took a sip of tea, not yet ready to turn the television on. She knew the movie almost by heart, so it wasn't as if she wouldn't be able to follow the story by tuning in late.

These quilts represented the sharing with friends as they stitched and chatted, exchanging pieces of their lives. Of the hundreds, well probably thousands, they had collectively quilted and given away for gifts and charitable causes, these were among the ones Helen chose to hang. Had they really been meeting for fifteen years? Phyllis was the only other original member left, although Carolyn Reynolds had twelve years in the circle. The others ranged from ten to the most recent, Rita, barely six months. A pleasant young lady if a bit quiet. Helen silently catalogued each quilt; one was the last one completed while Virginia Thatcher was still with them. She had helped with the assembly when the squares were finished, the two of them seated next to each other at the quilting frame on the weekends when the circle didn't meet. It was a lovely piece, Morning Meadow, with a field of green below, wispy clouds moving toward a pale sun in blue sky, and a profusion of wildflowers. A fawn was peeking from a clump of bushes in the bottom left corner and a red robin was in flight in the upper right.

Virginia's face was suddenly incredibly vivid, no doubt because of all the discussion about Gabriel. How could she not think of him as part of the quilts? Even if it hadn't been that his mother was in the original group, the truth was that almost a third of the women had been with Gabe for at least a little while. Helen remembered the night that Phyllis, outspoken about things she did, had popped off that if she was twenty years younger, she'd have taken up with Gabe in the snap of a finger. Helen, accustomed as she was to Phyllis frequently blurting out outrageous things, struggled to hide her surprise and poor Becky Sullivan had stabbed her finger with a needle.

"Oh piddle, it's not like we can't admit there's something devilishly attractive about him," she had breezily continued after whichever of Gabe's exploits started the conversation. "He came over a few evenings to help me out with gathering some of the family history that my sister, Jeanie, wanted when she was putting together that book." Her eyes had flashed a look of merriment. "It was that second bottle of wine on the night we finished up the project and I don't mind telling you that the thought crossed my mind more than once that if there were more men in town like Gabe Thatcher, I might change my mind about remarrying."

My, what a lively evening that had been! The other five women who had actually been with Gabe—no, at that point it was four others since Mary Lou Bell was later – hadn't taken the bait that Phyllis dangled. They had murmured that night, choosing not to confirm their own involvement as Phyllis hooted at their reticence. Each of them, however, had spoken with Helen privately, some before that night, some after, usually sitting at the kitchen table. As Helen explained to Justin, Gabe's effect on women was such that they nearly always needed to confide the emotions he stirred. When Mitch was alive, he joked that if Helen could get constructive college credit for every time women came to her to talk to her about emotional turmoil, she would have at least a master's degree in counseling. That also brought a smile to her face—his willingness for their kitchen to be a perpetual combination of sounding board and confessional.

And speaking of confessions, how was Justin going to manage this investigation? He was a bright young man and everything a mother could ask for, a sentiment that Mitch had echoed in sparser words. "Think Trish got herself a good one," had been his assessment. They had traveled to Baltimore while ostensibly on a trip to Washington, D.C., to meet Justin after their daughter's sudden pronouncement. Helen almost allowed her thoughts to drift to that and other trips with Mitch, but those memories could wait.

Justin, as dear as he was, had the same puzzling adjustments to make in Wallington, as did anyone who was not of at least two generations. In his case, it was compounded by having never lived beyond the boundaries of Baltimore. College at the University of Maryland couldn't really count as having experienced a cultural difference. She had no doubt that he was infinitely more streetwise than would be residents of Wallington plunked into a big city neighborhood, but he was still unaccustomed to many habits of small town life. You could tell that he had not yet adjusted to the common option of gun racks in trucks or that half the town's population really did attend the Fourth of July parade and then flock to the fairgrounds where men from the Lions Club had spent the night preparing huge pots of Brunswick stew and fall-off-the bone BBQ.

She, however, could help him as she did tonight to sort through some of the personalities. She would never dream of interfering without being asked, although she sensed that he trusted her as a source of information. Of the three men she suggested to him, she hoped that Paul Newton wasn't guilty. The Good Lord knew that Martha Newton had borne enough of a burden with her husband before he deserted them. Granted, the two boys were sometimes rough around the edges, but they had been hard workers from early on. If she were right about any of the three names she'd passed to Justin, she would prefer it to be Tommy Hillman. That whole family had a streak of bully in them, notwithstanding that his daddy and mamma hid behind a sanctimonious façade, keeping to their Christian values in a pig's eye. The two of them were nothing more than narrow-minded, judgmental prigs and everyone in town knew it. They were the kind that gave religion a bad name and Helen refused to do business with them.

Helen realized that her tea was now a tepid temperature and it took only a moment to decide to refresh it. One more mug would get her through the movie. It was time to let the antics of Rex Harrison as the ghost of the salty sea captain and Gene Tierney as the lovely widow amuse her.

CHAPTER FOUR

J ustin pulled into the station parking lot, mildly disappointed that the interview with Roger had been inconclusive. Lenny had met him outside the doublewide trailer that had seen better days. An older model red Blazer was parked at an odd angle barely two feet from the corner of the trailer. The burly man was inside with his brother, empty beer cans littering the stained coffee table in a room that smelled of leftover food and stale booze. The fact that the man was drinking coffee didn't do much to dispel the obvious effects of a hangover.

"Heard Gabe got killed and that's okay by me," had been Roger's statement, followed by his alibi of having gone by his sister's house after leaving the Suttons to borrow a wheelbarrow from his brother-in-law, but they weren't home. Could anyone verify that? Not as far as he knew, but a man didn't have to account for every minute of his day just 'cause somebody finally got tired of Gabe thinking he was God's gift to women, so best be that they leave him alone.

Justin resisted the urge to hassle him because a) he was right, and b) he didn't want to mess anything up at the beginning of the investigation. They departed with a warning for Roger not to leave town and ignored the expletives that followed them out the door.

Sheila was at the reception counter with Kelly Gleason, and the frosted glass double doors behind her were propped open as usual. She glanced up in the midst of showing Kelly something on the computer screen. "Sheriff got the fingerprint report; he left a message for Fletcher Brown, Gabe's cousin, and Lisa dropped off muffins and cookies."

"Thanks," Justin said, giving a quick wink to Kelly who rolled her eyes with Sheila looking his way. That meant either Sheila was trying to explain something to Kelly that she was well aware of, or Kelly was trying to explain something to Sheila that she didn't want to hear. Kelly had graduated from high school the year before and in addition to being a more-or-less assistant to everyone, she was as close to a computer technician as they had. That meant she was able to accurately assess when a problem was due to a human or they actually did need to call a technician. Fortunately, her personality was suited to the tasks. "Perky" was what always came to mind when someone said her name: short, curly black hair, a freckled nose, brown eyes that seemed to find humor in most things, and a trim body that should have belonged to a cheerleader, although Justin had never asked that direct question. She was taking online classes through the community college, getting required courses out of the way as she tried to decide on what she wanted to pursue as a four-year degree. She'd hinted that she might be interested in forensics and Justin thought they should arrange for her to spend some time with the county technicians.

The other four desks in the open bay were unoccupied and a white bakery box was sitting on the gray metal table next to the coffeepot. Justin looked into the sheriff's office. Two large windows in the wall facing the bay made it easy to see inside. There were blinds that could be lowered, although Justin had never seen them closed. Sheriff McFarlane was on the telephone so Justin took the coffee mug from his desk, filled it, and resisted the temptation of a chocolate chip muffin for approximately ten seconds. He wandered to the sheriff's door as he replaced the receiver and motioned Justin to come in.

"Coffee, muffin?" Justin asked before he sat.

"Got one, finished the other," Sheriff McFarlane said and held out a thin folder. "I left a voice mail for Gabe's cousin and don't know when we might hear from him. I guess we could try and track him down, but don't see any reason to do that just yet. Got multiple sets of prints from different parts of the studio— Roger Jenkins, Paul Newton, and two unidentified." He shrugged. "Problem is, of course, there's no way to know when they were made. Jenkins probably worked out there on a job. Couldn't lift anything useable from the cell phone."

Justin sipped his coffee as he read the short report. "Okay," he said. "It's easy to check if Jenkins ever had business there, but as a plumber, there's a good chance that he did. That shower enclosure in the studio looked to be fairly new. What's the story on Newton?"

The sheriff's face registered approval of Justin's assessment. "Newton works as a painter sometimes, so same deal as Jenkins— think Gabe might have had the place spruced up not long ago. As for the unidentified prints, that could take some genuine investigating." He paused and Justin waited, taking a bite of muffin. It was so moist that it didn't leave crumbs on the napkin. The sheriff swiveled his chair a little to the left. "Newton isn't at home or at work, but he's not a regular employee. Takes on handyman kind of jobs, no set schedule, and works for a couple of different places in town when they have overflow, plus he takes on stuff from people just calling him. The thing is that no one in his family knows where he is, or says they don't."

"Do you believe them?" Justin wasn't sure of the sheriff's tone.

"Could be," he said slowly. "Paul's always been an outdoor guy—could be off hunting and fishing just as easy as he could be on the run."

"If he is running, that gives him more than 24 hours head start," Justin said, careful to not sound critical. If the sheriff knew this last night, why didn't they put a bulletin out?

The older man drained his mug before responding. "Paul's not exactly a master criminal type, although they do have a branch of family down around Valdosta. Might as well put a bulletin out, strictly as a person of interest, okay? Let's don't be calling him a suspect yet."

Justin didn't understand the sheriff's reluctance, but he respected the man and before he could ask another question, Kelly rang through to say that the forensics computer technician had arrived. It took her less than thirty minutes to open Gabe's e-mail and check Internet sites he'd visited. Justin assured her he was fine to roam around inside Gabe's computer and he took it into the room that served for interviews, interrogations, training, and the rare meetings they had. He decided to start with only the past three months of e-mail. He wanted to see what he had before starting to print stacks of paper and both the quantity and detail in some were like reading a steamy novel. By his count, Gabe was corresponding with close to ten different women, about half who used addresses like "cutesmile@gmail.com." The county computer technician had said to forward those to her and she would see if she could find whom the addresses belonged to. There were several from a "MelissaN" that he assumed was

Melissa Newton, although compared to the text of some messages, it would seem that no physical intimacy had yet taken place.

Justin recognized two names of women in town, one of whom he was certain was married. If he was right and it was a situation similar to what Helen had described about Sheriff McFarlane, the husband would be another suspect, and a tricky one. He would have to ask the sheriff about the second name and any that the computer tech might identify. They would have to run each of them down as to potential husbands, ex-husbands, or otherwise protective males. He had to agree that it was unlikely the assailant had been a female, although he had seen his share of women in Baltimore who could throw knockout punches.

The last file Gabe had opened on the computer had been the morning of the murder. The heart, what irony of strength to love and yet what betrayal it yields. How can we begin to understand the path down which it will take us?

There had been no title or context. The beginning of a new piece? Was it to someone? About someone? His cell phone rang and when he answered, he saw that it was Tricia calling a few minutes before noon.

"Hi sweetheart," she said happily. "We did a late breakfast. I'm going to stop for gas, then head home. Traffic should be okay at this hour. What do you want to do about dinner?"

He loved the sound of her voice, even with the less than clear quality of a cell phone. "Uh, I hadn't given it much thought. Things have been pretty busy."

"With Gabe getting killed you mean? That will be stirring things up. Did Mamma give you an earful?"

"Well yes, she did," he said and felt his stomach rumble despite the muffin.

"She's known the Thatchers all her life, and certainly has had

Gabe's number since he was a boy. Listen, why don't I swing into Bess's on my way in and pick up that salmon you like?"

"Yeah, that sounds good," he said, thinking that he could catch the sheriff before he went to lunch and ask about the names of the women, so he could then plan out who to talk to and in what sequence.

"All right," her voice dropped off for a second, "...about three hours. Call if you get tied up and will be later than six."

"Sure," he said quickly. "Be careful driving."

She laughed, a melodious sound. "I've missed you, and I love you. See you this evening."

The sheriff was putting on his hat when Justin gave him a fast rundown about the e-mails. He didn't look surprised at most of the news. "Abigail Turner is the wife of Joe Turner. He has that Auto World over on Big Creek Road and I don't know him well enough to say how he might react. Bonnie Wallington, though, that could be a problem," he said, a slight frown creasing his forehead. "It sound like they were a current thing?"

"I'm no expert," Justin said, thinking that Helen's information appeared to have been accurate about the Turners. "It's not as...," he hesitated, "as detailed as some of them. Hard to tell for sure what the relationship might have been. If it was something to upset their marriage, is her husband the type to go after Gabe?"

If the question brought back painful memories to the sheriff, he didn't let it show on his face. "Walt played defense in high school. Didn't make the college cut, but still keeps himself in good shape. Even though he doesn't have the hair-trigger temper of a few that I can name, you never quite know how a man will react to something like this."

"He and his father are with the bank, right?"

"More like they are Oak Tree Bank, second and third

generation. His daddy is president of the chamber of commerce and former mayor, so take it real easy on that one," the sheriff said and settled his hat on his head. "Matter of fact, considering that can of worms, I wouldn't mind you asking if Helen knows anything."

"Helen?" Justin had been genuinely surprised with how much she had revealed to him, but he hadn't mentioned their conversation to anyone else.

Sheriff McFarlane stepped around the desk and Justin moved aside to let him out the door. "Helen knows as much about what goes on in this town as anyone and keeps to her own business better than about anyone," he said in a low voice. "Think of her as a civilian consultant. She doesn't need to be told everything that we have, but she might know about Bonnie. How to approach Walt will depend on if there was anything suspicious between Gabe and Bonnie. You want to come to lunch?"

"That's okay, thanks. I'll call and see if Helen is in."

The sheriff nodded, pointed for Justin to use his telephone, and left. Helen answered on the second ring and said that if he didn't mind anything more elaborate than sandwiches, she'd have lunch on the table in a few minutes. He verified that the bulletin had been issued for Paul Newton and drove the short distance to Helen's. The police department was one block to the east of the town square and bordered a small park. The opposite side of the park was one of the long established neighborhoods. Oak and magnolia trees shaded yards, rambling 1970s brick ranch style homes were mingled with 1950s bungalows, like Helen's. White clapboards had been updated with vinyl siding that gave the appearance of wood, but required little maintenance. The lawn was not large and a mature dogwood on the left side was balanced by a red maple on the right. Both had circular stone borders around them with purple and white pansies creating a bed of color. A line of trimmed camellia bushes ran the length of the porch, one of the features that Justin particularly liked. The porch gave a welcoming look with three wide steps leading up, flanked by a railing on either side. There were unadorned square white columns with a railing extending all around, and an oak flooring worn to a warmth that only real wood could give. The porch swing to the right was painted a dark green; two green rocking chairs to the left with a round tile-topped wrought iron table between them evoked scenes of relaxing with morning coffee—well, maybe a late afternoon beverage. They usually entered through the side, though, and he parked in the wide driveway behind Helen's silver Taurus instead of in the empty bay in the two-car carport. You never knew who might pop in to see her and he didn't want to be blocked in.

"Tricia called and is on her way back," he said by way of greeting.

"She can come over tomorrow and we'll get caught up," Helen replied as he crossed to the kitchen island to give her a peck on the cheek. She waved him to the table that was already set. A bowl of potato chips, a woven basket with slices of multigrain bread, a plate with sliced tomatoes, leaves of lettuce, and dill pickle spears were in the center, accompanying a small tray with slices of roast beef, turkey, ham, and Swiss cheese. A squeezable container of spicy brown mustard and another of light mayonnaise provided all the condiments he needed.

"Tea, cola, or water?" Helen asked as he politely waited behind a chair.

"Tea, please," he said, having adapted to the beverage not long after they moved from Baltimore.

Helen filled the glasses, brought them to the table, and waited until they'd fixed their plates. "Not that I don't always enjoy your company, but I assume there's an ulterior motive for today?" She bit into her sandwich, not taking her eyes from him.

Justin nodded as he swallowed. "Sheriff McFarlane thinks a lot of you," he said first.

Helen smiled and patted her mouth with a napkin. "We've known each other since his parents moved here when he was in the second grade. They came over from near Augusta, and bought the Reynolds' place." She lifted her sandwich, her eyes sparkling the way Tricia's did when she was trying not to laugh. "And?"

He might as well get to the point. "We have Mr. Thatcher's e-mails and there's a lot of correspondence from women; some we know, some we have to track down. You were correct, by the way, about Mrs. Turner. Another correspondent, though, was Bonnie Wallington, and the sheriff thought you might have an idea about her and Mr. Thatcher."

She raised her eyebrows, but didn't express surprise. "Ah, Norm is trying to keep things quiet and doesn't want you barging into that part of the Wallington family unless it's absolutely necessary." She tilted her head. "Does this also mean there's some question about the kind of e-mails between them? Could it have been affectionate without being romantic?"

Justin shrugged. "I guess that would depend on how you interpret phrases like, 'I will never forget how wonderful you were and how much it meant to me. Thank you for everything.' That was the only e-mail in the three months I went back through," he added.

Helen ate a potato chip before she answered. "Do you remember if it was about two months ago?"

He had written the date down for reference. "Yes, it was the twelfth of March. Why do you ask?"

"That was Bonnie's birthday," she replied, an expression of what seemed to be understanding crossing her face. "She was turning thirty and had been fretting about it something fierce for six months,

I'd say. Oh, in case you don't know, Walter, Bonnie's husband, is Wanda's nephew. Wanda owns Memories and Collectibles."

"Ah, that's the connection," Justin said, realizing that was the place where Helen taught quilting classes or worked part time or something.

Helen's voice sounded confident. "I do believe I can guess the situation. As I said, Bonnie is a pretty thing, former head cheerleader, homecoming queen, and all that, so she had this idea that thirty was a calamity. She started talking about eyelifts and that nonsense, and it about drove Wanda crazy. Then it couldn't have been more than three weeks before her birthday, her outlook changed. She said she decided we were right and she shouldn't be in such a fuss." Helen ate another chip and smiled. "Bonnie obviously is more discreet than I gave her credit for."

Justin shook his head, not able to see what Helen was getting at. "I'm sorry. I think you lost me."

Helen wiped condensation from her glass. "Gabe attends, well, attended, a writers' conference in Mobile they have in mid-February. It so happens that this year there was also a big antique show in Mobile that same weekend that had an emphasis on dolls. Part of Wanda's shop is devoted to dolls; it's something that Bonnie is fairly expert in, having her own collection—a really nice one, too."

Justin grinned. "Bonnie went to the show?"

"Not only did she go to the show, she went instead of Wanda. You remember I told you Gabe was especially attuned to women who were feeling vulnerable? That was Bonnie for sure. I'll bet you that they wound up running into each other and Gabe worked his charm to bring Bonnie out of her funk about her birthday." She held up one hand for Justin to let her finish. "This is what I'm talking about that people don't—didn't—understand about Gabe. The odds are that he just wined and dined Bonnie, let her see that her worries were silly, and she couldn't resist sending an e-mail as a thank you. She had no reason to think anyone else would ever see it."

Justin had eaten the last pickle spear while she talked. "So you don't think she would have told her husband about Gabe and he got upset about it? Could he have found out from someone else?"

Helen snapped her fingers. "I seriously doubt it, however, give me a second and it might not matter." She pushed back and went to the island where a newspaper was folded. She brought it back to the table and handed it to Justin. "Inside story, photo of men in suits."

He opened the paper and read the caption. He looked at her. "This branch is where?"

"Far side of the next county—the latest branch of Oak Tree Bank and the most distant. If they had the ribbon cutting at eleven, a tour of the facility, and then a luncheon, that means Walt would have been on the road by about nine thirty in the morning and not back until probably two o'clock at the earliest."

His schedule would have been extremely tight based on the estimated time of death, and Justin had to admit that the man cutting the ribbon for the new bank did not look as if he had anything on his mind other than the event at hand. He felt comfortable putting Wallington very low on the list of possible suspects. He didn't see a reason to interview either him or his wife at this point.

He set the paper aside and stood. "Thanks, Helen, I appreciate the lunch and the information." He reached for his plate and she batted his hand away.

"Go on, young man. You have a lot to do yet today. Tell Tricia to call me later tonight." She gave him a hug and a gentle poke in the shoulder. "Oh, were y'all able to reach Fletcher?"

Justin threw her a mock salute. "In a manner of speaking,

ma'am, the sheriff left him a voice mail. And if we don't hear from him soon, I'll set Kelly to searching the Internet for another way to contact him."

Helen nodded. "It seems to me that he has, or at least had, one of those jobs with a lot of traveling involved," she said as the telephone rang.

Justin waved, backing through the door, eager to get going. His plan was to return to the station, pass on the information about Bonnie to Sheriff McFarlane, send the list of e-mail addresses to the forensics computer technician, see if they'd had word about Newton, and try to interview the Turners and Mr. Hillman. He hadn't decided yet if he should try for both father and son or start with the son and see how that went.

CHAPTER FIVE

Helen laid the blue and gold striped napkins next to the forks, everything else in place. Glasses for tea and water, cups and saucers for coffee, and wine glasses for later were arrayed on the kitchen island where it was easier to manage beverages. The dining room opened off the kitchen and into the living room and looked as it had since the day they moved in. Except for a fresh coat of soft peach paint and deep cleaning the dark green area rug with a floral border, it had been left intact through the other remodeling and redecorating projects. The rectangular table that sat eight and the two corner cabinets had been her grandmother's. Her grandfather built all three pieces using wood from a black hickory tree on their property that had been struck by lightning when she was a toddler. The open shelves of the cabinets were allegedly so because he ran out of wood before he could make doors. Since he didn't care for chair making, he found ladder-back oak ones at a yard sale and stained them to a fairly close match. The table had served four generations and Helen was looking forward to when the fifth one would sit in the heirloom high chair that she kept in a corner of the guest room as a decorative piece until the day it would be needed.

Grandchildren were not really on Helen's mind, though, not with Justin's visit at lunch and the ladies due to arrive. There had been other occasions when crises or celebration had enveloped the circle, but Gabe's death was in a different category. Helen honestly didn't know how they might react and she was prepared for everything from bouts of crying to steady speculation about who killed him.

The front door opened without a knock or the doorbell ringing, which meant it was Phyllis. She was wearing her usual combination of a pair of twill slacks and a long sleeve front button blouse This was the sapphire blue ensemble of pants in a solid color and blouse in a print with tiny diamond shapes in silver. It was a wonderful combination with her blue eyes and white hair that she had decided to never color. She still worked as the office manager and bookkeeper for Dr. Cutler, the oldest dentist in town. Her passion for quilting was neck-and-neck with how she felt about gardening. She spent so much time outside that she declared maintaining the pageboy style of her hair was all the effort she wanted to expend in that matter, and trying to maintain blonde at her age wasn't kidding anyone.

"Food first," she said cheerfully, carrying in an oval platter. "Chicken salad finger sandwiches. Have they caught up with Paul Newton yet?" She set the platter in the center of the table and tossed her head. "I don't think the boy did it, mind you, but Sheila said they put a bulletin out for him. Person of interest—not for arrest."

"I was afraid that might happen," Helen started and was interrupted by Sarah's arrival. Like Phyllis, she brought food in before going to retrieve her quilting tote. "Chocolate Bundt cake with raspberry glaze," she said, giving Helen a kiss before she put the glass-domed cake plate on the table. "Do they know who killed Gabe yet?"

"Not as of a half-hour ago," Carolyn Reynolds said, coming through the arched opening with her tote across one forearm and a tray of cheese chunks, crackers, and apple slices in her hands. "Kelly Gleason was in the shop right at closing time. She said there was nothing yet."

Rita, Becky, Katie, and Mary Lou trailed in after each other, the front screen door barely closing before being opened again. It was a well-practiced choreography, only the number of members in attendance changing. There were eight of the dozen tonight, pecking cheeks in greeting, and it briefly crossed Helen's mind that half of them had been close to Gabe. She had the feeling that Phyllis was planning to get them talking and who knew what they might say?

Once dishes were deposited on the table and totes retrieved, the group gravitated to the quilting room to set up. Helen was at the table to continue working on A Garden Bouquet, a special design she'd created at Wanda Wallington's request. It was to be a surprise for her mother's ninetieth birthday—a celebration of the gardening she loved. Not quite two years ago "Miss Ruth," as they all called her, had reluctantly converted most of her raised beds to low maintenance flowering shrubs and kept only a handful of containers as arthritic knees and hands became too painful to ignore. When Helen had shown Wanda the design she was planning, she'd been thrilled with the theme. The background was ivory with a bouquet of white, yellow, and red roses in the center of the quilt, tied loosely with a gold ribbon. Individual sprays of purple irises, Stargazer lilies, gladiolas, and tulips graced the four corners. A birdhouse with climbing pink clematis and a section of white picket fence covered in honeysuckle ran along the top and bottom. It was an intricate undertaking, but Helen wasn't concerned about finishing in time. If she did run into unanticipated problems, there were many hands that would pitch in to help.

Phyllis and Rita preferred to sit on the sofa with their stitching. Phyllis's project was remarkably simple for her: a set of deep rose-colored pillow covers that would complete a bedroom makeover she was planning. Rita's stacks of squares were different types of leaves that would be put together as a quilt. It was going to be an anniversary present for her parents who had recently built a log cabin on a lake as a vacation home.

Becky took one of the chairs. She was halfway through a beautiful reversible table runner that would serve as an autumn festival on one side and Christmas on the other. She was considering adding a special gold binding instead of folding over the dark green as the simplest way to do the binding. She was using the tote bag by her side to hold the long part of the runner as she kept the portion she was working on in her lap.

Katie sat at one of the hoop stands, just beginning with the large center image of the Tybee Island Lighthouse. The quilted wallhanging would include the six Georgia lighthouses that her husband, Scott, had meticulously constructed in small scale.

Carolyn ordinarily also used a stand, but she sat at the table with Helen instead. She was experimenting with a quilted clutch bag, contemplating starting a line to carry in her store. The fabric was black with a rainbow of colors in diagonal stripes and she was quilting every other stripe to see if she liked the effect.

Sarah was hosting a baby shower for one of her nieces in June, and she had gathered pieces of leftover fabric from several family christening gowns. She'd cut half-circles to use in forming clouds that would be paired with stars on a midnight blue background. She'd originally planned it to be a crib quilt, but she thought she would have enough squares to make it a twin-size instead.

Whether or not to add a moon was still under debate. If she did, would it be a classic man-in-the-moon type or a crescent? There were opinions about all three options.

Mary Lou was building up a stack of squares featuring Victorian fans, some open, some half folded, from remnants of fabrics she'd found stuffed in a bag in their attic. The fabrics were paisleys, tiny floral prints, and a pink silk. She was undecided whether to make a quilt with a dominant fan theme or if she would put the squares away to be used as accent pieces in other quilts.

After they were settled, the room was gripped by an uncharacteristic quiet, as it seemed to Helen that everyone was concentrating too hard on their projects.

"Well, I'm just about to bust and I can't believe that y'all aren't as well," Phyllis said, breaking through the reserve as if popping a balloon. She clipped a thread and her eyes traveled around the women. "It isn't right, not at all. I've been racking my brain as to which woman Gabe could have messed with that caused this. I mean it isn't like most of them don't accept it as practically a rite of passage."

Carolyn hooted a laugh. "Rite of passage? Well, I've heard a lot of things said about Gabe Thatcher in my time, but that isn't one of the usual terms."

"Nonsense," Phyllis shot back. "Y'all want to sit here and act as if I'm the only one with fond memories of the boy, that's fine, but I think we all know better."

"Phyllis, honey, I'm not sure Rita has been with us long enough to hear what I think you're about to say," Sarah Guilford cautioned gently. She gave a questioning look to Rita who looked startled at the comment.

"I'm not a teenager, either," Rita said evenly, not lowering her eyes as she did sometimes. She held her needle in the fabric before continuing with the stitch. "I think that we would all like to know what Helen can tell us about the investigation before we say anything else. I mean with Justin being in charge and all."

"No offense intended, Helen," Katie said before Helen had a chance to respond. "I honestly don't understand why Norm felt like he couldn't head this up."

Mary Lou snorted in a way that was completely out of keeping with her petite figure and doll-like face. "Come on, you know good and well that it could turn out to be someone connected—someone like Tommy Hillman, for example. Between the politics that will stir up and Norm's own history with Gabe, I think it was smart for him to ask Justin to do it."

Becky turned her head to Helen. "Is Justin okay about this? Did he work homicides in Baltimore?"

This was going about as Helen anticipated. "I'm not completely convinced that Norm did need to hand it off, but I can see his reason for doing so," she said firmly. "Justin was surprised, as you can imagine, and of course they had all sorts of murders in Baltimore. He wasn't in the homicide department, if that's what you mean, but I can tell you that he's very thorough and is taking it quite seriously."

Sarah reached down and rummaged in her tote without taking her gaze off Helen. "How many suspects are there? The way names are being flung around, you'd think every male over the age of sixteen and under the age of seventy is on the list."

Helen was glad she was able to answer truthfully. "I honestly don't know. I assume everyone has their own list of suspects. It's all I heard being talked about in the checkout line today."

"It wouldn't have to be someone from here, would it?" Rita asked tentatively. "I mean, it's not as if Gabe lived in a secluded place that no one could find unless they were local."

"That's true," Mary Lou agreed. "I guess most murders are committed locally, though, and if someone came in from outside it couldn't really be about anything recent. I don't think Gabe had been out of town since maybe when he went to that writers' conference in February. I always read his column and when he's out of town, he usually writes something about that. I'm not saying that someone from a long time ago still holding a grudge couldn't have come here, but that just doesn't sound likely."

There was a moment of sudden silence as the women thought about the possibility, and then Phyllis spoke up again. "Going back to my earlier point. From what I heard, it was probably more manslaughter than an out and out murder, but it's still a shame. Prudes like Fred Hillman can say what they want and that doesn't change the fact that Gabriel Thatcher had a gift for making a woman feel special. I think we owe it to his memory and Virginia's, too, for that matter, to keep that in mind."

"You are right about that," Sarah said in a low voice. "His was a gift, one that I will cherish."

Phyllis chortled and waved the pillow cover like a banner. "That's more like it," she said. "We can make this as our own little memorial for Gabe. He deserves it and I'll start, then the rest of you can decide if you're going to be truthful, too."

Her voice held a poignant tone that Helen hadn't heard for years and an anticipatory quiet enveloped the group in place of the previous awkward one. Phyllis smiled fondly at Rita. "As Sarah mentioned, you haven't been part of the circle for long and you aren't even thirty yet."

"No one needs to hold back on my account," Rita said, lifting her chin a little.

Oh Lord, Helen thought. What can of worms was Phyllis about to open?

CHAPTER SIX

Despite her momentary misgivings, Helen realized that Phyllis was departing from the tart-tongue and outrageous antics that she was known for. The expression on her face was not somber—reflective was a more accurate word to describe it. There was certainly no telltale mischief in her smile as there always was before she let loose with one of her overly candid comments.

"Don't worry, everyone, I'm not going to be spouting off some of the stories about Gabe that I've heard," she said as she smoothed the pillow cover on her lap, having gotten everyone's attention. "Gabe was truly special, and no, I am not one of these women who ever for one minute would consider being with a man almost young enough to be my son. That's fine if some woman wants to go for it, but I can't personally see it for me." She let her eyes flicker from face to face. "I imagine at least some of y'all might have wondered when I was carrying on about him once before, but that was just talk about how he could affect a woman. I came to better understand what it was that could cause women to lose their senses over him.

It all started because my baby sister, Jeanie, had been after me for months to help her out with some information about the family history. I had two of the old Bibles, several albums, and a handful of letters that Mamma kept from when Daddy was in Europe during World War II. He was in Africa, and maybe Italy, and then Normandy, y'all remember. That was where he was wounded and later sent home." Most heads nodded. "Anyway, all that stuff was jumbled together and I'd been avoiding trying to sort it out. I was having lunch at Bess's with Denise Grigsby, and Gabe came in and joined us. This was, oh, maybe three or four months after Virginia, God rest her soul, passed away. Maybe that was what got the conversation going. You know, what with Stanley having been an only child and his parents not having kept much in the way of albums or letters, there was really a lack of their family history."

Phyllis had stopped stitching, holding the needle in her hand. "Y'all know me—I popped off as to how I saw Denise's point, but in other cases when you had a big old stack of stuff, it was hard to know where to start. That's when Gabe said he would be happy to come see what I had, if I liked, and he could help me get started." She glanced at the needle as though trying to decide what to do with it and continued to hold it between her thumb and forefinger. "That was fine by me and he came over a couple of evenings later. He brought a lovely bottle of wine and said there was no reason to make this dull." Phyllis cast a look around the group as the women waited to hear what she wanted to reveal about Gabe. "It was a very pleasant evening and that night we mostly took an inventory of what I had."

Helen felt a surge of affection for Phyllis. She was unfolding the story as a genuine tribute, and the room was respectful, waiting for her, hardly a chair creaking, but the women were still able to stitch if they chose to. And why not? They always chattered while quilting. That was as much a part of their bond as was the love of quilting.

"The thing that struck me about Gabriel that I had never really noticed was how well he listened—I mean actually listened," Phyllis said. "I had all sorts of photos, clippings, letters, and what have you covering the dining room table and in no time at all, he had me telling about people and things that I hadn't thought of since, well, since before he was born. It was as if that pile of stuff, as I'd called it, was important to him, important for him to draw the story out of me. This was our family's history, and I suddenly understood why Jeanie wanted to take the task on."

She used her left hand to brush at a strand of hair that had fallen across her cheek. "It was obvious that it was going to take two or three sessions to get everything organized, so I told him to come for dinner the next time. It was the least I could do and I was truly enjoying his company. Instead of getting into the family history, though, he wanted to talk about me while we were having dinner, and how I came to be the person that I am. It was the strangest thing how those really simple questions got me to carrying on about growing up here, my pathetic marriage to that snake of a husband, not having any desire to remarry, and treating my nieces, nephews, and pets like children because I won't ever have any of my own."

There was the tiniest catch to her voice at the part about not having children and Helen wondered if anyone else felt a sting of tears. Being open about her personal life was typical of Phyllis, but hers was a "join in the craziness, nothing is off bounds to talk about" manner rather than the gentleness she was displaying.

She laughed softly. "I know, I know, but that's what I'm

saying. Gabe, of all the men I have known in my life, Gabe touched something in me that took me completely off guard. We now come around to my main point about him."

Helen thought she knew what Phyllis meant, but Rita looked almost stricken. Perhaps she was expecting Phyllis to pour out a shocking detail after all.

Phyllis allowed a poignant smile. "I told y'all before, it was that second bottle of wine, and that's partially correct. We had finished organizing my stuff and were sitting at the table. I guess you'd have to say that we were sort of savoring the accomplishment. Maybe I had been feeling some kind of extra connection, and we were right next to each other, shoulders no more than an inch apart. Gabe's voice was like melted chocolate and he started thanking me for the privilege of having shared myself with him." She paused. "And that was when I saw how easy it would be for any woman to get drawn into that voice and those blue eyes of his. It was a feeling right that moment of him being completely centered on me as a person, that every word I said mattered."

Another smile curved her lips. No matter what his reputation was, I could tell that Gabe wasn't a man just looking to make conquests; it was that he genuinely wanted to devote himself to whatever woman he was with at the moment for whatever that reason could be. In fact, the next day he sent a bouquet of a dozen yellow roses with a card that said, 'Thank you for sharing your history with me.' Believe you me, I haven't tolerated anyone saying an unkind word about him since then."

She picked the pillow cover up from her lap, apparently ready to begin stitching again. What had been almost a daze seemed to clear from everyone's faces. Phyllis looked around the circle as she had at the beginning, her eyes not lingering on any single friend. "Well, those are my feelings about Gabe, and I say again that it's a crying shame someone took him from us. I understand how he could rile a man, has riled more than one, and I suppose it shouldn't come as the shock that it did, but that doesn't change that it shouldn't have happened."

Carolyn Reynolds broke the quiet that seemed to be ebbing and flowing among them. Her voice was reflective as Phyllis's had been. "Since I'm the only one here tonight who has never been married, and I was a few years older than Gabe, my perspective might be a little different from anyone else's and maybe I should go next." She gestured to the dining room. "Mine won't take long and then it could be time for a break."

"Thank you," Phyllis said with a smile, "for both suggestions."

CHAPTER SEVEN

Helen hadn't been certain if any of the other women would speak up, and if Helen remembered correctly, Carolyn was two or three years older than Gabe. Not that Carolyn looked her age, but in all honesty that couldn't be said about Phyllis. Part of that was Carolyn's preference for indoor hobbies, instead of being like Phyllis who spent hours in her garden. Even with hats and sunscreen—which Phyllis by her own admission wasn't diligent about—the outdoors could take its toll. Carolyn also had a different image to maintain with having a clothing store on the town square. Knowing she couldn't compete with larger stores, she had consciously made The Right Look: Ladies and Children's Apparel into the place in town to go for professional attire, Sunday and cocktail finery, and adorable clothes for children. That choice meant she, too, should project fashion flair—classic styles rather than trendy. She kept her overhead low by having only two assistants in the store. She personally knew every customer's tastes, the ones who were really a size 16 instead of the 12 they claimed, and how to accessorize for those who wanted a fresh look on a tight budget. Carolyn also understood that a woman sometimes needed a nudge to try a new style or color, and she had an unerring eye for that precise shade that made the difference in enhancing a woman's features or missing the mark. Another business practice that set her apart was her willingness to special order. The arrangements that she'd established with suppliers allowed her to keep her inventory at a manageable level while simultaneously offering a wider variety than most stores her size.

There was no question that she was the most stylish woman in the quilting circle with flawless make-up, manicured nails that always coordinated with whatever outfit she wore, and understated jewelry for that perfect touch. She usually came to the circle directly from the store, and the dress she wore tonight was a sleeveless, dark red scooped-neck sheath with a short-sleeved bolero jacket of the same material with black piping. A short strand of onyx beads, small onyx oval earrings, and a watch with a band of interwoven gold and silver were her only jewelry. In fact, the fabric she was using for the clutch bag she was quilting would be a wonderful match for the outfit. Her short, layered hair with enough natural curl to preclude needing to perm was the exact cut for her oval face; the frosted blonde look had long ago replaced the dishwater blonde of her middle school years. Helen didn't know if her contact lenses had any sort of tint, although her gray eyes had a slight blue that might not be completely natural.

Helen caught her mind from wandering as Carolyn spoke again. "I know there are people who don't have a clue as to why I've never married, and that's fine—it isn't any of their business," she said with a wry smile. "But it does bear on my remembrance of Gabe. Most of y'all know that I was engaged back in college and thank the Lord I called that off. Bruce was everything I was supposed to want, and it wasn't until we were talking about who to invite to the wedding that I realized what an overbearing, controlling horse's behind he was. After I told Mamma what I'd done, she gave me a hug and said she was glad I'd come to that conclusion because they hadn't liked him in the first place." She waved a hand dismissively. "So, I came home and took a job at the bank and that's when I found out that Laura was looking to sell. Y'all remember that she'd really let the place get run down."

All but Rita's head nodded. Most of the women in the quilting circle had patronized Laura's Dress Shoppe out of loyalty, the decline of the shop being a frequent topic among them.

"It was a real risk for me to take on the store and it was my mother who urged me to. She was positive that I could give it the right look, which is where the name came from, and Daddy, bless his heart, did an incredible amount of the remodeling to save me a bundle." She smiled fondly. "There honestly is a point about Gabe in all of this."

"You take your time, honey," Becky said and frowned slightly at the stitch she'd just made.

Carolyn held the partially completed purse in her lap, having secured the needle carefully in the top of the fabric. "There was so much work in the beginning that I was putting in at least fourteen hours a day, and then it turned out that being successful meant every bit as much work, if not more. I loved it, though, making decisions about what to carry, how to market it correctly, practically everything about it." She smiled faintly. "It isn't the kind of place where I get many men my age shopping, though, and between the store and buying my own house, there never is a lot of spare time to go out and meet men. And the truth is that there are still a lot of men who are intimidated by successful women." She shrugged. "A year or two slipped by, then another. Before I knew it, there I was coming up on my fortieth birthday and not a serious relationship in sight," she flashed a quick smile, "male-wise, I mean. Y'all know I love this circle."

Head nods again, to include Rita this time. "So, Gabe comes in one day not long after he moves back to town. Virginia wasn't getting around much at that stage, and he came to talk to me about maybe taking several outfits home for her to try and then he would bring back what she didn't want. I thought that was the sweetest thing for him to do. I mean, how many men would even think to do that? Virginia loved it and when he returned the items she didn't want, he came in at closing time and asked me to dinner. I was surprised, and I didn't give it much thought—I guess I thought it was sort of a thank-you. He suggested that if I didn't mind the drive we could go to Magnolia Inn, and that really did take me by surprise."

Helen felt a flash of nostalgia. Magnolia Inn was almost thirty miles east, a beautiful plantation home set within sculpted gardens that was especially popular for weddings. She and Mitch had often celebrated their anniversary there as an overnight indulgence.

"No, he had not booked a room in case you're wondering," Carolyn said with a hint of a smile. "That was part of why Gabe was so special. He truly wasn't in a hurry—he did want to talk, or rather to listen. I have never met a man as attentive as he was." Her voice drifted for a moment. "It really was a perfect evening: a wonderful meal in a lovely setting and not the slightest pressure for it to be anything other than that." A tiny sigh escaped her lips. "I suppose on some level that Gabe not making a play was a tiny bit disappointing, although the rational part of my brain chalked it up to the age difference. Anyway, when he dropped by a few days later and suggested I come to dinner at his place, I was definitely taken aback. I asked him point blank why and he said, 'Because you're a fascinating woman and a marvelous dinner companion. I hope you like French cuisine.' I will tell you that I had never been so flabbergasted in my life and it was the most natural thing in the world to say yes."

She sighed louder, a poignant sound that floated within the room. "There really was something magical about it—not in the going crazy over him kind of way, but in the sense of how you enjoy a great vacation somewhere that you've always wanted to go to. Even though you doubt you'll ever go there again, it's this terrific memory that you will always have."

She looked down at the material in her lap and briefly made eye contact around the circle, her eyes soft with fond memory. "We were together only four times. I understood it for what it was and Gabe let me be the one who said it wasn't going to work. He also gave me what I can only describe as an incredibly endearing affirmation that not having a man in my life was okay. I had a full life with work that I love, friends, and family, and there simply might not be a place right now to add more." Carolyn lifted her hands to figuratively embrace the room. "It was classic Gabe and he was absolutely right. It isn't that I don't believe I will never meet the yet-to-appear Mr. Right, it's that I'm okay with waiting. And if it doesn't happen, that's okay, too."

Helen suddenly remembered the night they celebrated Carolyn's forty-third birthday, and how she had laughed with delight at the array of candles on the cake. There had been no question that she was a woman happy with her life. She smiled at the recollection and pushed her chair back from the frame. "We love you too, darling. Now, I think we need some refreshments."

CHAPTER EIGHT

Notwithstanding the element of murder and Gabe's role of the town's Don Juan, the rhythm of the circle was unchanged. The first part of the evening was quilting. Then they broke to enjoy food, tea, and coffee; then back to quilting for another hour; then wine and perhaps a bit more nibbling. Skilled hands stitched, clipped, and suggested design or color changes as conversations flowed in the friendships that had seen joy, sorrow, births, deaths, divorces, and marriages. Needles were pretty well put away as the wine was poured, and, other than Phyllis, Helen never knew who might linger. Each one of the women, the ones tonight and those who were absent, had looked to her virtual sisters for comfort during crises, to share celebrations, to vent frustrations, and to laugh at their foolishness when that was needed. Rita hadn't experienced much of that closeness considering how new she was and Helen sensed that perhaps tonight was a bit overwhelming for her. Although they enjoyed her company and she was a better than average quilter who had been taught by a great aunt, they didn't know her all that well. Helen hoped this frank discussion of Gabe wouldn't cause her to rethink being a part of the circle.

"I'm opening the wine early tonight," Helen announced as half the women started at the table and the others came into the kitchen for beverages. That was the easiest flow and had become an automatic routine. Phyllis took the glasses to the ice dispenser and handed them to Becky who set them next to pitchers of tea and water. Coffee was already made and Helen would turn on the teakettle if anyone was in the mood for hot tea. As she suspected, wine was the popular choice except for Katie who was a tolerant teetotaler, and Rita, who said she was too much of a lightweight to drink and drive, much less drink and quilt.

The rule about food was it had to be edible with one hand, preferably bite size since everyone tended to stand and eat like at a cocktail party. That was another pattern that emerged years before as they discovered that if they sat down at the table, the eating time stretched out and if they waited too long to eat, the cranky factor was raised. By an apparently unspoken agreement, the subject of Gabe was suspended for the twenty minutes they ate, replenished beverages, and returned to their seats.

"If we're going by age, as we seem to be, that makes me next," Sarah Guilford said with a half smile. "The truth is that when Gabe came along as soon after my divorce as he did, I felt a little guilty because it never occurred to me that I would want to be with another man that quickly. It just isn't what I would have thought of as me," she added quickly when Rita once again looked slightly askance, although she didn't make a comment. Sarah had finished the square she was working on before the break and she didn't reach into her tote for the fabric to start a new one. "Larry and I married too young to be honest—not young like you, Rita—

young like the month after we graduated from high school," she said. "That was Gabe's freshman year and even then he had girls my age considering him over senior classmates. Although I will admit that he was a good-looking kid, I was Larry's girl—had been since the ninth grade."

Helen felt a twinge of age when she suddenly remembered having attended a football game as part of their fifteen-year high school reunion, and Sarah was a senior in the marching band—flute, if she recalled correctly. She was the type that hadn't changed too much since high school. She was not quite as tall as Helen, but she had Mary Lou by a good three inches. Her fine brown hair needed a perm to keep any sort of shape and she enhanced her thin eyebrows with a good quality pencil. The new gold wire-rimmed glasses she'd switched to were better for her wide-set brown eyes than those brown plastic framed round ones she had favored for a while.

"I wasn't one the girls headed off to college. No, it was a June wedding for us, and Larry was working at the John Deere dealership. We moved into the old Fitzpatrick house over on Pine Street and, oh yes, I thought my life was set. I can't say that I ever gave a thought to Gabe, especially not after Larry Junior and Laura came along practically on each other's heels."

She paused and took a sip of tea. "You know, you hear terms like, 'growing apart.' You read something in a magazine and you don't ever think about that applying to you. And of course I didn't realize it for a while. I wasn't working outside the home, but I volunteered in the church and at the library since I always loved to read. Larry, though, well it never occurred to me that Larry would be one of those guys who stayed stuck in high school—poker with the boys, hunting, sports on TV, real guy stuff—although he was good with the kids." She smiled in a way that moved around the circle. "I suppose that at some point I knew it wasn't right for us any longer, but it wasn't until they found that lump that it came into focus. That was probably no more than six months after Gabe moved back. I knew his reputation—who didn't? But that had nothing to do with me."

Her voice wavered for only a fraction of a second before she continued, another smile spreading to encompass the group, her hand out in a gesture to them. "Most of y'all were with me through that—your wonderful support that helped so much." Heads nodded and half smiles of affection matched hers.

Helen heard a brief shading of sadness in Sarah's voice, not knowing who else might have picked up on it. She had been appalled at Larry's behavior, Sarah not letting the other women in on the depth of his insensitivity. The man had actually faulted her for not keeping up with housework when she was so exhausted she was lucky she could sit upright. It hadn't been a cruel comment on his part, but rather an utter lack of understanding of what his wife was going through. He made no effort to find out what he could have done to help her.

Sarah shook her head sharply. "Larry, though, Larry didn't want to believe it. He wanted to pretend it wasn't happening, that I was being overly dramatic. The biopsy, thank God we caught it early, the treatment—he didn't want to acknowledge any of it." She lifted her shoulders and let them drop. "Even that wasn't enough to make me see Larry's immature selfishness and his genuine disregard for me as anything other than the wife, mother, and housekeeper that I was supposed to be. I guess that in his adolescent view, I was now flawed despite the fact that I didn't have to go through surgery. The poker nights came more frequently, the stopping after work for a beer took longer, and I realized that I didn't care. The kids were older, didn't need him around the way they had when they were little, and the less he was in the house, the better. I had my family, friends like all of you, and I increased my volunteer hours at the library."

She paused and took a breath. "It wasn't as if I didn't try at all with Larry. On our anniversary, which he forgot, by the way, I told him that this was why we had to make some changes. I asked him to go to marriage counseling with me or maybe go on a romantic getaway. He thought I was experiencing the change of life early and said that if I couldn't see how good I had it, then maybe I was the one who needed to be talked to. He left for a three day fishing trip and I went to see Boyd Gilbert about a divorce."

Sarah's voice dipped for a moment, then strengthened. "Funny, when I brought up the divorce, it was almost as if Larry was relieved—as if he'd wanted it all along and didn't have the courage to ask for one. He certainly didn't fight it and the kids didn't seem to be too upset either. So here I was, a new divorcée, and I suddenly realized that it wasn't a role I had honestly seen myself in. That was when Gabe stepped into my life."

Helen had heard this story at her kitchen table when her emotions were still conflicted. That had diminished over time and she was glad Sarah was speaking with nostalgia instead of pain. "Virginia always loved books, and Gabe would bring her and let her spend as much time as she wanted making her selection. He would come in and get books for her after she was house bound, and read to her for hours when she wasn't able to do it for herself any longer. He was incredibly devoted to her no matter what else he was, and we started talking about different books that she might enjoy. Then one day we went for a drink after work and we had a wonderful conversation. It didn't matter that I hadn't gone to college or traveled more than to Orlando the year we took the kids to Disney. There was never a hint of a condescending attitude, and the day when he invited me to his place to look at a couple of first editions he owned seemed like the most normal thing in the world."

Sarah paused briefly, her eyes glistening but not watering. "Magical is the right word to use when describing Gabe." The expression on her face was one of reflection. "The relationship didn't last long, of course. I wasn't interested in affairs. Even in that short time, though, what Gabe did for me was to remind me that I was a woman who should be appreciated and cherished and if I wasn't, then it was time for me to rethink my life."

She sipped more tea before continuing and pushed her glasses up with one finger. "And the other reason that I didn't want to stay with Gabe was that I didn't want people to get the idea that he might have had anything to do with the divorce. It wasn't remotely related, but you know how people can jump to conclusions, especially when it came to the subject of Gabe."

Becky Sullivan was shaking her head, although in a thoughtful way, not negatively. "You know, listening to y'all has really brought back memories. "I was with Gabe for almost a whole summer, a long time ago. Even then, no older than I was, I think I understood that he was an incurable romantic—that he would never be able to settle with just one woman."

Seven pairs of eyes turned to her and she laughed softly. "Oh, I guess it's my turn now."

CHAPTER NINE

"It was the summer that I turned nineteen and Gabe was going into his junior year—of college, I mean," Becky said. "I was fine with the idea of attending Abraham Baldwin, but Gabe of course was off up north. He was home right after finals and my, that year he was filled with ideas for short stories and poems. I don't think he'd started on a novel yet." She wrinkled her forehead. "Hmm, I need to explain about high school first. Unlike a lot of girls, I didn't have a crush on Gabe because horses take up a tremendous amount of time and I didn't really move in the same circles as he did. For me, he was this good-looking guy who was pretty popular and not too much more."

People who did not know Becky's love of horses would nonetheless think that she was engaged in some type of outdoor or athletic career. Perhaps a physical education teacher would come to mind. At the same height as Helen, she had a sturdier build, a face that was neither round nor quite oval, and ash blonde hair that was similar to a pixie cut although not as short. Her hazel eyes tended to reflect green when she wore her favorite color, as she did tonight. A square-necked cotton knit sweater in forest green with three-quarter length sleeves topped her khaki slacks, and a gold horse head pendant hung from a gold chain. Her thoughts of veterinary school had fallen by the wayside between strained family finances and falling in love her senior year of college, but she still taught riding part time and was a substitute teacher. She particularly loved introducing children to riding and how to properly care for animals. She'd told Helen that while she appreciated the beauty and intricacy of dressage, that wasn't something to which she had ever aspired. The relationship between horse and rider were what she cared about, especially the older horses that were beyond their prime show years. She often talked about the possibility of establishing a horse therapy program, although Helen wasn't certain as to how serious she was about it.

Becky rested her wine glass on her knee. "That was the summer that Gabe's mamma decided to have the house remodeled and even though the major construction was finished, there was all the interior decorating to do. There were workmen in every day, paints to choose, window treatments, and some new furniture to bring in. It was pretty distracting and Gabe needed a quiet place to write. That was also the summer that Dr. Cotton convinced his mother to move into town from her house, the one with the pond that was across the road from the stables. They weren't sure what they wanted to do with the house, so Mrs. Cotton offered to let Gabe use it as a studio. By late in the afternoon when he was about done writing for the day, I would be finishing up with the horses."

Becky gave a half smile, although whether it was for Gabe or the horses was hard to tell. "It had been a hot, sweaty day as usual and I had put the last horse in. Gabe might have been watching from the porch because I was barely out of the barn when he ambled over— that's the best way to describe it, looking cool in a pair of jeans and a short-sleeve blue cotton shirt, a curl of golden hair falling across his forehead. He had two glasses in hand and he said, 'Becky, if a woman loves horses as much as you do, you're bound to love a good mint julep, too,' and I took that icy glass and held it right up to my cheek. Lord, I think I drank it in two swallows."

She touched her cheek lightly with her fingertips. "He invited me to come for a refill and it was as pleasant as it could be. Mrs. Cotton had that pond to the right of her house and it was a sweet little place. It was a cottage really, white picket fence and all. There were pink and white azaleas on the far side of the pond, with dwarf crepe myrtle coming around, and blue hydrangea that made up like a horseshoe. The open part of the horseshoe, to use that description, closest to the house was graveled, though, so you could be right at the edge of the pond without standing on the grass. There were two wooden chaise lounges with a little side table and two big old stumps that had been hauled over to sit on. She had rocking chairs on the porch, of course, but with the sun headed down, it was nicer to be at the pond."

Becky lifted her wine glass for a sip. "I think that might have been the first time I ever truly looked at Gabe, him being right there next to me like that. It was like everyone else has said, though. Gabe got me to talking about the horses, not that I ever needed encouragement to do that. I didn't stay long that day, maybe an hour. I didn't think too much about it either until the next day when I was done, there was Gabe again. I hadn't seen him before then. This time it was a bucket of iced-down beer and he even had a couple of sandwiches in case I was hungry. I didn't have a lot of experience with guys, but I did know that was more considerate than most would be. I was curious about his writing and asked what he was working on."

She put a finger to her lips and giggled. "The next day was

chilled wine, chunks of cheese, and a loaf of bread. It was real bread from the bakery, not sliced white bread. I started looking forward to the end of the day. Even at that age, Gabe was not in a rush, not pushy. I look back sometimes to how he was and I think that he was so sure of himself with girls, and later with women, that he just didn't feel the need to pressure you." Two faint spots appeared on Becky's cheeks. "I had so few dates in high school that I guess I didn't realize Gabe was romancing me. He was just so smooth about it and, well...Gabe was, I mean, I was..."

Helen could see that Becky was struggling. She supplied the words gently. "You hadn't been with a boy yet?"

Becky shook her head quickly and the surge of affection that flowed from the women seemed to lift her past that point. "I don't know that I'd ever really thought about who or when, or if I was supposed to be saving myself for marriage. I can tell you that I had never imagined that Gabriel Thatcher would show an interest in me. It's important for me to say that he wanted me to understand that he was leaving after the summer. He wanted to assure me that he wasn't asking for more than just friendship and that I could be comfortable with the idea that our afternoons together didn't have to involve anything else."

"Were you falling in love with him?" It was Rita's quiet voice.

Becky exhaled deeply. "No, I can't say that. I couldn't put it into words then, but in listening to Gabe, his stories, his poems, there was a...a feeling, I guess, of a man who wanted to love every woman in the world—not love as in 'marry' and not simply using the word 'love' as a magic way to seduce a woman. Goodness, that's an old-fashioned word, isn't it?" Becky's face was a study in tenderness. She paused and, much as Sarah had done, she allowed her gaze to touch on each of her friends before she continued. "Remember, I was coming over after working all day with horses, sweaty and sticky. Aside from having booze and snacks for me, Gabe brought in one of the collapsible basins like for camping and he would have it filled with clean water, a washcloth, and a towel waiting for me along with our happy hour. There just weren't many men that would think of doing something like that. We did make out on more than one occasion, and I have to say that it was Gabe who taught me what a kiss should be." She paused for a smile that seemed turned inward. "Bless his heart, though. He never once tried to go beyond that. He told me repeatedly that the idea that virginity was old-fashioned was nonsense, and no girl should feel pressured to do otherwise."

Her eyes were soft with the memory. "And that was it, my summer with Gabe, although it was really more like six weeks instead of the whole summer. He went back north just as he said and I met Bob when we had a class together. Gabe called me and we had dinner one evening that next summer, but things were getting serious with Bob and I didn't want to risk confusing myself. Gabe said it was wonderful and he hoped we had all the happiness in the world." She looked at the wine glass as though surprised to see it was empty. "You could tell that he meant it and wasn't just saying the words. He genuinely wanted me to be with the right guy."

"And he did," Mary Lou Bell said. "That was a part of Gabe that was truly special. You're correct about him wanting to love all women, or rather the essence of women. That's why he didn't care about age or anything else. Gabe was a man who could see beauty in a woman that had nothing to do with her physical appearance."

Helen fleetingly thought that with Mary Lou's strawberry blonde hair, robin's egg blue eyes, heart-shaped face, and figure that did not bear signs of having two children, Gabe wouldn't have any lack of physical beauty to see. Then again, Mary Lou had been in a fragile place when she was with Gabe.

CHAPTER TEN

Mary Lou gave a wry smile and moved her gaze from Helen, to Katie, to Rita. "Unless I've missed something, I do believe that this will make me the last to speak of involvement with Gabe. Rita, you haven't known us for very long. Are you doing okay with all of this, honey? We're not upsetting you, are we?"

Rita looked properly startled, and if she had been as fair-complexioned as Mary Lou she might have blushed. "I'm okay, just a little…"

"Surprised at how women our age can be carrying on like this?" Katie interjected with an edge of humor. "As the only other one in the room who didn't grow up here, I had no history with Gabe, and didn't know a thing about him. When he moved back and I started hearing of some of his escapades, it did make me wonder if they could be true. It does seem like something you'd read in a romance novel, and if you think of it that way, it's easier." She lifted one hand toward Mary Lou. "My apologies for interrupting, and the floor is yours."

"You're correct, of course. Being with Gabe was like being in a romance novel," Mary Lou said softly. "That was the whole point. That was what he did. He had the ability to talk with a woman and see what exactly it was that she needed in order to experience that feeling." She gestured around the room. "That's what we all understood about Gabe. When you were with him, you were the center of his world. You were all that mattered to him right then." Heads nodded, smiles flitted.

"I was a freshman in high school when he went to college, but there were photographs of him all over the place and a lot of girls still talked about him. Do you know that he took four girls to his senior prom?"

"Oh Lord, I had forgotten about that," Helen said, not meaning to speak, the words tumbling out. What a memory that was! "Virginia was so proud of him and Stanley thought he was a little crazy, but let him take the Cadillac because it had more room in it."

"That's right. It was in the paper," Phyllis chimed in. "Bless their hearts, they were the bookish kind of girls and I don't mean that unkindly. Somehow or other, Gabe found out that none of them had a date for the senior prom and he asked them to all sit with him at lunch one day and said that if they didn't mind, he would like to invite them together as a quartet."

"No one had ever heard of such a thing," Becky added. "My mother was working at what is now Forsythe's and Gabe came in, ordered four wrist corsages, each in a different color, no ordinary white. He had called to check on the color of each girl's dress to get a match and acted as if it was the most normal thing in the world. He paid an extra charge to have them delivered to the girls' houses, too."

"That's what Mary Lou means," Sarah chimed in. "Gabe didn't care that it had never been done or that no one else would have thought of it. The reason that he acted as if it were the most normal thing in the world was because it was for him. These were girls that had been overlooked and he didn't see why it should be that way. It might have seemed foolish to other people, but I'm willing to bet that none of them have forgotten that night."

"You don't forget being with Gabe," Mary Lou said. "No matter that a relationship with him wasn't supposed to be permanent, it was memorable." She took a shuddering breath and released it. No, maybe it was more like a cleansing breath.

"I was bordering on depression when my marriage was coming apart. Anna was barely two years old. From the outside, my marriage and life looked perfect. We had the nice house, Lance had a good job, and Anna was a lovely child with the sweetest disposition. She obviously didn't get it from her daddy." Her voice caught and she waved a hand to signal that she was okay.

"The truth was that Lance had always been sarcastic and quick to criticize people. He hid it in public and then it would all come out when we were alone. He got so bad that I couldn't do anything right. From the time he woke up in the morning until he turned out the light at night, he was chastising me for one thing after another. I hadn't taken up quilting just then and my circle of friends had shrunk to practically nothing, because I dropped out of doing almost everything when Lance kept being so ugly about my friends. I kept thinking that maybe he wanted my attention focused on just him, the baby, and the house, and if I did that, it would make him happy.

It got to where I could hardly eat because my stomach was in such knots, and I lost so much weight that Mamma wanted to drag me to the doctor for a checkup. I had to finally tell her the truth and that I couldn't stand it any longer. She had a hard time believing it until I broke down and squalled like a baby. I could hardly stop to breathe. It was sort of like purging my system, though. I didn't know what to do and she sat me right down and said there was no reason for me to stay in a marriage with a man like that."

Mary Lou shook her head sharply, with a look of determination passing across her face. "There have been nastier divorces for sure, but it was as bad as I ever want to go through. I was so anxious to get out of that marriage. All I wanted was the house and child support for Anna. I didn't care about alimony. The only saving grace was that Lance was offered a job in Atlanta, and he left town after telling me what a pathetic, stupid whiner I was. In a way, he was right. I was a whimpering mess by the time we got through it."

"Honey, it wasn't your fault," Carolyn said with a note of alarm in her voice that Mary Lou would think of herself in those terms.

Mary Lou shook her head again. "I appreciate you saying that, but what I mean is that I hadn't stood up for myself when I should have and I was leaning hard on my parents for support. Mamma was taking care of Anna who, thank God, was too young to understand. Daddy negotiated with the bank to refinance the mortgage and he talked to Bobby Wallington, which is the real reason I got an administrative job in the utilities department." Her smile grew stronger. "That was a boost, of course. Then, thanks to you two," pointing her chin at Helen and Phyllis, "I came into the circle. Thank God, y'all gave me the kind of sister support I needed. I didn't have to get into details, I just soaked up all the friendship that I had been missing." That brought both smiles and dampened eyes.

Mary Lou blinked rapidly. "In thinking about Gabe and y'all, I suppose the best description is like someone who's been in an accident, in my case emotional, going through physical therapy. You're really weak at first, but you regain the strength in your muscles. My job and this circle all helped. But there was still the hole that Lance had left—that sense of loss not for what we had, but for what we should have had, and a fear that maybe I wouldn't ever find it. Men asked me out a few times, and I was scared to say yes. I was scared to think that if I had misjudged Lance so badly, what was to say that I wouldn't make the same mistake again? Those were things that I couldn't put into words at that stage."

She fortified herself with the wine and everyone waited patiently. "Funny, it was a Friday the thirteenth when Gabe came into the office. He was home for a visit and there had been an error in Virginia's bill because of a problem with some new meters. It was real close to quitting time and I'd told Gail and Lillian to take off a little early. They had something at the church that evening and it had been real slow all day, so there was no reason that I couldn't handle the office alone. Anyway, Gabe was looking handsome as usual, with those intense blue eyes of his and that curly golden hair. We were chatting the way you do, and of course he was complimenting me on everything from the style of my hair and the outfit I was wearing to how efficiently I was taking care of the problem."

It was as if laughter and poignancy were woven together in her voice. "I think the radio must have been on and the DJ said something about it being Friday the thirteenth, and Gabe gave me one of those smiles that make your knees feel funny.

"He said, 'It can't be an unlucky day if I get to spend part of it with a beautiful woman like you.' Then he snapped his fingers, pointed to the clock and said, 'Of course, it would be even luckier for me if you would honor me by joining me for dinner.' I thought at first he was joking. He assured me he was serious, and then he asked me when was the last time that I had dressed up and been treated to the kind of romantic dinner that I deserved.

"It was such an off-the-wall question that I blurted out

something like it had been so long that I couldn't remember when." She shook her head slightly. "The next thing I knew, I was calling Mamma to see if she could baby-sit and headed home to go through my closet trying to figure out what to wear.

Exactly like you said, Carolyn, he took me to the Magnolia Inn for a perfect night and he was a perfect gentleman. All he wanted to do was talk about me, about what courage I had in leaving my husband, and how well I was faring as a single parent. When he drove me home, he didn't ask to come in. We stood on the porch and he held my hand and said that he was only going to be in town for another four days. If I could make arrangements, he would love to make the next three nights magical for me."

Mary Lou gave a quick giggle. "Magical! He actually used that word. I honestly wasn't sure what to do; I mean, I had Anna to think of. He said to give him a call to let him know, and then he gave me this kiss on the cheek. It was the sweetest thing in the world."

The color in her cheeks heightened momentarily. "Mamma brought Anna back early in the morning. We stuck her in front of cartoons and talked in a way that I thought might be embarrassing as I tried to explain what Gabe had suggested. I was sure Mamma would tell me to come to my senses, but she didn't. She said she thought Gabe was right and that she and Anna would treat it like a little vacation, and that I could drop her off every afternoon.

"I called Gabe and he told me to be prepared for a surprise each night and to not worry about a thing. Sure enough, he drove us in a different direction each night, finding those darling little inns they write up in travel pieces. Oh, he did start by bringing me a lovely bouquet, a box of Godiva chocolates, mind you, and three bottles of champagne—one for each night when we would return from our sojourn, as he called it. You can't get more like being in a romance novel than that unless you do go away to Paris or some exotic island."

"That was classic Gabe," Sarah said.

Mary Lou nodded once. "And it worked. In those three nights, Gabe told me over and over that this was the way any man with half a brain should treat me. Even though I knew good and well that there wasn't another man around here who would do this, and maybe nowhere else either, it was the best possible therapy that I could have had. I felt a genuine pang when he left town, but he had a bouquet delivered later that day. The note said: To a beautiful woman who deserves a beautiful life."

Her mouth curved into a smile. "I met Waylon about a month later at the Rotary Club banquet where we'd done that quilt for their raffle. Y'all remember? It was the quilt of the town square."

Everyone except Rita nodded. Half or better than the quilts they made each year were in response to requests for raffle prizes. "He seemed like a nice guy, but he was a little shy, too. In a way, though, him not being all glib and flirty was attractive. When he finally managed to ask me for a date, I was ready." Her smile widened at describing her husband. "Waylon can't compare to Gabe in the romance department and that's not important. He's good about birthdays, anniversaries, that kind of thing, and I couldn't be happier."

She picked up her wine glass from the floor. "That's what Gabe gave to me and it's a terrible shame that whoever did this didn't understand what kind of man he really was."

"Well, amen to that," Phyllis said firmly and they all joined as she lifted her glass in a toast.

Helen grabbed the tissue boxes she'd anticipated a need for and passed them around as Becky let the first teardrop trickle.

CHAPTER ELEVEN

Helen eyed the wine and decided that a cup of tea was a better choice. The house was almost echoingly silent after the emotional meeting. Everyone insisted on helping clean up. The conversations carefully moved from the topic of Gabe with the tacit understanding that what needed to be said had been. The farewell hugs seemed to last longer than usual, although no one stayed after. In a way, Helen was glad. She suspected they were all feeling a bit drained with the catharsis of the evening. None of them were strangers to sorrow, but none of them had faced ircumstances like these either. Gabe's reputation, whatever one thought of it, was indisputable and plenty of households had been touched by his, well... him, during the time since he'd begun to be the him of his reputation. Helen wondered how often a similar scene like the quilting circle's had been played out around town since the news of Gabe's death. How many other memories had spilled from women who had been involved with him in whatever manner?

Helen drifted into the den with no intention of turning on

the television. Mug of tea in hand, she went instead and stood in front of the child-size quilt hanging to the left of the window. If the time came, it would come down, be cleaned, and presented to either Ethan and Sharon or Tricia and Justin, depending on which one had a grandson first. An adorable pink one that was in the guest room would herald the birth of a granddaughter. Virginia, Gabe's mother, had helped her design the quilt for a baby boy and given her pieces of fabric from linens in Gabe's room when he'd outgrown the little boy look of nursery rhyme characters.

She and Virginia had been the youngest women then in the quilting circle. It rotated between four houses. She and Mitch had put an offer on this house, hoping they could be completely moved in before the baby was born. They didn't have a lot to move from the two-bedroom cottage they'd been renting and having the quilt ready for the crib that had been handed down from Mitch's side of the family was important to her—not that she didn't love the quilt that her mother had already completed. It was a familiar Noah's ark with a splendid parade of animals. She wanted something she personally designed, though, not a pattern that she usually followed. Although Helen worked full time, the insurance office closed early on Wednesdays and Virginia often came over for afternoon coffee. Naturally, the discussion usually turned to fabrics or ideas for quilts and Helen mentioned what she wanted to do.

Virginia immediately said that she was redecorating Gabe's room and had curtains, sheets, and a bedspread she was planning to cut up for quilting projects and she would be glad to share. She also suggested that Helen ask around her family and see if there were old linens or clothes she could use as well. What a clever idea that had been. She called her mother and mother-in-law later that same day and her sister the next day. Why not have pieces from grandparents, aunts, uncles, and cousins that would all be part of the extended family? The end result was enough fabric in multiple shades of blue that she used to create an inside border of triangles, alternating the direction of the point. Inside the border on a field of light blue were a yellow sun with rays shooting from it, a puffy white cloud, a man-in-the moon of palest green, and a rainbow. They were all cheery symbols with enough colors so they would match whatever color she finally decided on for the baby's room.

That was in the days before parents routinely found out about the sex of the baby beforehand. The fact that she'd carried the baby high and experienced kicks and squirms from early on were all supposed to be signs of a boy, but she wasn't confident enough to decide on blue paint. Ultimately, she'd accepted Mitch's suggestion for him to paint the lower half of the room and the chair rail in blue and the upper half in rainbow stripes. He'd done such a great job that the paint lasted through Tricia's infancy, too.

Lord, the memories that were seeping through her! This was a quilt that she had worked on at home rather than at the quilting circle. As much as she enjoyed and admired the older women, she thought they might want to offer their own advice for design and she wouldn't have known how to politely decline their suggestions. No, Virginia had been the only one to see the quilt in progress and to sit with her in the cozy living room. That was when the room doubled with its original purpose and before Helen established, well, inherited was a more accurate term, the current quilting circle. The light had always been better there than in the family room and it could comfortably hold eight people, up to a dozen with careful arrangement of chairs. The quilting frame was kept folded against the far wall, taken out when they needed it; but back then she hadn't had the nice wall unit to conceal it from view.

The dining room table served for laying out, cutting, and

marking fabric, and as the base for the portable sewing machine that she kept in the closet along with the iron and ironing board. Of course, that meant putting those tools away after she'd used them, since quilting could certainly generate clutter if she didn't keep it under control. She did have a wonderful handcrafted wooden blanket chest at the foot of their bed to hold a lot of her fabrics and patterns.

Funny, she couldn't recall what project Virginia had been working on while she was making the crib quilt. Helen closed her eyes for a moment, bringing back the picture of the two of them. Helen was in the rocking chair that she was breaking in and Virginia was in one of the dining room chairs that she preferred to use. Helen saw it then, the panels of lilies of the valley that Virginia was quilting into an altarpiece for the church. The fabric had been a spectacular purple polished cotton that Virginia bought at a shop in Atlanta. She had gotten extra of the deep green backing fabric that matched the leaves and stems of the flowers. That way, she could use the same fabric for the sashing as well as the binding.

Helen was almost startled to hear the sigh that escaped her, a sound that was filled with affection and sadness. Really, when you thought about it, how tragic it was that no one in the Thatcher family had lived the average life span. Stanley had been maybe fifty-seven, Virginia only sixty-four, and now Gabe. Granted, her husband, Mitch, hadn't made it to sixty, but there had been no known history of pancreatic cancer in his family. The doctor explained that in many cases, it had nothing to do with heredity and there was no reason to fear for Ethan or Tricia. Helen shook her head sharply, bringing back the love and friendship that the quilt represented, not the pain of loss that she didn't want to dwell on.

The tea had cooled and, rather than rewarm it, she thought

that perhaps she would change into her gown and robe and read in bed for a while. She usually kept two books going at a time, one in the den and one by her bed; that way, she wasn't running around the house trying to remember where she'd left her book. The magazines always stayed in the rack, whatever page she was on bookmarked with one of the advertisement postcards that were inevitably stuffed inside.

She meandered back into the kitchen. There was just enough room in the dishwasher for this mug and her breakfast dishes. If she didn't add dishwasher tablets to the grocery list, she would be doing them by hand within a day or two. She kept one of those shopping list pads next to the telephone for this very reason. It was so much simpler to write things down as they occurred to her instead of trying to do it on the way out the door. The pen was still in her hand when the telephone rang, immediately putting her on alert. It was unusual for anyone to call past nine o'clock, and when she heard Father Singletary's voice, she tried not to panic. He couldn't possibly be contacting her unless there was some kind of problem.

"Helen, my dear, it's Father Singletary and I am sorry to call at this hour, but I would like to ask for your help. Although it's not too bad, young Mrs. Raney, Rita, has had an accident and her husband is out of town," he said calmly. "Her injuries are fairly minor, but she does seem to be quite upset and she doesn't have any other family here."

"Are you at the hospital? Of course I'll come," Helen said quickly, thankful that she had switched from wine to tea. Wine, oh goodness. How much had Rita had to drink? She told Father Singletary she could be there in twenty minutes. She thought back to the evening. No, she was certain that Rita had passed on the wine as she usually did. She grabbed her purse from the mudroom where she kept it on top of the dryer, hoping that the priest's definition of fairly minor injuries was not an understatement. Helen was Episcopalian, but all the major churches in town were clustered close together and most participated in the same community events. Father Singletary had been the priest at Saint Mary's Catholic Church for twelve years or so. He was well liked by the parishioners and the community at large. Helen didn't know if he had been at the hospital for visitation or if Rita had called him. She knew that he was often on the hospital grounds. Well, really it was more of a hospital complex now and quite an interesting one in a town no larger than Wallington.

In addition to the hospital, there was an independent living apartment building, as well as another H-shaped building that had a skilled nursing facility in the center and assisted living and long term care services on either side. Father Singletary spent a good deal of time participating in activities with the residents and patients. He might well have been at bingo or with the chess group, then gone by the emergency room on his way out, as was his habit.

Helen was glad she caught almost every traffic light on green and was relieved to see that the emergency room parking lot was nearly empty. She hurried inside, unsure of what she would find.

CHAPTER TWELVE

Helen had seen the hospital go through two major rebuilding projects and watched as the other parts of the complex were added during the past decade. Colorful quilts brightened a room, were useful, and easy to transport. She had long ago lost count of how many quilts she and other members of the circle had contributed to the hospital or, in some cases, helped residents with. The independent living community on the far side of the complex had its own circle, and women in the assisted living facility often quilted as individuals rather than in an organized club. The assisted living population was more fluid, so the number of quilters ebbed and flowed, yet those who were still capable of quilting were always eager to exchange stories, ideas, and fabrics. Members of Helen's circle and other quilters in town frequently dropped by to share the special companionship of spending an afternoon working on projects with women who might no longer be fully mobile, or who were perhaps slowed by dimmed eyesight and stiffened fingers. Limited physical capabilities in no way diminished their love of the craft.

Father Singletary was talking in a low voice to the young nurse at the reception desk and he looked up as Helen approached. He straightened his tall, thin frame, stepped forward, and drew her to the side, where they could speak privately. The bright fluorescence of the open tiled room and the armless chairs with padded vinyl seats, some in green, some in blue, looked like any other emergency room. It was a space intended to be transitory, not comforting. The sole occupants of the waiting room were a middle-aged couple Helen didn't recognize who were both seemingly intent on the magazines they were reading.

"Thank you for coming," Father Singletary said, clasping her hands in his long fingers. "Rita is not badly hurt, but more shaken up and quite distressed." He loosened her hands, his narrow face calm, brown eyes beneath bushy eyebrows concerned, but not distressed. "She apparently swerved her car to miss a dog that had wandered into the street, lost control, ran into a tree, and the air bag deployed. I was in the hospital meeting with the Griffith family; bless them in their hour of need. I always stop by the emergency room on my way out to say hello and to check and see if I can be of any assistance, and this is one of those times when it proved beneficial. Rita appears to be far more upset than the accident calls for, and I thought that perhaps she might like another woman to talk to. I didn't think you would mind me calling at this hour."

"Of course not," Helen said immediately, glancing across the hall to where two of the six cubicles had curtains closed around them. "Does she know I'm here?"

Father Singletary hesitated. "Once I realized that her husband was out of town, I asked if there was anyone I could call for her and she shook her head no without stopping crying. She mentioned that she was coming from the quilting circle as part of the in processing, and I asked if it would be all right for me to call you. She managed to say, 'I wouldn't want to bother Helen,' but I promised her you wouldn't mind."

"Of course not," Helen repeated. "Are they going to release her?"

"They offered to keep her overnight for observation, but she shook her head at that, too, and I think she's probably correct in that her injuries don't really warrant it." He gave a half smile. "I don't know why she's so upset, but I don't think she should be alone just yet and they are processing the paperwork for her release."

"Let me see what I can do," Helen said quietly. "You go ahead and if there's anything else you can help with, I'll call."

"Bless you, Helen, you're a good woman," he said in parting.

Helen didn't know the nurse on duty, but after a quick consultation to explain who she was, she was allowed to poke her head into the curtained cubicle to see if Rita was willing to talk with her. The young woman's delicate frame and cap of dark curls made her look scarcely older than a teenager. Her long sleeved pale yellow tunic top was splotched with who knew what, but it wasn't ripped. Ethan's childhood inclination to copy superheroes had included multiple trips to the emergency room, so Helen was familiar with the triangle of skinned places on Rita's face—bruising that would turn to nasty shades of purple, black, yellow, and green. Her makeup was a messy smear and her eyes puffed red, but Helen had certainly seen worse. At least there were no broken bones or stitches required.

"Helen, you're here," Rita gulped, tears still trickling as Wanda Wallington's granddaughter, Betty, stood patiently with a clipboard.

"Hi, Helen," Betty said, a question in her voice.

"It was quilting circle night," Helen said looking affectionately at Rita. "Steve is out of town and I thought another friendly face might be helpful."

"That is so sweet," Rita said shakily, "but I don't want to trouble...."

"Mrs. Raney, I've known Helen my whole life. Believe me when I say she wouldn't be here if she didn't want to be," Betty said with a coaxing smile. "It would be better for you to be with someone for a little while than to take a cab home."

"Truly, Rita, I'm glad to be here. I can get you home and make sure you're comfortable. You've had a terrible fright."

Rita nodded without speaking this time and reached her hand out to Helen, a slight trembling that stilled when Helen squeezed it lightly.

"Good," Betty said, coaxing transformed into a brisk nurse kind of voice. "I have the discharge instructions and a sample packet of a pain killer that Dr. Turner prescribed. These pills will get you through the night so you don't have to deal with getting the prescription filled until tomorrow."

Fifteen minutes later, Betty rolled Rita out in a wheelchair as Helen brought her car around. Helen was glad to see that despite her disheveled appearance, Rita was sitting upright, her purse in her lap. "I can't tell you how much this means to me," she said, stifling a sob. "I feel so stupid and embarrassed."

"There's not one thing for you to be embarrassed about," Helen said, handing her a packet of tissues that she'd taken from her purse. "You live near here, don't you? In one of the newer developments?"

"Azalea Park. Magnolia Street—427 on the corner of Holly," she said before she sobbed again. "How am I going to tell Steve? The whole front of the car was smashed."

"Honey, cars can be repaired. The fact that you weren't hurt worse than you are is what's important. When does he come home?" Helen assumed she was correct about what Steve's reaction would be, although she hadn't actually had a conversation with him. They'd met in passing at a few social functions, not a setting for deep philosophical discussions.

"Day after tomorrow," Rita choked out. "It isn't the car, it's…" Her voice trailed off and she sobbed again.

Was this the first time Rita had ever been in a wreck? After all, she had never had the experience personally, thank God, and she might be equally upset if she found herself in Rita's place. Losing control of a car in the dark to barrel into a tree would distress anyone.

"The garage is jammed with stuff so we park in the driveway," Rita said wiping her eyes. The outside light shown yellow across the car. "I know it's asking a lot after your coming out like this, but do you think you could come in for a few minutes?"

"Of course," Helen said. "I had no intention of just dropping you off. Let's get you in and settled." Now that she'd shut the engine off, she heard a dog barking—it sounded like a small breed.

"That's Toffee," Rita said. "He's a sweetheart and will stop as soon as he knows it's us. Are you okay with a dog? Oh, and there's Smoky, the cat. He probably won't come out, though."

"I'm fine with both," Helen said, jumping out to get the door for Rita. "Do you need to lean on me?"

Rita slowly swung her legs from the car and passed her purse to Helen. Her brown leather flats meant she wouldn't have to try and wobble on heels. "I have to move carefully, but if you can take this, the keys are in the bottom. They always wind up down there, don't they?"

Azalea Park was one of two new developments in town that boasted a clubhouse and a pool. The houses were a mix of single and two-story homes in either brick or vinyl siding, fenced backyards, and small front yards. The entryways were recessed rather than having front porches. The Raney's house was a gray vinyl-sided ranch with dark red shutters and raised beds running the width of the front. Roses took up the part of the bed that was visible in the pool of light. A modest-sized magnolia tree would someday cover most of the yard. Helen unlocked the dark red paneled front door to the sound of excited barking and she stepped back to let Rita enter ahead of her.

The introduction to the golden-colored terrier mix involved several excited yips and sniffing and clattering of toenails on the ceramic tiled entryway. Helen decided it was time to exercise a little maternal prerogative that comes with having grown children. She persuaded Rita to let her brew tea while she took a hot shower, Toffee scampering at her heels.

The kitchen was nicely laid out in a neutral palette of beiges, creams, and browns; stainless steel appliances, as was all the rage; granite countertops with a travertine backsplash; and maple cabinetry. There was space for an island if they decided to add one, although for now there was a round oak pedestal table with four armless chairs featuring rush seats. Recessed lighting was supplemented by a frosted glass pendant over the double stainless steel sink. The stove had one of the stainless steel vent hoods that was more modern looking than Helen cared for.

The smallest in a set of square canisters in dark red enamel was labeled Tea in black script, and Helen easily located cups, saucers, spoons, and napkins.

"In the cookie jar there are some more of the bar cookies I brought tonight," Rita said when she came in, Toffee still at her heels. "I think it would be better for me to have chocolate for comfort than a glass of wine."

"Especially if you've taken a pain pill," Helen agreed, glad to see that Rita's tears seemed to have stopped. "You sit, I'll get them," she instructed.

"The shower worked wonders. I'll do the pill later," Rita said, easing into a chair and patting the one to her right. Toffee hopped up and reclined with his head toward Rita. She was bundled in an ankle-length yellow terry cloth robe, and pale green brushed cotton pajamas showing through where the robe was open. Her towel-dried curls clung damply to her oval face, her eyes brown like dark roast coffee, a faint olive tone to her skin. Hadn't she once mentioned that her grandmother was Italian?

Helen delivered the plate of cookies first, then brought the tea and took the vacant chair to the left. Rita sighed deeply. "I think I owe you an explanation as well as my thanks," she said, her voice more stressed than Helen had hoped.

"You don't owe me a thing," Helen said warmly. "This is what friends are for."

Rita nodded, mixed sugar into her tea, and reached for a dark chocolate, almond, and coconut bar that had been a hit only a few hours before. "Then maybe what I should say is that I would really appreciate it if I could talk to you. I hate to ask with everything else you've done tonight." She took a tissue from her pocket and dabbed at the corner of one eye. She hadn't looked directly at Helen yet.

Helen softened her voice. "Rita, all of us in the circle have sat in one another's kitchen at some time or the other feeling sad, angry, foolish, or lost. You haven't been with us long enough to know that, but I think you got the idea with all that was said earlier. I'm right here if you want to tell me something."

She nodded and lifted her eyes to Helen's, the tears spilling over as she caught them, then sniffed loudly. "Well yes, that's part of why I so much need to talk. You see, it wasn't at all that I didn't understand about Gabe and the effect that he'd had on women. It was, oh God, it was just the opposite and I couldn't say anything." Her voice quavered and Helen reached her hand out to touch the sleeve of Rita's robe.

"Honey, it's okay, believe me. I hate to see you in such a state. You can tell me as much or as little as you like because there is not one thing you're likely to tell me that I haven't heard before. From what I'm seeing, though, it might be better to get whatever this is inside you out into the open. I can almost promise you that it won't come out sounding as bad as you think it will."

Rita's sigh was so forlorn that Toffee lifted his head and whimpered for a pat. "It's okay, boy, Helen is right. I need to get this out." She lifted the cookie and held it to her mouth. "I can't tell this without a little chocolate for strength."

Helen smiled encouragement, took a bite of cookie, too, and waited for Rita to unfold a story that she suspected was neither unique nor as bad as the young woman imagined. She savored the taste of the treat and Helen was willing to bet they came from Lisa Forsythe's bakery. Not that she thought Rita couldn't have made them, but with working full-time at the veterinarian's office, she might not have had time to bake before coming to the circle, and these tasted fresh.

Rita ate the entire cookie and drank a swallow of tea, then brought her gaze to meet Helen's. Her red, puffy eyes were dry. "Steve and I had our second anniversary four months ago, right after I joined the circle. There was a while, though, when I wasn't sure we were going to make it that long." A pensive look crossed her face.

"Lots of people refer to us as practically newlyweds, and I suppose in a way that's true. I don't know if I ever mentioned that we met about six months before we got married. Steve was with a manufacturing company in Cincinnati and I had my first job as a vet's assistant. One of the animal shelters was having a fundraiser that included a 5-kilometer run/walk/bike kind of thing. The company president's wife was on the board, so a bunch of people from Steve's company came out to support the event." She shook her head. "I'm rambling already."

"Take your time," Helen said. "I'm fine, really."

"Well, to get past that part, Steve and I hit it off and we had a fairly short engagement period. We rented a house while we were thinking about exactly where we wanted to live. He's from Akron and not as close to his family as I am to mine, but I knew that we might move as part of his career. Things were fine starting out, the whole newlywed bit for sure, even though I hadn't realized that Steve could be as moody as he was." She turned the cup on the saucer, not drinking from it. "I'd come home all bubbly about this or that in the clinic, and at times it was like Toffee and Smoky were the ones I was talking to. Steve could go for days with hardly a word, and when I would try to get him to tell me about work, he would just shrug and say he'd rather watch TV."

"Men can bottle things up," Helen said quietly.

Rita almost smiled. "That's what my mother told me. It was all right, though, and then the father of one of Steve's college roommates had the chance to buy into the factory here. I don't understand all of it, but because of the expansion they have planned, they wanted someone with a strong logistics and distribution background. That's what Steve does, you know."

Ah, there was that wifely pride in her voice.

"No offense, but I'd never heard of Wallington and it was going to be my first time to leave home. I didn't mind that," she said quickly. "It's an adjustment, though."

"Of course it is," Helen said, remembering some of those early calls when Tricia left home.

"It's lovely here, I had a wonderful time getting the house arranged, and it took me no time at all to find a job with Dr. Dickinson." She lifted her eyes to Helen and tapped the edge of her cup with her forefinger. "People here are so friendly, but they're also, well, I mean, when you don't grow up here..."

"It's very much like being the new kid in school, isn't it?" Helen supplied gently.

Rita nodded rapidly. "Yes, and I'd never been through that, and didn't realize what it would be like to not know anyone. Even though there are a number of activities at the church, and Father

Singletary is a good priest, I haven't become involved with any groups. Most of the women my age have babies or young children and that keeps them really busy."

"Was Steve traveling from the beginning?" Helen thought she saw where the story was going.

Another deep sigh from Rita. "Yes, and then there was the part that I didn't know." She looked at her empty cup. "May I get you a refill?"

Helen rose. "You sit. I left the burner on low so the water is still hot. I'm listening."

Rita pushed her cup forward. "Thank you. Okay. What I didn't understand, and as it turns out, and Steve didn't know, was that there was some kind of internal arguing going on in the factory. His friend's father had been allowed to buy in over the objections of this one man, and he was causing problems. Not surprisingly, since Steve was an outsider too, not to mention being brought in by the new investor, he was giving Steve a hard time. Him being on the road a lot more than we thought was a piece of it."

Helen brought two fresh cups of steaming tea to the table. "I imagine that was Ross Lawrence, Raymond's brother."

Rita looked startled. "How did you know that?"

Helen smiled. "Ross has always been the complete opposite of Ray and from what little I understand, they had a real disagreement about how to run the factory after Ray Sr. passed away. Ray Sr.'s wife, Maureen, had never liked the place, said that Ray Senior had always put the factory ahead of her as a priority, and she went to Savannah to be near Cheryl, their daughter. Ray Jr. finally bought Ross out about three or four months ago, if I remember correctly."

Rita nodded rapidly. "Yes, and that's all a part of this. See, I didn't know about those problems. What I knew was that Steve was gone a lot, and when he was home, well, he was moodier than ever. I tried to ask him what was wrong and he would say, 'Nothing that we can do anything about, so there's nothing to talk about,' and he'd go into the den to turn the TV on, or into his office and play computer games. I mean, everything was supposed to be so good for us, and it just wasn't that way."

Toffee stirred again, the pitch in her voice rising. She stroked the dog's head. "It's okay, boy, I'm almost done."

"It was my birthday and Steve was out of town again," She held the cup before she took a sip. "He'd forgotten, Helen, he'd forgotten my birthday. Not even a card."

"Oh," Helen said without further comment.

"Yeah, and I was so angry that I said, 'Fine, I'll go out to dinner myself,' and I went to the Wallington Inn." A sip of tea, then it was as if she were gaining strength as she talked. "You probably know that was one of Gabe's favorite places and here I was at the bar after dinner, feeling, well, I guess abandoned is the best word. That night it was as if I were questioning everything— the man I married, us moving here, what was the point? What was I supposed to do about it?"

Helen nodded, picturing the scene in her mind. This was indeed a scene that had been repeated many times around Gabe.

"There had been a man sitting between Gabe and me, and when he left, Gabe asked if he could move next to me. I wasn't what you would call in the mood to be hit on, but he didn't come across that way—more like, well, I'm not sure how to describe it."

"He was smoothly charming with a slow smile that took your breath away," Helen said quietly.

Rita gave another sigh, wistful this time instead of the previous sadness. "Yes, that was it, exactly like everyone talked about tonight. I'm not sure when I admitted it was my birthday and he ordered us a bottle of champagne—champagne from a man I didn't know. It was a weeknight and the bar was practically empty by eight o'clock, so it was like we were alone in this little bubble. He started telling me all sorts of amusing stories and showering me with compliments. God, it was precisely the kind of attention that I needed. I'm not that much of a drinker and I'd already had two glasses of wine, so when we finished the bottle, I wasn't in shape to drive home. Gabe insisted that he drive me and said I could get my car the next day."

Her look at Helen was calmer. "I was feeling as giddy as I can ever remember feeling, and when we got here I invited him in for another drink. I did not want this man to go away, and I can't honestly say what I really intended. We went into the living room and I poured us both a brandy. I never drink brandy, but it seemed like such a fitting thing to do. I kicked off my shoes and curled up on the couch next to him; I wasn't making the first move, but there was no way that I wasn't sending a message."

Helen reached her hand out to grasp Rita's. The tears trickled, running down her chin. "Do you know what Gabe did, though? He took me into his arms and held my head against his chest. He said that I was beautiful and tempting and he would be honored to taste the sweetness of my lips. Who talks like that? But he didn't think that was what I truly wanted."

Rita removed her hand so she could retrieve another tissue from her pocket. "I pulled back and the look in his eyes was so sympathetic that I did this," she said and lifted the tissue. "I burst into tears. I mean it was a waterfall. That man pulled me to his chest again and just let me cry it all out."

She ruffled Toffee's ears. "I'd locked poor Toffee out in the backyard and after I finally stopped crying, Gabe said, 'How about if I let the dog in and make us some coffee?' It was crazy. Like it was the most normal thing in the world for him to pick up this woman in a bar, take her home, and instead of, well, you know, he's comforting me and making sure my dog is all right."

"That sounds like Gabe," Helen said, not overly surprised.

"So, he makes the coffee and brings it in. Toffee hops on the couch with us, and the next thing I know, instead of us, well, you know, it's like he's listening, really listening to me pour out all this worry and anxiety."

The tears stopped and a tentative smile started at the corners of her mouth. "When I finally ran out of things to blubber about, Gabe said that most men had difficulty expressing their feelings and that he had the sense Steve was probably worried that he was letting me down."

Helen briefly remembered how intuitive Gabe could be, but then perhaps that was why he was a talented writer. "How was that?"

Rita set the wadded tissues on the side of her saucer. "It's funny. I asked him the same thing. He said that if Steve had moved me away from my home, brought me to a place where we were supposed to have this great opportunity and it wasn't working out, then he might think that he had made the mistake, and that I was disappointed in him. He might be afraid of losing me and did not know how to bring up the subject. Gabe said that he would find it easier to clam up rather than to try and talk about his fears."

"It is difficult for most men to express feelings like that," Helen agreed.

"As silly as this is going to sound, it really was like the cartoons where the light bulb comes on over your head. I thought about how instead of continuously asking Steve what was wrong, maybe I could tell him what I liked about being here and that I wanted to help make it happy for him." Rita straightened her shoulders. "When Gabe left, he gave me the sweetest kiss on the cheek and said that he thought things would work out for us."

"And then?"

"I was off the next day since I was scheduled to work Saturday, and I slept really late. I woke up when Steve called all apologetic about missing my birthday, saying that he hadn't called the florist in time. About an hour later this huge bouquet was delivered, and I decided that when he came home I was going to try my new approach."

Rita's voice had grown stronger. "I fixed his favorite meal that night and said that forgiveness for missing my birthday would cost him one hour of talk time." She reached for another cookie. "You could tell he wasn't thrilled with the idea, but we did it and Gabe was right. Steve was worried that the politics within the company might go the wrong direction and that he would be tossed aside. If that happened, there wouldn't be an equivalent job here and our plans for the house and for starting a family would all be up in the air."

She waved the cookie like a little baton. "I told him that none of that mattered and that we would find a way to deal with it if we had to." She lowered the cookie. "It was maybe a month later that Mr. Lawrence bought his brother out, the whole atmosphere in the factory changed, and Steve was put in a new position where he didn't have to travel anywhere near as much."

She reached out a cookieless hand. "That was about the same time that I saw the beautiful quilt the circle had made for the church raffle, and you invited me to come join you."

"And we are so glad you did," Helen said, waiting for the final piece to tonight's drama.

Rita nibbled the cookie. "Not nearly as glad as I am, but the thing with tonight was this: I've always wondered if I should have confessed about Gabe. I mean, if he had been a different kind of man, I would have been guilty of cheating on my husband. It all came flooding back when everyone was talking and I kept feeling like I was being a terrible hypocrite for not saying my part. That's why I was so distracted driving, and then having Father Singletary showing up in the emergency room like that, well, it was just too much."

Helen extended her hand, comfortable now with what she needed to say. "Honey, what you also heard were women who have known each other for a decade and more. Not that anyone would have thought badly of you, but it's understandable that you couldn't say all of this at the circle." She squeezed Rita's fingers again. "As for confessing, well, I've always thought that was sort of an advantage of being Catholic. I can promise you that Father Singletary has heard more than one confession about a woman having impure thoughts about Gabriel Thatcher. I'm touched that you've confided in me, but I tell you with all my heart that I don't think you are deceiving Steve in any way by not telling him about Gabe."

The return squeeze of Rita's hand was more expressive than her face. Her voice was low and questioning. "Really? That's how you see it?"

Oh my, to be twenty-something again! Helen spoke in as loving a tone as she could. "Absolutely. You were going through a rough patch that happens in a lot of marriages. If talking to Father Singletary will help you put this behind you, then sure. Otherwise, try and let it go."

The anxiety had not yet left the young woman's voice. "You don't think that I was subconsciously trying to punish Steve?"

Helen gave one more gentle squeeze. "First, I believe you're being too hard on yourself. And second, I will let you in on a secret about Gabe that should make you feel better." She paused as a puzzled look crossed Rita's face. "Gabe didn't mess around with married women."

Rita was so startled that she released Helen's hand and pressed her fingers to her lips. "What? After everything I've heard about him?"

Helen allowed a tiny sigh to escape. "That's what so few

people know—knew about him. Like someone said, for Gabe it never was about making conquests. Oh, he absolutely would flirt with a married woman—buy her drinks, take her to dinner even—but he drew the line there. If he were here to ask, I can guarantee that what he saw in you that night was the need for someone to lean on, talk to, and, okay, unburden yourself to."

Rita nodded once slowly. "That is what happened." She tilted her head. "His reputation? Was it a lie?"

"Oh, I wouldn't call it that," Helen said softly. "You felt his magnetism and you heard everyone earlier. With Gabe it was easy to mistake what he was really about, and he never bothered to correct the impression. The only reason that I know is because his mother, Virginia, and I were good friends. During the last weeks she was alive, I spent extra time with her.

One day, Gabe and I had this genuinely candid discussion over a cup of tea when Virginia had drifted off to sleep. I finally asked him why on earth he let people think what they did about him, and he laughed. He said that it was usually too difficult to change someone's mind once they set it; after all, as long as he knew the truth, that was what mattered. So you see, what Gabe picked up on was your emotional distress, not anything else."

Rita's smile was a welcome sight, "How can I ever repay you for tonight?"

"By not worrying about it," Helen said and stood. "If you're think you're able, then I imagine a pain pill and sleep are what you need."

Rita rose and Toffee sat up expectantly. She pushed her chair back and stepped to embrace Helen. "I'm so glad I found you and the circle."

Helen held the girl, as she would have hugged Tricia. "Like I told you, this is what friends do for one another."

CHAPTER THIRTEEN

Justin was glad that Mrs. Turner was able to see him early. He'd been by the station to double check that he hadn't somehow missed a report on the whereabouts of Paul Newton. No luck, though, in sighting him or his truck. At least three people told him this was not unusual, that Newton had been running the woods since he was old enough to walk and he often took off for days at a time. Okay, but how often did he do that following the only murder the town had seen in twenty years—especially after the murder of a man that Paul was suspected as having been angry with?

As an added step, Sheriff McFarlane had personally contacted a friend of his with the Georgia Wildlife Resources Division. "All those guys know the Newton boys and if Paul's gone deep in the woods, they're the ones likely to run across him," he said when Justin gave him a status update.

The county forensics technician had been quick in tracking down the real addresses of the women from Thatcher's e-mail account, none of which yielded likely suspects. Mike Gabler was eliminated because he and a cousin had left for a bass tournament in Louisiana two days prior to the murder. That left Mrs. Turner, or rather her husband, Joe Turner, and Tommy Hillman since the sheriff said there was no way in his experience that Fred Hillman would have gone to see Gabe in private. He was a man who preferred to do his mouthing off in as public a forum as he could find—be it in speaking or a constant stream of letters to the *Wallington Gazette*.

Mrs. Turner stepped onto the stoop of their white painted brick house and waved for him to come in the front door. Like Helen's neighborhood, this was an older one—a mix of hardwood and pine trees in the yards with houses that all looked to have been built in the 1960s to maybe the 1980s. There were a few split-level models, but no two-story ones, on a short street with no traffic.

"Do come in, officer. I have coffee made if you'd like some— oh, and cinnamon rolls if you haven't had breakfast." She held the screen door open; the white wooden door with a large etched-glass oval inset was propped open with a heavy looking metal green frog. "I have us in the living room," she said, motioning him to either chair or couch. Coffee items, napkins, and a plate with two cinnamon rolls were neatly arranged on the coffee table.

Abigail Turner was of average height, mid-thirties, he would guess, and pretty in the way that would usually make a man look twice when passing her on the street. Her shoulder-length hair was a wheat blonde shade and her blue eyes showed just a trace of anxiety. She had to know why he was here.

Justin took the stuffed easy chair and Mrs. Turner perched on the edge of the pale blue fabric couch. "I would rather do this over a cup of coffee," she said holding the plain white china carafe.

"Black is fine," Justin said, relieved that she was going to be direct.

She stirred sweetener and cream into her cup, both of them ignoring the rolls. If he hadn't been listening for it, he would have missed the squeak in her voice that she hurried to make sound calm. "How... how do we do this?"

He took a sip of coffee. It was quite good. He then set the cup down to take up his notebook. "The timeline of your... relationship with Mr. Thatcher, and whether or not your husband was aware of it, are our main concerns," he said, watching her body language. She had that shoulders-back-legs-crossed-at-the-ankle posture many of the women in town seemed to adopt.

She exhaled slowly. "Relationship? Well, you couldn't really call it that, I don't think. It hadn't progressed to, well, to that." Anguish crossed her face. "I'll explain in a minute, but I presume the real question is if I think that Joe could have been responsible for Gabe's...Gabe's death." Her voice faltered briefly, although she didn't break eye contact.

"Yes ma'am, that is the main question."

"Let's see, it's motive, opportunity, and means, isn't it? That's what's in all the detective books and on television." She was stating a fact, not mocking, and didn't wait for his response. "Joe is certainly in good enough physical shape and he's never backed down from a fight. As for opportunity, he owns a used car business and he often takes test drives or is otherwise gone from the office for extended periods." She said the last two words with an odd emphasis before she continued. "Motive? Well, if you mean, when did he learn about Gabe? That would have been about a week ago, although I would say my...my encounters with Gabe were very brief and ended almost two months ago."

She drew in a deep breath and exhaled. "You see, it wasn't that

Gabe and I were ever together alone, it was actually some long lunches."

Justin didn't show his surprise at the statement. "How was it that your husband found out and what was his reaction?"

She gave a half smile. "It's one of those stupid things you don't think of as ever happening, and we had a nasty fight because of it." She held her cup in her right hand and lifted her left. "However, my being with Gabe was my reaction to Joe spending way too much time with Miss Big Hair, Wears-Her-Jeans-Way-Too-Tight, Ruby Greer." She lowered her hand. "The fight was as much about that as the other."

"If you could clarify that a bit, ma'am," Justin tried again, still not quite following her.

Mrs. Turner finished her coffee and glanced at his left hand. "How long have you been married, officer?"

"A little over four years," he said patiently.

"You're Tricia Crowder's husband, aren't you? Helen's son-in-law? And please stop ma'aming me. It's Abigail." She waved her hand for him not to say anything to that. "You're right—let me answer the question in a useful way. Joe and I are coming up on our fifteenth anniversary. We were high school sweethearts. His daddy started Auto World. I work out of the house, by the way, selling Avon and Tupperware both. Joe has always had a tendency for flirting, although what happens when he goes off on fishing trips with his brother I neither know nor want to know."

Justin almost reminded her of getting to the point, but thought he would give her another few minutes.

"I've known about Gabe all my life. What woman raised here doesn't? I was a big fan of his writing. It was common knowledge how a woman who wanted to get involved with Gabe Thatcher could hang around the Wallington Inn, Herb's, or a couple of other places.

My point is this: we're an ordinary family with two kids—a boy and a girl—and everything that comes with a nice, small town, middle-class life; I can't say when, but the truth is that I suppose Joe and I both forgot that 'ordinary' was not a bad thing. Miss Big Hair worked at the Quail Roost Bar where Joe and his friends go, and apparently she started hanging all over him and no matter what his real intent was, he seemed to be enjoying himself. I found out from a friend who saw them together and decided I should know."

She shrugged, her expression neutral. "I was angry, of course, and thought about all kinds of things to say and what to do. Then I decided that what was good for the goose was good for the gander and I would just see what this was all about. Joe went off on one of his weekend fishing trips and I got myself all dolled up and took myself right on down to the Wallington Inn. Later that night I was having a lovely dinner with Gabe."

Justin coughed. "Well ma'…Abigail, I see how it started, but you said your husband didn't know then?"

She shook her head so hard that her gold teardrop earrings swung. "I will tell you that Gabe Thatcher knows how to make a woman feel appreciated, but about the time we had two or three lovely lunches together, Miss Big Hair ran off with some trucker and Joe suddenly started coming home earlier from his boys' nights out. I figured that things could get out of hand with Gabe, too, and told him how much I had enjoyed being with him, but I wouldn't be seeing him again."

She tapped her fingers against the rim of the empty coffee cup. "In looking back, the e-mails I sent to Gabe did make it sound like there was more going on than there was and I should have deleted them." She flicked her gaze away and brought it back to Justin. "Like I said, about a week ago, Joe's computer was giving him problems. He came home to get some things, and while I was out of the house he went into my computer. I guess I left my e-mail open and he just couldn't help taking a look."

"Did he confront you that day?" This was what Justin needed.

She nodded. "He was pacing up and down this floor to where I'm surprised he didn't wear a hole in the carpet. I hadn't been in the door more than two minutes when he started in about how I could do this to him." Indignation flashed through her eyes. "The kids were at school, of course, and I let him have it right back."

"Did he threaten harm to you or to Mr. Thatcher?"

She paused for a moment, a small frown creasing her forehead. "He had some harsh words about Gabe, but I can't recall him threatening to do anything to him, especially not when I told Joe it was his fault that all this got started in the first place." Her smile was a little sad. "I guess we must have yelled at each other for twenty minutes or so and then we both sort of ran out of breath. Joe, to his credit, took the first step and said that maybe we needed to calm down."

"And that's what happened?"

Abigail flexed as though to stand. "Yes, we started talking like adults and a lot of things came out—things that we're working on. If we're being honest, I suppose we both recognized that we had a choice to make. We could try to get through this or we could walk away. It was hard and there are moments when we realize that we're not totally past it, but we are mostly there, I think."

Justin stood and closed his notebook. "Is your husband at his office this morning?"

"Yes, and, if I may ask, how much of this has to go into your report or whatever it is you do?" She wasn't able to completely hide her concern.

"Abigail, we'll keep this as quiet as we can, but I can't make any promises."

She saw him to the door. "I understand, and is it okay if I call Joe and let him know you're on the way? It might save you some time when you get there."

"That's fine," Justin said, thinking that if Joe left the office rather than wanting to talk to him that would be a point of interest. He mentally reviewed what Mrs. Turner had said, knowing from too many domestic calls that a man can claim to be okay about something and that not be the case. It can either fester like a splinter in the finger or a later remark can reignite the anger. A week wasn't a long time since learning about his wife's flirtations with Gabe. The questions were if Mr. Turner had an alibi and if he would be willing to have his fingerprints taken. They needed to determine if his was one of the two unidentified sets.

The sheriff had explained that Joe Turner's Auto World wasn't the kind of used car places of bad jokes. It was the kind of place where you didn't have to worry about something falling off the car when you drove it from the lot. There were only two salesmen other than Mr. Turner, and they worked on salary, not commission, so there wasn't the pressure to talk someone into a vehicle they might not want. Mr. Turner's father had started the business after World War II based on honest dealings. And with his son's marketing skills, it tripled in size after the current Mr. Turner took over.

Joe Turner was waiting by the front door when Justin got out of the patrol car. He might not be a typical used car salesman, but he did look like one. He wore a light blue short-sleeve shirt with a navy blue and green striped tie, navy blue slacks, and polished black lace-up shoes. He was Justin's height with a stockier build, dark brown hair cut short, and gold wire-rim glasses. Justin also noted his brown eyes and a nose that had been broken, although not recently. His eyebrows looked a little like fuzzy caterpillars and a small jagged scar was by his left earlobe. He was in good shape without being muscular. Justin guessed him to be a golfer.

"Officer Kendall," he said in that voice that salesmen were known for, with the wide smile and a firm handshake to match. Was that something they taught you or were those natural characteristics that led you into sales? "It's a pleasure to meet you, I mean, not under these exact circumstances, you understand."

Justin immediately added good poker player to his assessment of the man. "Is there somewhere private we can talk, sir?"

"Joe, call me Joe," he said and looked over his shoulder. Both of his other salesmen were out of hearing distance with potential clients. He cleared his throat. "Sure, my office is right inside. Get you a cup of coffee, cola?"

"No, I'm fine," Justin said, following him into the rectangular red brick building that was filled with light coming through the two large windows, despite being covered with lettering about the business.

The layout was functional with standard décor. Dappled beige short pile carpet covered the floors, and light blue paint was the choice for the walls dominated with NASCAR posters. Three offices were to the left and a reception desk was to the right, with two more desks behind that. One desk had a telephone and computer, the other only a telephone and an empty in-box. A woman was speaking on the telephone, her face not clear because of the angle at which she was sitting. Blue metal filing cabinets lined the far wall and a perpendicular wall blocked what Justin assumed was another area of the office.

The woman at the reception desk looked vaguely familiar, although Justin couldn't place the name. She was fiftyish, on the plump side, wore glasses with a dark-colored frame, and wore her graying brown hair in a twist. She, too, was on the telephone, an expression of utter boredom on her round face.

"Have a seat, and let me close the door," Turner continued casually as he then took his place behind a desk devoid of stray paper. The desk held a telephone on the corner, a computer to the left, and an inbox on the right with a single file folder in it. "Abigail called right after you did," he said evenly and dropped the salesman pitch voice. "What is it I can answer?"

"Your wife indicated you both had a pretty intense argument about Mr. Thatcher," Justin said forthrightly.

"We did," he acknowledged, clearing his throat. "Abigail gave as good as she got, too," he said. "She tell you that?"

"Yes, and also that you had some strong words about Mr. Thatcher. Did you contact him about the situation?"

Mr. Turner was shaking his head before the question was finished. "Nooo," he drew out the word. "No, sir, not at all. I was mad. I'll admit that and if Gabe Thatcher had walked in the door, I'm not going to say I wouldn't have punched him in the nose." He hesitated. "Well, I mean, it's a natural reaction."

Justin nodded.

"Abigail told you right, though; we got through the yelling part and we're working on trying to put this behind us. I can see how a man would have it in for Gabe, but it wasn't me."

"You were here all day on the twelfth?" Justin had his notebook out.

The other man looked uncomfortable for the first time. "Well now, no, I wasn't. I had the Rotary Club lunch at eleven thirty. Then Mrs. Blackwell, who's been a customer since my daddy owned the place, was thinking about swapping her car so I went out to her house like I always do. She prefers to do business over her kitchen table."

"And that was what time, please?" Justin noticed that

Mr. Turner briefly looked away before he regained eye contact.

"That was a little after one o'clock, but it's kind of a leisurely thing with Mrs. Blackwell. Have a cup of coffee, piece of pie. So, it was pushing three o'clock, I'd say, before I was back here."

Justin pointed his pen. "I see you have a scrape on your right hand."

Mr. Turner rubbed it self-consciously. "I'm in the used car business. I check every car out personally and pretty much always have scrapes and scratches on my hands."

"I can understand that," Justin said smoothly. "Would you be willing to come down to the station and let us take your fingerprints?"

Mr. Turner looked startled at that. "Uh, well now, well, it isn't that I have anything to hide." He looked out the window of his office. "The problem is, I do that and won't everybody see me, I mean, getting fingerprinted? Town like this, word will get around fast. You know what I mean?"

Justin held his pen over the notebook as if ready to make an entry. "It would help with the investigation," he said without inflection.

Mr. Turner sighed. "Okay, I guess it will be best. Can I come down after lunch? You know, not being seen leaving right away with you?"

Justin thought rapidly. They couldn't get immediate results anyway and a couple of hours wouldn't hurt. "One o'clock, then?"

"Sure, yeah, sure thing," he said, as the telephone rang.

"Go ahead and take that," Justin said and stood. "I'll let Sheriff McFarlane know you'll be coming in."

Mr. Turner half stood, grabbing the telephone with his left hand and extending his right for a shake.

Justin couldn't decide whether to laugh or shake his head in exasperation when he got into his patrol car. While Joe Turner didn't feel right for Gabe's murder, there was motive, little doubt about means, and he did not have an airtight alibi. That made him at least a person of interest, if not a suspect. The idea that he agreed Turner could come in later for fingerprints would have gotten him laughed at (or more likely screamed at) for being an idiot in Baltimore. Maybe Sheriff McFarlane's style was rubbing off on him.

CHAPTER FOURTEEN

Justin stopped briefly at the station. Sheriff McFarlane hadn't been surprised about the Turners. There was no word yet about Newton, and Justin was on his way to see Tommy Hillman. Of all the men impacted by Gabe Thatcher, the connection to the Hillmans seemed to be the most tenuous except that the sheriff agreed with Helen. "Tommy's got a mean streak in him, always has had," he'd said. "He's never crossed the line as far as throwing a first punch, but he's goaded plenty of fights. That's usually his style, but Gabe wrote some pretty provoking words about Fred, so it's worth checking up on where Tommy was at the time of the murder."

The Hillman Insurance Agency was one block off the historic town square in what was referred to as the "modern section" of downtown, although Justin felt that the idea of 1970s-style commercial buildings as "modern" was a bit of a stretch. It was a standard red brick strip of four offices with a shared parking lot, each office suite identical with double plate-glass doors and gold lettering designating the business name. If he remembered what Tricia had told him, Helen had been at the agency with the original owner and she retired when he sold it to Mr. Hillman.

Justin stepped inside. The carpet was a better grade than at Auto World, gray with blue undertones, and the walls were two-toned, medium blue on the bottom half and creamy white above. No posters here—the décor was more decorous, if you were in the mood for a pun. Hanging on the wall to his left were framed photographs of Wallington that were positioned to the left and right of a colorful quilt that featured a depiction of the town square and Wallington June 1, 1827 sewn below it. Ah, that looked like something Helen would have made for the office. He didn't understand the whole interest in quilting, but it seemed as if practically every older place in town had a commemorative quilt to announce some sort of anniversary.

"You must be Officer Kendall," the woman behind the desk in the reception room said, rising from her chair. A nameplate in the center of the desk read "Doris Strickland," and she offered her hand. She was in her mid-to-late fifties with short, wavy hair much too black to be natural at her age, and Justin couldn't help thinking that if it had been a lighter color, she could have been a double for Aunt Bea on the old Mayberry television series. To be honest, he often thought of characters from that series as he went on patrol around town. Well no, Mayberry never claimed to have a character like Gabe Thatcher, as far as he knew, and for sure they didn't have an episode with a murder.

"Yes ma'am, I'm here to speak with Mr. Hillman."

She removed her tortoiseshell readers, pale green eyes appraising him with a flinty edge that cancelled the Aunt Bea image. "I'll let Tommy know you're here," she said, pointing to a door on the left. Directly behind her was a large room with another set of double glass doors where Justin saw four desks. The muffled sounds of talking and telephones ringing leaked through. The four women inside all looked to be busy.

Mrs. Strickland, assuming that was her, held the door open for Justin. Tommy Hillman was halfway around the desk, thrusting a hand at him—a right hand that, like Joe Turner's, had bruising across the knuckles.

"Tommy Hillman. Justin, isn't it?" he said with a tight smile. "Married to Tricia Crowder, aren't you? Helen's daughter?"

"Yes," Justin said, deliberately returning the hard grip that was obviously intended to broadcast that Hillman was a man's man despite working behind a desk. While he was better dressed than many of the neighborhood thugs Justin had dealt with in Baltimore, the way he carried himself was similar with that immediate sizing up of another man. Hillman topped him by at least an inch with broader shoulders, although the slight belly on him offset the image of a man in top physical condition. This was a man that if he wasn't careful would go to fat instead of muscle. His thick brown hair was losing the battle with premature balding, exposing a broad expanse of scalp. He was attired much as Turner had been, except in a crisp white cotton short-sleeve shirt, gray pants, and a University of Georgia tie. A navy blue sports coat was on a hanger on the coat rack to the left of his desk.

"Do have a seat," he said, gesturing to one of two black leather armchairs in front of his desk; he went back around and sat down in his black leather chair that looked to be one of the expensive ergonomically designed types. "I guess you'd be here to talk about Gabe Thatcher. Can't say I know as to why. The man tomcats around town in a shameful way—women always going on about his writing, his looks, and his charm, and some guy finally gets tired of his ways. Not saying he should have been killed, but this isn't the first time Gabe's taken a punch or two."

There was a gloating edge to Hillman's voice. He had a gleam of satisfaction in his brown eyes. Justin opened his notebook and clicked his pen. "From what I understand, Mr. Thatcher and your father often exchanged differences of opinion in the paper."

Hillman guffawed. "That's what this is about? Y'all think I might have gone after Gabe with the crap he's allowed to say about my daddy?" He leaned forward, hands as fists against each other. "The Hillmans have been in this town for four generations, and been on the city council for every generation beginning with the first one. I'm not saying I always agree with Daddy. I mean, I've got nothing against selling liquor on Sundays, but Gabe had no reason to describe Daddy as a 'sanctimonious, unenlightened, holdover from the last century' in that editorial he wrote last week."

Justin watched Hillman's nostrils flare, and then he must have realized the anger he was projecting. He unclenched his fists and leaned back a little. "Daddy's right, though, about Mr. Fancy Pants Gabe Thatcher being a blot on this town. He's made a laughingstock out of half the men and everybody lets him get away with it." This was followed by a smirk, the kind that was typical of schoolyard bullies. "Gabe's ways caught up with him is all, and let me tell you— y'all find whoever did it and 'less they pack the jury with women, he's liable to get off no problem."

Justin nodded once. "Where were you from say, 11:00 a.m. to 2:00 p.m., on the twelfth?"

Hillman chuckled, which was not a pleasant sound. "I'll say where I wasn't. I wasn't at Gabe Thatcher's beating up on him. I wouldn't, and haven't, darkened his doorway. And since I wasn't there, my whereabouts are none of your or Norm McFarlane's business."

"I notice you have bruising on your right hand," Justin

said pointedly.

Hillman shrugged. "Lots of ways to bruise your hand without it being because of smacking another man around."

Justin scribbled in his notebook without looking at it. "We'd like you to come down to the station and be fingerprinted," he said as if they were having a routine conversation.

"And you can kiss my behind," Hillman said, his face taking on a challenging look. "Unless you've got somebody who's lying about seeing me anywhere near Gabe's place, you've got no call to be asking for my fingerprints." He stood. "I'd say there's no need in us taking up anymore of each other's time. I'll walk you to the door in case you might want to hang around to try and talk to Doris or one of the girls because they have nothing to say to you either."

Justin stood, keeping his eyes locked on Hillman's. There was nothing that angered a bully more than someone who wouldn't back down. Apparently, in Gabe's case, he'd stood up to the Hillmans with words. "It's been my experience that people who have nothing to hide tend to be a little more cooperative, Mr. Hillman."

Hillman strode to the door, yanked it open, and stood to let Justin pass him. "That may be, but being uncooperative is hardly illegal. And speaking of lawyers, mine is Dewey Lambert. Sheriff McFarlane knows how to reach him. Any more talking about this will be done with him in the room."

Justin stepped out and noticed that Doris was watching silently. He nodded to her politely as Hillman opened the outer door. "You have a nice day now," he said with a smirk as Justin was tempted to bump into him on the way out. Well actually, he was tempted to punch him in the belly. That, however, would be best not done in front of a witness.

He contemplated the difference in Hillman's and Turner's

responses to the same questions as he drove to the station. Turner's motive was certainly stronger, but there was no doubt in Justin's mind that Hillman had the personality to fit the crime. The problem was that Hillman was correct. Being an uncooperative jerk of an individual was not illegal and Justin was not allowed to pick a suspect based on personal dislike. On the other hand, he was allowed to further investigate for a possible alibi since there was motive, means, and the question of opportunity had not yet been answered. It would be imprudent of him to not check as much into Mr. Hillman as he could until the lawyer screamed about harassment.

"Tommy Hillman is cut from the same cloth as his daddy," Sheriff McFarlane agreed when Justin relayed the conversation. "Whole family thinks this town couldn't exist without them." He lifted the receiver to the telephone and fingered through his Rolodex. He stopped at a card, pulled it out, and started punching in numbers. "The only reason Tommy Hillman never got arrested for some of the stunts he pulled in town was because the sheriff before me was way too friendly with Fred Hillman. I'm willing to bet a dollar to a donut hole, though, that when Tommy was at Athens he got himself in trouble with the law."

Justin didn't doubt that. Mix a college boy like Hillman and booze, and the odds were there was a disturbing the peace or assault charge somewhere in his history. Athens, the home of the University of Georgia, was far enough away that he could have been arrested and people in Wallington would not have known about it.

"Thanks, Danny, I appreciate it, and if you can get it to me right away, that would be good. You bet, we'll do that." Sheriff McFarlane cradled the telephone and grinned. "Oh yeah, disorderly conduct, resisting arrest, and assault and battery. Charges were dropped after restitution was made and the prosecutor didn't want to mess with it, but fingerprints are on file. We should have them sometime tomorrow."

Justin shifted in his chair. "No word yet on Newton?"

Sheriff McFarlane ran a hand through his hair. "Nope. My friend called in from talking with his boys about keeping an eye out for Paul. They all know him, of course, and somebody did a run by one of his favorite camping sites over by Big Rock Creek, but no sign that he'd been there."

Justin was careful to keep his voice neutral. "Should we broaden the search? We're into our third day."

The sheriff fished into his pocket for a pack of gum and placed the pack on the edge of the desk for Justin. "I know that Newton is our best suspect, but I also know that he can easily disappear for up to a week at a time. He does it often enough so that it isn't out of the ordinary. He knows those woods as well as anyone around here because back when he had to grow up a whole lot faster than a boy ought to, he put food on the table for the family with fish and game. Plus, the kind of home life they had, the woods was a better place to be most days."

Justin heard the reflective tone in the sheriff's voice, took a piece of gum from the pack, and waited.

"Martha Newton is a good woman, but it's hard when you start off poor and come from a family that's mostly trash. She was no more than seventeen when Slade got her pregnant, and I suppose you could say he did right by marrying her. Truth is, if she'd come from a decent family, she'd probably been better off not marrying him. But that's one of those sad cases of one choice is no good and the other worse. She wouldn't have had help with a baby from her kin. You know the kind I'm talking about."

Justin nodded. He'd seen his share in Baltimore: addict parents using welfare money for drugs or booze instead of food and clothes, and too many teenagers who didn't have the support to wrench free from the cycle of dependency and despair. Bureaucracies and programs that were allegedly designed to break the cycles resulted instead in children slipping through the cracks.

"Matter of fact, Martha was the only decent one of the lot and, judging by her getting tangled up with Slade, I guess there's some validity to repeating the mistakes of your own parents. Slade Newton was a no-account drunk who couldn't hold a job for more than a few months at a time. Martha had the three kids and, if it hadn't been for folks like Helen and some of the church ladies, things would have been a lot worse for them than it was." He put the pack of gum back in his pocket. "Family was too proud to go on welfare. Martha cleaned houses and took castoff clothes and shoes; Paul learned how to hunt and fish when he couldn't have been more than seven or eight years old. The only thing I'll say for Slade was that while he was a drunk and didn't provide, he was a whiney, feel sorry for himself drunk, not one to knock the kids or Martha around. He disappeared right after Paul's thirteenth birthday—no idea where he went or what happened to him."

Justin wasn't sure how this made Newton less of a suspect.

"Paul and Virgil were pretty close in age, Melissa several years younger. I think Martha lost a baby before Melissa was born. With Slade taking off, Martha was able to keep more of the money she made and she can find a bargain where no one else can. When he got old enough for a work permit, Paul hired himself out as a general helper to Scott Nelson's construction company so he could earn money and learn a trade. Worked every weekend and summer from the time he was sixteen. Virgil had an old bicycle and took on a paper route soon as they'd let him, then he went to work at the grocery store. Neither boy was a lot on school, but they've never caused trouble either."

"If there was something going on with their sister and Mr. Thatcher, that would seem to be a strong motive," Justin pointed out.

The sheriff sighed. "Yeah, and the boys have always been protective of Melissa. She's a smart thing, pretty like Martha was, and all of them have set money aside to help her go to college. She's got a scholarship for Georgia State, but you know that doesn't cover near all the expenses."

He rubbed his chin. "What it comes down to is this: that family shows that you can be poor and still hold your head up, and I'd sure hate to see it come apart if Paul is the one. It would mean prison for Paul and Melissa would never forgive herself. It would be a terrible shame." He looked at Justin and grinned. "Not that I'm saying if it was Paul that he shouldn't pay. I can't believe he went there planning to kill Gabe, though. It would have been manslaughter at the most. You saw the body well enough to know that the beating could have been a lot worse than it was."

Justin stood. "Hillman said that whoever goes on trial would probably be acquitted if he can manage to have an all-male jury."

Sheriff McFarlane reached for the telephone as it rang. "I hate to agree with Tommy Hillman about anything, but he could be right on that." He spoke into the phone, held his hand over the mouthpiece, and inclined his head to indicate that Justin could leave. "How about going over for a chat with the assistant DA and see what he says about Tommy Hillman. I won't mind hassling him just for general principle if we can find a legal reason for doing it."

Justin waved his hand in acknowledgment and admitted that among the three men they were looking at, it wouldn't bother him a bit if Hillman were the one.

CHAPTER FIFTEEN

Helen had one leaf to the table in the up position to accommodate the quilt laid out. With the center and left bottom squares completed, she was debating about positioning the other squares and if she should add in a few more features.

Harriet Healy, a friend who painted primarily in watercolors and specialized in flowers and birds, told her that she sometimes began a piece with such a vague notion of where she was going that she would start with a sky to see how the picture would develop in her mind. Dawn colors might move her in a different direction than a hued sunset and the hard brightness of a cerulean sky with no more than wisped clouds brought other ideas. "I don't always know exactly where I'm going when I start, but that's the magic of art, unless it's a commissioned piece. Every time you begin, it's your own creation."

Although Helen learned quilting from her grandmother and mother, she had not been experimental with design until she created the crib quilt for Ethan. That hadn't been complicated, but it had raised her comfort level for working with design. She continued to use patterns, of course, and occasionally used preprinted fabrics for what they all called "cheater" quilts when she was either in a real hurry or it happened to fit a theme perfectly. In all fairness, though, she'd been surprised how much time was saved on the first occasion when she'd followed only the lines of a preprinted fabric. It was a wonderful way for novice quilters to begin. It was in that same vein that she machine stitched quilts when time was a factor. As much as she loved the feel of the fabric with her needle in hand and drawing the thread through, speed was called for in other situations. She'd yet to meet anyone who could hand stitch a binding as quickly as with a sewing machine.

She was glad she had the luxury of doing A Garden Bouquet by hand as an extra tribute to Miss Ruth, Wanda's mother. Helen as satisfied with the balance of colors, and all of the flowers depicted were varieties that Miss Ruth had once cultivated. Helen was rethinking the size of the birdhouse with climbing clematis and the honeysuckle-covered white picket fence. Should she widen them a bit? Should she come up with two other similar ideas to run vertically? Would that be too busy and distract from the initial design? There was an element that wasn't quite right and she couldn't put her finger on it. By placing the sketch on the quilt and looking at the design again as a whole, it might come to her. She stood back a few feet to take it in. Oh, of course! Butterflies! She didn't have a single butterfly, and what garden was complete without them? She could fix that with appliqués.

Helen breathed in deeply, remembering scents from the profusion of flowers that Miss Ruth had nurtured as lovingly as she had her children. The front door was open with the screen door closed to allow fresh air in, the way she preferred the house except for in the depth of summer when the air hung heavily humid. The house had been built in the days when only rich people, the movie theater, and a few stores had air conditioning. This house, like many others in the neighborhood, had made the transition from window box fans to the noisy window unit air conditioners to a central air conditioning system that Tricia's generation took for granted.

Helen often laughed when she caught herself saying, "Back when I was young..." for whatever the topic happened to be. How she had rolled her eyes when her mother or grandmother started a conversation in that manner, and yet, here she was, doing the same thing more often than she had thought possible. It was one more example of how she'd learned that wisdom did come with age, or perhaps the correct word was *could* come with age. The crotchety crowd that refused to acknowledge the value of certain progress, be it technological or social, seemed to have learned little in their many years on earth.

There was no question in Helen's mind that her own advancing age was the primary reason she increased the amount of time she spent at The Arbors, the assisted-living residence. Although she periodically visited the quilting circle and friends who were residents at Tall Oaks, the independent living/active retirement community, she could offer more to the residents at The Arbors, especially to the quilters. They were in that transition stage where they were no longer able to do at least some basic functions that enabled them to be truly independent, and, in a few cases, they were only a matter of weeks or months from requiring the higher level of long-term care. For the long-term-care residents, a quick visit to say hello, pat a hand, or perhaps bring a lovely new quilt was all the interaction they could cope with in their bedridden state that frequently included some type of dementia.

The assisted-living crowd, however, was usually able to converse, relate stories of their youth, fill in gaps of history about the town or region, attend events, and in general enjoy themselves as long as their reduced mobility and other physical limitations were taken into consideration. One of the great benefits of quilting was that there was no need to travel, so the issue of maneuvering walkers or wheelchairs in and out of a vehicle wasn't a factor. The Arbors facility was designed with all private rooms, each with a small sitting area by a window that looked out onto the carefully tended garden with wisteria-covered arbors at each of the four entrances. Light filled the sitting area and it was a wonderful spot for quilting. Other times, quilters gathered in the main recreation room that opened onto the dining room. The leisurely act of quilting and the natural companionship that flowed among quilters made it an ideal sedentary activity. Residents who had impaired vision or crippling arthritis could frequently still participate at a slower rate, leaving their love of discussing quilting undimmed.

Helen's mind drifted to this subject, thinking about how Miss Ruth had adapted her home and her habits to remain living independently in the house she had lived in for more than seven decades.

Her thoughts were pulled away at the sound of a car in her driveway, then a pause before a car door slammed. She started to rise from her chair when Martha Newton's voice preceded her up the porch steps. It was unlike her to come by for anything other than her cleaning day.

"Helen, I'm sorry to bother you, but I sorely need your help," she said, opening the door a crack.

Helen motioned her inside. "Of course, Martha, come in, and tell me what you need." It had to be about Paul.

Lines etched into Martha's thin face told of a life spent

battling against hard luck punctuated by poor choices. What Helen and the other women who employed Martha knew was that rather than wrap herself in victimhood, Martha had looked into a mirror one day and said instead, "My upbringing was a burden I was forced to bear; my choosing a man too much like my father was an act of foolishness, but I will find a way to make a better life for my children."

Her body was lean from constant hard work, and both boys, Paul and Virgil, had taken their work ethic thankfully from her instead of their father. Neither was inclined to school beyond the basics, yet they looked to their baby sister, Melissa, with pride. You could see the pretty girl that Martha had once been when you looked at Melissa and she, too, had taken to working at a young age—babysitting, then working part time at the Sandwich Shop when she was old enough. The difference between Melissa and her brothers was that as Martha accepted used books in the same way she did used clothing, Melissa showed a genuine interest in reading. Watching the girl devour books fired Martha's determination that Melissa would be the first in the family to attend college. The girl, in turn, like her brothers, understood the sacrifices their mother made for them and understood her insistence of "Being poor doesn't mean you have to be trash."

Melissa took her studies seriously and sought help from teachers when she didn't understand something. She kept her grades high, and even though she couldn't participate in afterschool activities because she worked instead, she seemed to recognize that for her, high school was a means to an end— nothing more than a temporary period on the way to achieving a higher goal. She looked to her future rather than resenting that she was not, and could not be, a part of the "in" crowd.

"The quilt is going to be awfully pretty," Martha said with a nod to Helen's handicraft. "You should enter the competitions. No matter what Rachel Jackson thinks, you're a better quilter than her any day of the week."

"She can have the ribbons," Helen said with a gentle smile, trying not to react to the drawn look on Martha's face. "Why don't we go into the kitchen and I'll make coffee or a cup of tea."

Martha hesitated as though regretting she'd come. "Maybe it's not my place to be here," she said, her brown eyes beneath pale eyebrows glistening with tears that she was holding back.

"Nonsense," Helen said crisply. "We've known each other too long for you to say that. Come on and tell me about Paul. I would imagine that's why you're here."

Martha reached into the pocket of her faded yellow print cotton dress, pulled out a tissue, dabbed her eyes, and attempted a smile. "That's always been one of the things I've admired about you. There's no beating around the bush or getting into a flutter when there's a problem to be solved."

Helen smilingly patted Martha's arm and led the way in, asking with her hands as to whether they should sit at the table or the kitchen island. Martha perched on one of the stools at the island. "It's on account of your son-in-law doing the investigation," she said and nodded when Helen pointed to the coffeepot. "I can't say that I know him, but he seems to be a good man."

"He is," Helen said over her shoulder as she prepared the coffee, brought out mugs, spoons, sugar, and napkins. "I have some wonderful bar cookies left from the circle the other night. They're in foil in the cookie jar if you'll get them. Don't bother with a plate."

"I know your boy Justin and the sheriff are looking for Paul, but I don't know exactly why that would be—something about his truck being seen near to Mr. Gabe's house that day and that maybe he had hard feelings toward him. I don't understand how that could be, seeing as how they don't have much of anything in common." Her voice had as much question as declaration and Helen drew her breath in, not wanting to be the one to tell Martha about Melissa.

Her silence must have alerted Martha, though, because as soon as the two women were seated, Martha straightened her shoulders and the look on her face said that she was prepared for bad news. "You know something about Paul you can tell me? I'd rather hear it from you than from someone who takes delight in other people's troubles."

Helen hesitated. For a moment, she wished she'd never seen Gabe and Melissa together. "Martha, I am so sorry to be the one to tell you, and it may be nothing at all, but you know that Gabe regularly comes into, I mean, came into the Sandwich Shop?"

Martha's eyes widened and she lifted the coffee mug a few inches from the counter. "I can't say that I do, and I can't say that Melissa ever made mention of it." She took a sip of coffee as though thinking about Helen's question. "Mr. Gabe was near to forty-three and Melissa's only been eighteen for a couple of months now. I know all about him and women, but Melissa is not much more than a child. I've never heard tell of him messing around with a child like that."

Helen pushed the foil packet of cookies to Martha who absentmindedly took one and laid it on the saucer. "You saw something going on with Melissa and Mr. Gabe?" Her voice held a note of controlled panic and Helen suddenly thought of what it must have been like for Martha when she discovered she was pregnant at seventeen.

"Not the kind of thing that you're thinking," Helen said quickly. "They've been, I mean, they were talking quite a bit."

Martha shook her head slowly, her voice heavy. "I don't want to believe Mr. Gabe would do that, but if there's a chance it looked that way and Paul knew, he'd get up a head of steam for sure. This can't be right, though. It can't be that I've raised these kids and it comes to this."

Helen shot her hand out and laid it on Martha's arm, much as she had done for Rita. Was that only two nights ago? Good Lord, what drama had been unleashed with Gabe's death! "Martha, I know this is hard for you. Justin and the sheriff are fair men and they don't want any harm to come to Paul if he's not involved. His disappearing doesn't look good, though."

Martha sighed and looked at the mug of coffee, a tiny tendril of steam rising from it. "Paul can fade back into those woods for days at a time for all sorts of reasons." She lifted the coffee, took a sip, and as she raised her eyes to Helen, the glistening returned. "I swear that Melissa has never said a word about this and I've seen nothing. She's got that little computer, though, that she won in the essay contest. You think she could have sent him letters or whatever that is they do on computers?"

"That's possible," Helen said quietly.

Martha shook her head again, broke off a piece of cookie and ate it before she steeled her voice. "I've come to accept the life that I've been given, but I've done all I could to see that my kids would have it better. If it turns out that Melissa and Paul are messed up in this, that their lives could be laid to ruin, that's a cross that will be awful hard to bear."

Helen wanted to weep for Martha's sake, but she didn't think that was what the woman needed. She knew that if it hadn't been her who told Justin about Paul, it would have been someone else. That didn't stop the flash of guilt, though, that perhaps she should have kept quiet. "We really don't know what happened, Martha, and maybe there's no connection with Paul going off like he did. The sooner he gets back, the sooner they can talk to him and maybe clear it all up."

Martha ate the rest of the cookie and nodded as if to an inner conversation. "Thank you for your time, Helen. I think it would be best if I have a talk with Melissa now. I hate to think the girl has been up to what she may have been, but there's no sense pretending it can't be true. Depending on what she tells me, I'll sit Virgil down and find out if he's hiding anything from me. He and Paul are close-like and when I asked Virgil about where Paul was, he had that look like he might not have been telling me everything he knows."

"Martha, I'm so sorry about this," Helen said softly. "All I can tell you is that Justin won't try and make Paul look guilty. He's not that kind of man."

Martha's smile indicated that she might not be as certain of that as Helen was. "I sure hope you're right about that." She slid from the stool, taking her mug, saucer, and spoon to the sink. "I appreciate your time. Why don't I wash these things up for you since I'm here?"

Helen stood. "Thank you, Martha, but I'll put everything in the dishwasher." She hesitated, not wanting to offend the woman. "If you can find Paul, I think that would help."

"Virgil don't know the woods like his brother does, but he does know some of his favorite places." She turned, her back to the sink, her face questioning. "I heard tell, though, that your Justin has been in to see Mr. Turner over at the car place and Mr. Hillman—the younger one."

"He isn't telling me about that kind of thing," Helen said. "He's looking into all the possibilities and he's working hard to find out the truth about this."

Martha moved toward the mudroom. "I'll go out the back way and thank you again for your time."

Helen held out her arms. The smaller, wiry woman gave a hug that was brief yet intense and left with no other comment. Helen returned to the kitchen, tidying up. She felt a heaviness for Martha, as much because she was afraid that Paul was guilty as for any other reason. She didn't think for one moment that Paul intended to kill Gabe; it would have been a confrontation that got out of hand. And while it truly wasn't like Gabe to turn his attention to someone as young as Melissa, perhaps she had merely misinterpreted his irrepressible flirting and developed a crush on him as so many other women had done. The problem with that was it didn't eliminate Paul's motive, especially if his view was that he was intervening just in time.

Helen was startled to hear herself sigh. What a tangle there was surrounding Gabe! Of all the eccentric characters that a town was likely to have, he had been one of the more colorful ones. He was the type people loved to gossip about; he provided fodder for who knew how many conversations. Helen understood why he reveled in his reputation although she couldn't say that she approved of it, and now it had come to this. Could the tragedy have been prevented? Could Gabe have changed his ways?

She finished in the kitchen and returned to the quilt. If she was being honest with herself, of all the men who might be suspect in the case, she preferred that Tommy Hillman would turn out to be the guilty one. You weren't supposed to wish ill of anyone, but there was no denying that Gabe was dead and Martha was right. If Paul did it and he went to prison, Melissa would probably never forgive herself, or perhaps never forgive her brother. A decent family that had scratched to dig themselves from poverty and wretchedness would be torn apart.

Tommy, on the other hand, was a bully who'd been allowed to get away with his nastiness all of his life because of his family. He was smart enough to taunt without technically instigating a fight, to goad and belittle until someone else's anger would get out of control. Even when he didn't provoke actual fights, he was expert at the type of humiliation that left people wounded from his sneers. The problem was that unlike a purely physical bully, he was expert at masking his brutishness when it suited him. He was the dark side of the good-old-boy image, as his grandfather had been and father still was—the type that felt people had their place in the world and that they, the Hillmans, were obviously a part of us and not them.

Neither Fred nor Deborah Hillman had an ounce of Christian charity in them, no matter how much they donated to their church or how many committee and community positions they held. They might not be the most hypocritical people Helen had ever known, but they were surely in the running. Tommy's sense of superiority came directly from them, and their refusal to allow anyone to fault the child for anything simply reinforced that view. They reveled in their status as big fish in a small pond.

Helen had been appalled when Larry Shipley, as decent a man as you could ask for, told her he was selling the business to Tommy. She'd helped Larry build the company from his little two-desk office starting out until he was the most successful insurance agent in town. He was a man who truly cared about his clients. Larry had been older when he broke away from being a regional sales manager for a national company to open his own independent office. His hopes for passing the business to a second generation faded when Jesse broke the news that he wanted to be a lawyer.

The fact was that when Larry decided to sell, he offered her the company, but that was barely a year after Mitch had died. It wasn't a step that she wanted to make and Larry confided that Tommy was not his first choice as a buyer, but it was the best business decision. He insisted, however, that she accept a large bonus. When she added that to the life insurance policy on Mitch and their investments, she had the option of retiring. That was the phrase they all used, despite the fact that a number of people understood her real motivation for leaving. Larry and Alicia bought a lovely, low mileage RV and were touring the country, returning every few months with stories of their travels.

Helen wasn't the least bit surprised when Tommy brought in that dour Doris Strickland to take her place, or that not one of the women stayed long in the office after the transition. These thoughts unfolded in her mind as she moved from the quilt to the armoire to see what she might do about butterfly appliqués. She thought she had some left from another project, but that had been a year or so back.

She was glad that Martha dropped by and she hoped she had helped. She also hoped that Martha could locate Paul and they could get to the bottom of this whole sad business.

CHAPTER SIXTEEN

Justin paused in the doorway of Sheriff McFarlane's office, a fresh mug of coffee in each hand.

"Don't mind if I do," the sheriff said and nodded to the empty chair. "Any breaking news?"

Justin blew across the liquid in his mug before answering. "Not unless something came in while I was pouring the coffee." He looked over the rim of his mug. "The more I talk with people, the more I'm puzzled about Gabe Thatcher. I've met a lot of different kinds of characters, but I can't say that any of them have been like him." He waved his hand. "I'm not referring to men who constantly chase after women. Those are commonplace. What I don't get is the hate-him-and-love-him kind of thing that I keep hearing."

The sheriff gave one of his rare chuckles. "Well, there are a couple of reasons really. You ever have any dealings with a house inspector?"

"Uh yeah, sure," Justin said, puzzled at the question.

"Okay, you know how you look at a house and it seems fine,

you're all set to buy it or want to sell it, so you get an inspector in and next thing you know, he's pointing out all sorts of problems that you didn't realize you had. Or, you knew and had forgotten about them because you thought it was no big deal—some problems so small that you can take care of, maybe some major, maybe something really serious."

Justin nodded.

The sheriff twitched his mouth. "You go through with him or get his report and how do you react when it's news you don't want to hear?"

"You're mad because of what he tells you?" Justin was beginning to understand the analogy.

"Most often, even though you know it's not his fault. He happens to be really good at what he does and tells you the truth about things you either didn't know or didn't want to know." The sheriff lifted his mug like a toast. "Gabe was like that with women. He was an expert in romance and there are a whole lot of marriages and relationships out there with problems, like mine was."

"I'm not trying to pry," Justin said quickly.

"It's okay," his boss replied. "It makes for a good example. Cindy and I got married for all the wrong reasons and if we could have said the words to each other, we knew early on that it was a mistake. We did okay in the sense that we didn't fight much, but the truth was that neither one of us was what you'd call happy. We settled into what was a workable arrangement because it was easier than trying to do anything about it. Think of it like having a little crack in the foundation of your house that starts small and it doesn't get better over time by ignoring it." He paused for a sip of coffee. "Gabe comes back into town for good and starts making his rounds and Cindy was looking for something that I'm not giving her. Next thing I know, she's going on about all sorts of issues we should talk about, mostly changes I should be making."

"How was that?" Justin watched as amusement played across the sheriff's face.

"Talking about issues doesn't set well by most men and the truth was, her bringing that crap up was no more than an excuse to get at the fact that we were stuck in a marriage that wasn't what either of us needed. Was I mad that she was hanging around the Wallington Inn having drinks and sometimes dinner with Gabe? No question about it, but by the time the divorce was final and Cindy took off for Philadelphia to be near her sister and find herself, we knew it was the best thing for both of us."

Justin shifted in his chair. "That was sort of what Joe Turner said."

The sheriff nodded once. "In that case, though, it sounds like repairs can be made. Anyway, there are two other parts about Gabe that I might as well say since we're on the subject. One is that he did right by his mamma coming back, whether or not she was the real reason. Virginia was in bad shape the last few months of her life and Gabe was there with her every day, helping take care of her. Wouldn't see her put into a hospital. He managed the nursing care and did a lot of the work himself, too. You have to admire a man who's willing to do that." The sheriff drained his mug, followed by a slow grin. "Then you have to take into account that all small towns, and especially small Southern towns, need to have at least one character who is either outrageous or so eccentric that it's worth talking about. Local color, I suppose you call it."

"I would say that describes Mr. Thatcher," Justin agreed. "Outrageous more than eccentric."

"Yep," the sheriff said, holding his empty mug over the desk. "Guess we'll have to depend on Miss Bea instead now that Gabe's gone." Beatrice Wallington, the eldest of the town founder's family, had recently taken to dressing in period clothing and walking around the town square providing impromptu and somewhat garbled history lessons. With six generations to represent, she had quite a wardrobe to choose from.

Justin stood and took the mug. "She is a good candidate. By the way, we should get the results on Turner's fingerprints sometime today and if there's a match I'll go after the alibi. I hope we get Hillman's in, too."

His cell phone rang and he was surprised to see it was one of his former bosses calling from Baltimore. He excused himself and went into the only room other than the sheriff's office that had any privacy. It was a rectangular, multi-purpose room that served for interrogations, training sessions, celebration space when Sheila acknowledged birthdays or whatever, and extra workspace.

"Hey there, Justin," Louis Becker's voice rumbled through the telephone. "You doing okay down there in Mayberry?"

"Funny you should mention that," Justin said. "We have a murder and it's too complicated to get into, but I'm heading the investigation."

"I imagine it's because they recognize your vastly superior skills learned here in Charm City."

Justin laughed at the banter. "That could be. How are you?"

"Couldn't be better and I'll get to that in a minute. How's Tricia? You guys starting a family yet?"

"She's fine. We've been getting the house fixed up; she's enjoying her job and being around her mom. No family yet, although I'm pretty sure my office at the house is on tap to be a future nursery."

"No regrets about leaving the big city?"

There was a momentary exchange as if someone else was talking that gave Justin a chance to wonder at the question.

"Sorry about that," Louis said. "I've got the door closed now.

So, are you missing good crab cakes yet?"

"That I am," Justin laughed. "I've almost converted to grits, though, and I have to admit that a pulled pork sandwich goes well with a cold draft."

"You got a suspect for your murder? Think you can wrap it up soon?" There was a subtle shift in Louis's voice.

"Another two or three days, I think," Justin said. "I know you too well, Lou. You didn't call out of the blue to ask how I'm doing. What's up?"

"No, I didn't," the other man acknowledged. "In fact, this cell number will still be good, but I'll need to give you another office number. You call me a week from today and you'll be connected to the new chief, homicide division."

"Whoa," Justin said, sitting straight up. "Are you kidding? That's great, man! Congratulations!" It was a stunning development since Louis had been in homicide for barely three years. Normally a promotion of that level would go to someone far more senior.

"Yeah, there have been some internal adjustments and political maneuvering," he said, and Justin imagined his broad shoulders shrugging, or a grin across his wide face. "As part of the arrangement, I have the opportunity to bring on a couple of new guys. How would you feel about being one of them?"

Had he heard Lou correctly? "Jumping right into homicide? How could you do that?"

Lou laughed. "Not right away. You would be assigned to a special task force for a short while, take the right exams that I have full confidence you will pass on the first try, and be fast-tracked into homicide. I'd expect six months, could be as long as a year depending on different things. I know this is kind of sudden, but it's a serious offer."

Justin's mind jumped into high gear. Homicide in Baltimore?

Never mind the promotion—that was icing on the cake. Being a homicide detective in Baltimore was practically every police officer's dream. "Geez Lou, I don't know exactly what to say."

Another chuckle was heard, the kind when you've pulled off a successful surprise. "Listen, I know this isn't something you can agree to without talking to Tricia, so I won't press you for an answer right now. I will need to know by the first of next week, though. You okay with that?"

"Sure, sure," Justin said trying to keep the excitement from his voice. What an opportunity! "I really appreciate this, Lou—I guess I mean, sir."

"Yeah, well, you give Tricia a hug for me, and tell her that I know the move will be disruptive, but I really would like to see you take this."

"I'll let you know as soon as I can, three days tops," Justin promised and they spoke briefly of other friends and acquaintances before Lou rang off. Justin sat motionless as he replayed the conversation in his head. The thrill of the offer careened into the reality of the two, maybe three conversations he would need to have. Tricia, of course, the sheriff naturally, and in all fairness, probably Helen, since it was her daughter he would be taking away again.

He stood, feeling almost giddy with anticipation, and shook his head sharply to bring the here and now back into focus. He had a fleeting sensation of guilt at realizing that identifying Gabe Thatcher's murderer would be the perfect springboard for the move. The headline of "First Small Town Homicide in Two Decades Solved by Big City Police Officer" flashed through his thoughts before he could stop it. "Take it easy, fellow," he admonished himself. "You aren't in charge of this investigation because the sheriff wasn't capable of handling it."

The sound of his cell phone interrupted his dialogue and Tricia's voice was teasing. "Hey listen, our in-school training finished early and I wanted to see if you had time for lunch today."

Justin hesitated, wondering if lunch would be appropriate for this conversation—not in a public place, that was for sure.

"I mean, I know you've got the case going and all, but I thought I would check anyway," she said, misinterpreting his silence.

"Uh, I may be able to," he said. "I have to verify the status on a couple of things. Tell you what. If I break loose, how about I swing into Smokin' Hot to pick up BBQ and meet you at the house?"

"I'm closer," she said, apparently calling from the car. "I'll get the BBQ and if you can't come home, we'll have it for dinner instead."

"That's good," he said, stepping into the sheriff's office to find it empty. He went to the dispatch room, which was one of three places he might find Sheila.

The woman who was the unofficial but openly acknowledged glue that held the office together, no matter who was elected as sheriff, looked up as she held the microphone to her chest, either ready to transmit or having just finished. "No word on Newton yet and Lenny and Dave are on patrol."

For a woman who was sixty-three, barely five foot five, and couldn't weigh more than 120 pounds, she had a stare that could intimidate any man in town. When her brown eyes fixed on you with an expression that was like a cross between your mother and your first grade teacher, you wanted to swear you had nothing to do with whatever it was you were about to be chastised for. Cyrus, closest to her age, swore that they once had two skinhead wannabees in custody for vandalism at Sheila's church. Sheriff McFarlane was fairly new to the job and he let Sheila have a go at them when they spouted off a racial slur while being processed. Allegedly when she was done with them, they had volunteered to help repaint the church inside and out. She could be remarkably comforting, though, when people came in distraught; more than one dispute between aggrieved parties had been settled by Sheila sitting them down for a cup of coffee and donuts.

"Thanks," Justin said. "Uh, did the sheriff leave for lunch?"

Sheila didn't have to check. She knew the sheriff's schedule for the entire week better than he did. "Rotary Club lunch today and it's a special program so he's not likely to finish there before one thirty. Time for jawjacking with that bunch, and it'll be around two o'clock before he gets loose; but if you need him, he'll have the cell phone on vibrate."

Justin lifted his hand. "Nothing that can't wait. Uh, I'm going to the house for lunch in case we get word in."

Sheila didn't comment as the radio squawked, and she made the shooing motion with her hand that was her usual way of dismissing people.

Justin drove home, mindful of the series of events that led to their departure from Baltimore. Tricia's father's death from pancreatic cancer had occurred only months after their wedding. No one believed it would move as rapidly as it did and he died within three weeks. As much of a shock as the news had been, at least she had the memory of what had been a perfect few days of family and friends with her as a beautiful bride on the arm of her father gliding down the aisle of the historic Episcopalian church filled to capacity. Mitch and Helen had been wonderful hosts to his parents, sister, brother, and their families who traveled from in and around Baltimore for the June wedding and festivities.

It was sometimes difficult to reconcile that laughter-filled weekend with the rush back for Mitch's final few days and the funeral. The pastor of the First Methodist Church had gently suggested to Helen that their sanctuary would be better able to accommodate the large crowd that came to pay their respects. Helen had borne up well, surrounded by those who cared for her.

Tricia arranged to take a full week from her job as a high school biology teacher, and when her older brother, Ethan, offered to stay as well, the two women lovingly told Ethan that there were things he could come and help with later. Justin was also dispatched and Ethan confided his relief as he drove Justin to the airport. "You'd be amazed at how many widows of all ages are here and female support is probably what's best for her right now."

Tricia and Helen had talked often after that, and despite Helen's assurances that she was coping, he always had the sense that Tricia hadn't quite believed her. She flew home to spend part of each summer with her mother, and that third summer a man who had been one of her favorite high school teachers contacted her before she left. Wallington High School was scheduled for a major renovation and there would be more than facility changes involved. He was to be named principal and his vision for the school was to bring in dynamic math and science teachers to steer the curriculum toward what would eventually be a center for science and technology. It was a project he was working on with a team from the Georgia Institute of Technology, her father and brother's alma mater.

Justin remembered her excitement and his willingness to move for her sake. The transition in the school was proceeding smoothly and, in truth highly qualified math and science teachers had flocked to the openings. Rumor had it that there was literally a waiting list of teachers who would gladly take Tricia's place, so he wouldn't have to be concerned about letting Principal Taylor down. Plus, she had liked the school in Baltimore that generously promised her a position if they ever returned. If only it had been longer than a year, though, since they moved. As great a chance as

146

this was for him, in a way, he almost wished it hadn't come so soon.

A major point in his favor, however, was that Tricia had admitted Helen was doing well, or as well as anyone did under the circumstances. Her own strength of character and the phenomenal support network among her friends saw her through the grief to acceptance of a loss that had no rational explanation. Tricia had of course worried at the idea of her mother retiring, afraid she had made the decision too hastily, but Helen soon showed that she was not about to spend a great deal of idle time sitting around the house. The quilting classes she taught were a minor part of her many quilting activities and, if he understood correctly, she and one other lady had recently begun to recatalogue the library at the church. He also knew that Helen was glad to have Tricia close by, yet wouldn't want to be the reason that Justin turned down a career advancement that would probably never come his way again.

He turned onto their street, trying to think how to break the news to Tricia. Blurting it out as soon as he saw her might not be the right way, but he didn't want to beat around the bush either. He wasn't overly concerned about the fact that they had really only settled into the house. They both agreed that this was a starter home until they had a chance to really decide what they wanted. It wasn't as if he would be asking her to give up her dream house, even though Tricia had spent a lot of energy decorating it with Helen. He mostly stayed out of the way and took care of the handyman work that he enjoyed. It wasn't the first time he was glad he'd been raised in his father's electrical business. He wasn't a bad carpenter either, although rebuilding a toilet and snaking a drain was about all he knew when it came to plumbing.

Fortunately the three-bedroom, two-bath ranch they'd bought was only ten years old and had been solidly constructed.

Other than Tricia wanting extra ceiling fans put in, the work had been routine maintenance. The yard was an easily manageable size, with a green-coated wire hurricane fence around it, honeysuckle growing along one side, and a single pecan tree providing both shade and a nice crop of nuts in the fall. The concrete patio off the sliding doors of the den was large enough to hold his grill. A round black wrought iron table with four chairs and a wooden two-seater glider made up for not having a front porch.

Tricia's blue Ford Fusion was in the driveway and he parked the black and white cruiser in the spot where his green Mustang would be later. Like most people in the neighborhood, their two-car garage was devoted to storage: a lawnmower, their bicycles, and the assortment of tools and miscellaneous items that every home seemed to need. Talk of sorting, clearing, and organizing the accumulation hadn't made it high on the priority list. That could change pretty quickly depending on how the conversation went.

CHAPTER SEVENTEEN

I assumed you wouldn't have a lot of time," Tricia said when he came in, the enticing smell of BBQ enveloping the open containers. She was transferring sandwiches, coleslaw, and dill pickle spears to paper plates. A bowl of sour cream and onion potato chips was already on the table along with napkins and forks. She lifted her face for a kiss and handed him both plates. "Tea is in the fridge, or do you want a cola?"

Lou had been right on target when he asked if Justin missed crab cakes, and he might as well have asked about steamed crabs too. One of his earliest family memories was his dad taking a bushel of blue crabs steamed in Old Bay seasoning, dumping them out on a table covered in butcher paper, and giving everyone wooden mallets and plenty of paper towels. BBQ, however, was something that he had merely thought he appreciated until he tasted his first bite of local pulled pork. What he had thought of before as BBQ couldn't compare to what everyone in the area served up. Although he wasn't going to say that he preferred it to crab cakes or steamed crabs, it did make for a good meal.

"A cola, please," he said, carrying the plates to the small rectangular table pushed to the side of the wall where three could comfortably sit. Unlike Helen's house, the eat-in nook to their kitchen was for convenience, not the homey sense of gathering around the hearth. Of course, their entire house was barely 1400 square feet and while laid out with a functional flow, extra space was not part of the plan. He and Tricia did want children, but whether they wanted two or three was still a debate. The number of children would impact the size of the house when the time came to move. Justin briefly thought about his own upbringing in a row house in Baltimore, the park down the street serving as the real playground for kids who had limited backyards.

"Is there a big break in the case?" Tricia set the glasses on the table and took her usual chair on the right. "You look like you have something important to tell me. I mean, is it something you can tell me?"

Justin finished swallowing the bite of sandwich and looked at her with exasperated affection. "How do you do that?"

She held her sandwich ready. "What?"

"Know when I have something special to tell you?" He bit in again, still not certain that lunch was the right time for the conversation. The problem was there wasn't a reason to rush back to the office unless there was a break, and Tricia was off the rest of the afternoon. What if he postponed, then had a break and couldn't be home at a regular time? He sensed that waiting until tomorrow to tell Tricia would not be a good move.

She laughed, that sound that he loved. It had been her laugh rather than her face that he'd noticed first that night they met at a friend's party. Her back had been to him, a shapely back in a simple sundress of some color, blue maybe, her long brown hair with sort of reddish highlights that he later learned was called chestnut spilling down past her shoulders. He was approaching their hostess and Tricia was laughing at something she'd said. "Oh hi, Justin, glad you could make it. Tim is in the backyard at the grill. This is Megan, we went to high school together, and Tricia Crowder, up from Georgia."

"Well hello, Justin," she'd drawled, extra syllables in each word. Her smile matched her laughter with straight white teeth and lips that were full without quite being pouty. She had sable brown eyes and a nose with enough of an upturn so that you wanted to kiss it for no other reason than it was incredibly cute. He was no expert on women's makeup, but he had the idea that she wasn't wearing much and the scent she gave off was a light floral. Everything about her seemed like a summer day as the sun arced in the sky, the morning breeze keeping the oppressive heat at bay, and all you could see was the brightness that beckoned you to call in sick instead of going to work. This was a girl meant for picnics in a meadow or a barefoot stroll on moonlit beaches. He didn't care how many clichés he was using to describe her.

He remembered behaving normally and wondering if anyone else could tell that he'd fallen in love without the slightest warning. He had practically stumbled into the backyard for a beer, wanting to blow off the party and whisk her away somewhere private.

Tricia's voice changed slightly as she looked closely at him instead of answering his question. "Sweetheart, are you okay? You have the strangest expression on your face."

He laid his sandwich on the plate and exhaled deeply, closing his hand around the glass. "It isn't the case. I, uh, I got a call from Lou, Louis Becker. You remember him?"

Tricia stopped eating. "He's not a guy you forget—not at six four and shoulders like his. He always reminded me of a football player." She tilted her head. "What's going on, Justin?"

"Lou had some great news," he said, and then paused for a gulp of drink. He continued. "It's hard to believe, but he's been jumped over no telling how many guys and is going to be promoted to chief of homicide next week."

The look on her face was cautious. "That certainly is news worth sharing. Is there more to it than that?"

Justin cleared his throat, trying to hold his excitement in check. "Well, yeah, there is. He gets to pick a couple of guys to add to his team and…" He stopped as she raised both hands.

"He wants you to come back and be in homicide?" Her voice was hard to read.

"It would be a special task force at first," Justin said, wanting to reach for her hand and not being sure if he should.

She exhaled a long breath and placed her left hand on the table where he could grasp it. "I gather this would be right away? What did you tell him?"

Justin laid his hand on top of hers, squeezing it lightly. "That I had to talk to you, of course. This isn't a decision I would make on my own."

Her hand didn't move and her wide eyes didn't register an emotion he could read. Slowly, she ventured, "I'm trying here, sweetheart, I am. I understand what a big deal this is, I do. Well, I probably don't, but I have a good idea. But, it's so sudden and we haven't even been here for a whole year."

He lifted her hand this time, bringing it to his lips, glad she didn't resist. "I know, I know, and I wish the timing could be better. I know it's a lot to ask and that we can't come to a decision right this minute."

She smiled tremulously in a way that he thought was a good sign. "Did you tell the sheriff?"

He shook his head immediately. "No, no, you're the only person, as you should be. I... shoot!" The cell phone ringtone of *Another One Bites the Dust* meant it was the sheriff.

"Go ahead and take that," Tricia said, slowly removing her hand and looking at her unfinished sandwich as if trying to decide about it.

Justin answered the phone as he stepped into the combination dining room and living room. There was a fair amount of background noise on the sheriff's end.

"McFarlane here," he said unnecessarily, "I'm still at the Rotary Club lunch, but got word that Martha Newton wants to come into the station around two. I think she sent Virgil off looking for Paul."

"Should I take back up and go to her place?" Justin couldn't believe it. Delay after delay in looking for Newton and it happens right this minute. It obviously wasn't his day for good timing.

"No need for that," the sheriff replied. "Martha says she's coming at two. We should respect that. I wanted to make sure you'd be around is all. It'll be another half hour or so before I can break loose."

"Yes sir, I'll see you there," Justin said and let the sheriff hang up first. He reentered the kitchen, glad to see Tricia's mouth curved into a warmer smile.

"That did sound like a break in the case." She gestured to his chair. "Look, let's finish lunch and get you on your way. We can talk about this tonight when I've had a little time to process it. Okay?"

He stretched his hand out to touch her cheek. "Of course, whatever you want."

"Uh huh," she said, the smile diminishing. "Come on, eat your sandwich. Do you want another one?"

He grabbed a fistful of potato chips. "No, I'm good. I'll call you if whatever this is about keeps me late," he said. They spent the next ten minutes with Tricia telling him about her workshop that morning. She didn't mention the impact of a move on her job, a sign that he wasn't sure how to interpret. Her good-bye kiss to him was as loving as usual and she stood in the doorway watching him get into the patrol car.

What a day this was turning out to be—the telephone call from Lou that could skyrocket his career and what sounded like the chance to get their hands on Paul Newton. With the way things were going, maybe the fingerprint report for Hillman and Turner would be in, too. He stopped for a red light. There was no reason to hit the siren and blast through. He thought about Tricia's reaction. He'd learned the hard way that she had a quick temper about certain topics and the fact that she hadn't treated him to an angry blast was a positive sign. She also hadn't given him an immediate that's-fantastic,-you-so-deserve-this,-I'll-start-packing response that he couldn't have realistically expected, although that would have been nice.

In a way he was sorry they'd been interrupted, but maybe giving Tricia the afternoon to absorb the news was a better approach. He rolled into the station parking lot thinking that in all likelihood, Tricia would call Helen and spend the afternoon there. He let that thought tumble around in his head, realizing that conversation was going to take place no matter what. He counted himself lucky to have a mother-in-law who was the exact opposite of all the jokes, and there were occasions when he felt a flash of regret at not having the opportunity to have known Mitch for longer. Reflecting on Helen's loss gave him a moment of hesitation about asking Tricia to move away. His sister and mother had a close relationship and he'd seen the same sort of unspoken affection between Helen and Tricia. It was different than father and son, he thought, even though he couldn't define it.

One of the characteristics that Justin admired about his mother-in-law was her practical view of life despite being more than a little softhearted—like in that movie his mother and sister always cried over. What was it? A flower title. Oh yeah, Steel Roses, no, *Steel Magnolias*. That was it. Anyway, Helen was definitely that kind of woman and he didn't think she would lay a guilt trip on Tricia about staying for her sake. After all, one of the advantages of Tricia being a schoolteacher was that she did get summers off and she could spend four or five weeks of the summer with her mom like she'd previously done. Not that he enjoyed being separated from Tricia, but that would be the fair thing to do. Naturally, Helen would be welcome to visit them anytime she wanted.

Sheila was at the reception counter with Kelly, and the older woman looked up. "Sheriff get hold of you?"

"He did," Justin said and Kelly lifted a packet.

She smiled at what must have been an eager look on his face. "This came from the Athens Police Department addressed to you or the sheriff."

"Fingerprint report is in your in-box, too," Sheila called after him.

Justin nodded his head to indicate he'd heard her, pushing through the double doors with his left shoulder, and opening the packet. He noticed the bay room was empty. Everyone must still be either at lunch or on patrol. It didn't take long to verify that neither Hillman nor Turner's prints matched the two unknown sets taken from Thatcher's place. That didn't necessarily eliminate them as suspects, although he hadn't suspected Turner for it anyway. There had been something painfully honest about the man's admission of weakness of his marriage and something hopeful about his assertion that they were working things out. Justin hadn't leaned on Hillman about his alibi, but with no fingerprint match and no witness placing him anywhere near the crime scene, what cause did he have to pursue him? Being a jerk was not in fact a crime, and his motive was nowhere near as strong as Turner's. That left them with Newton still being the primary candidate unless someone came forward with new information.

The room was quiet and Justin checked his watch. He had maybe fifteen minutes before Sheriff McFarlane arrived to explain what was going on with the Newtons, so he used the computer to check the Baltimore paper's website. Multiple homicides, drug arrests, armed assault, assault and battery, robberies, a home invasion—they were routine crimes in the sprawling city. It was like most major cities and the results would have been similar if he'd checked the Atlanta site instead. When he remembered the mix of petty and hardened criminals he'd encountered daily on the streets, it made him wonder briefly how it could be so different in a town like Wallington. How could a place inhabited by human beings have such a low crime rate? They had no doubt covered the topic in the sociology course he'd been required to take as part of his criminology and criminal justice major at the University of Maryland. He supposed that part of it was having so many people knowing your business. There was also a genuine respect for the police rather than the constant suspicion of police that was prevalent in many big cities—not that reluctance to cooperate with the police was without merit.

During his second year on the job, he'd been placed onto a small task force that mounted a sting operation against a group of cops on the take and it had shaken him more than he wanted to admit. That had been when his dad took him for a weekend fishing on the Chesapeake. The two of them were on a charter boat and there was plenty of cold beer in the cooler. There was a workingman's tavern on one side of the motel where they stayed and a ramshackle crab shack on the other. Justin's faith in his job was restored and Lou Becker had transferred in to be his boss.

Sheriff McFarlane strode toward his office, waving his hat to Justin. "You get the fingerprint information?"

Justin switched the computer to his homepage, grabbed the report, and entered the sheriff's office. "No match for Hillman or Turner," he said, waiting to hear about Newton.

The sheriff sat on the edge of his desk instead of in the chair and Justin opted to lean against the doorframe. "Martha Newton called. Said she was figuring Virgil would be back soon with news about Paul and they'd come down to see us." He ran his left hand across the top of his head. "She didn't say Paul would be with them, so that means Virgil has narrowed down where he might be and hasn't found him yet, or he found him and there's some kind of an issue."

Justin was curious. "Which do you think it is?"

The sheriff shrugged and moved to his chair. "Hard to say. Either is likely, but we'll know before too much longer."

Justin hoped they would have Newton in custody within hours. He really was the only viable suspect, no matter how badly the sheriff and Helen wanted it to not be true. After everything Justin had learned about Gabe Thatcher, he agreed that it was probably a case of manslaughter rather than premeditated murder. If a man like Thatcher had been seen with his sister when she was eighteen, he might have confronted the guy and pounded on him, too. Understanding that didn't make it legal, though.

CHAPTER EIGHTEEN

Helen wasn't overly concerned when Tricia called and asked if she could come over to talk, although the tone of her voice spoke of something important. There were no tears in it, however— not the suppressed wail of a major argument with Justin. Thankfully, Tricia had never been the drama queen type. She was a mature young lady by the age of twenty. Not too serious, Tricia had a good balance of common sense and the idealism that most college students possess in their belief that they can change the world for good. Tricia's desire to inspire middle or high school students to pursue a life of science was commendable and achievable under the right circumstances. Helen did wonder idly at the time why Tricia chose biology instead of engineering as her science inclination. After all, Mitch had been an industrial engineer and Ethan was a mechanical engineer. Perhaps it was due to her preference for living things versus metals and wiring.

With Ethan settled in Augusta, Helen had hopes that Tricia's first teaching job would be in Macon or at the new magnet school in Lawrenceville. The idea of her moving to Baltimore hadn't come as a total surprise, though, after she'd called to talk about meeting Justin at a party. She'd gone to visit a former roommate right after graduation and Tricia asked if Helen believed in love at first sight. Yes, Helen confessed she did, as long as Tricia understood that love wasn't necessarily the correct word for that wobbly-knee, intense feeling. Since Helen and Mitch had fallen in love somewhere between seventh and eighth grade, it was difficult for her to insist that you could only find your soul mate by going through years of failed searches.

Tricia called her again after the first date with Justin; while it might have been mere afterglow, there was no mistaking the surety in her daughter's voice during that nearly hour long discussion. Well no, it had been a listening session on Helen's end. Yes, taking her on a sunset cruise of the Baltimore Harbor, then dinner at a cozy side street restaurant in Little Italy did sound romantic. A day trip planned next for the Eastern Shore of Maryland was certainly a lovely follow up, and a trip to the zoo complete with picnic in the park and later the Twilight Tattoo ceremony and concert at Fort McHenry would indeed give her a broad view of his native Baltimore and Maryland. How nice that he wanted to show her all these things. And he was a policeman, she said?

Mitch had been cautiously approving of the unknown Justin, since Tricia had been selective enough in the few boyfriends she'd previously chosen. Her judgment about men was not in question, but talking about marriage having known the man for less than a week could certainly be questioned. Hearing that the friend whom she'd gone to visit in the first place had put her in contact with potential teaching positions in Baltimore was what propelled Mitch to suggest that perhaps he and Helen should make that trip to Washington, D.C. they'd been talking about. Well yes, he could book them on a really good deal through Baltimore-Washington Airport for an afternoon flight. They could spend the night in Baltimore, and then drive into the capital for a couple of days.

Justin had done one better than merely meeting them. If they didn't mind, his mother had invited them all to dinner and he'd taken the liberty of booking them into a bed and breakfast on the opposite side of the neighborhood park. Had it been nothing more than coincidence that the woman who ran the B&B was a fourth-generation quilter? The public rooms and their bedroom had a fabulous collection from tea cozies to the queen-size quilt on their beautiful four-poster mahogany bed.

And as soon as Justin's father discovered that Mitch was an industrial engineer, he insisted on a quick trip down to his nearby store, a thriving electrical business that he had bought from his boss. Justin's mother sent "the kids" to pick up a bushel of steamed crabs and invited Helen to join her in the kitchen for a glass of wine. Yes, it looked as if Justin and Tricia were in love, or at least they thought they were, and like Helen and Mitch, Sue and Lloyd had been high school sweethearts. Sue was complimentary of Tricia and it had been a pleasant evening with no awkwardness.

At least "the kids" had agreed to have a long engagement and nothing in those ten months caused Helen to think that Tricia and Justin had been mistaken in their assertion of love at first sight.

The sound of Tricia's car pulled Helen from her thoughts and her daughter came through the mudroom as Helen rose from in front of the quilting frame. She was mildly surprised to see Tricia's quilting tote and the hug Tricia gave her was fierce.

She looked carefully into her daughter's face when they broke the embrace. "I was going to offer you tea, but would a glass of wine be better?"

Tricia set her tote and brown leather shoulder bag on the

floor next to the quilting frame. Her mouth faltered in giving a smile and she allowed a tiny sigh to escape her lips. "I suppose it isn't quite a wine-in-the-afternoon situation. I'm not trying to be mysterious, but let's get the tea and start quilting and I'll explain."

Helen tucked her arm into Tricia's and gave her a gentle pull. "Okay, and is there a topic we can discuss in the meantime?"

Tricia laughed, a good sign. "It's related actually. Justin came home for lunch and then had to rush back to the station with some sort of break in the case."

"Oooh," Helen said switching the burner on as Tricia took mugs from the cabinet. "Something to do with Paul Newton?"

Tricia shook her head. "He didn't say." She paused with the silverware drawer open. "Why would you ask that? Do you know something?"

Helen opened the tea box to allow Tricia to make her selection. "Martha came to see me and all I did was tell her that if they could possibly find Paul, it could help clear everything up."

"Do you think he did it?"

"It would be a real shame if he did and, if it was him, all of us who know him can agree that he didn't intend to kill Gabe," Helen said quietly. "For Martha's sake, I really hope it wasn't him, though." Despite Paul as a logical choice, perhaps there was something she didn't know that would lead to a more viable suspect. The kettle vibrated slightly to indicate the water was heating and the two women added sweetener and tea bags to the mugs in anticipation.

"Why don't you set up the TV trays and I'll bring these when they are ready," Helen suggested.

"Okay," Tricia said and Helen could hear the sound of the trays being pulled from the rack in the corner of the room. The set of four faux-antiqued wooden folding trays were decorated with different decoupaged quilt photos. They had been a present from

Tricia after the living room had been transformed. It was both a thoughtful and practical gift.

Helen still had the table extended with the sketch to the side and the completed medallion of the rose bouquet and the squares of purple irises laid out. Unfinished squares of Stargazer lilies, gladiola, and tulips were in their place based on what she'd sketched. Helen found the butterfly fabric left over from a previous piece. She hadn't decided yet if she would quilt that or do new appliqués. She'd folded the fabric into small squares and set them down to see the effect. A rectangular compartmentalized plastic container for the threads Helen was using was on the corner of the table to the left of the sketch. Tricia had set the trays on either side of the table and was looking at the array.

"I like it," Tricia said, her hand hovering to reposition the square with yellow butterflies to where the tulips were to go.

Helen had them by the Stargazer lilies, but Tricia was correct. They were practically the same shade as the yellow tulips and it was a better balance. "I agree," Helen said and moved the fabric to the new spot.

Tricia reached into her bag and pulled out her needle and the pewter thimble that Helen had given her from Mamaw Pierce's collection. Tricia had only vague memories of her great-grandmother and the thimble was a lovely link passed down.

Helen sat, her needled poised, to continue stitching the square she'd been working on and glanced affectionately at her daughter. "Whenever you're ready."

Tricia slipped the thimble on, but anchored the needle into the square of the tulips, her mind obviously not on the project. "I'm not sure where to begin. It's jumbled."

"Justin came home for lunch," Helen prompted.

"Yes," Tricia said and blinked rapidly. "I knew he was excited about something, so naturally I thought it was a break in the case."

Helen doubted they would be doing much quilting. She tried a sip of tea, a tiny tendril of steam curling over the rim. "I thought you said he did have to dash back to the station because of the case."

"Yes, but the call was unexpected and it came after Justin told me about the call from Louis Becker, his old boss in Baltimore."

"Ah," Helen said and waited.

"It's…it's a good thing for Justin," Tricia said, reaching for her mug. "No, it's a great thing for him from a career perspective."

It wasn't too difficult to imagine what Tricia was trying to say. "Something to do with Baltimore, I gather," Helen said in an effort to make it easier.

Tricia shifted her chair slightly and turned her face to Helen, frustration in her eyes. "I don't know what I am supposed to feel. God, you could see how much this meant to Justin. I mean, I do understand. Why now, though? Why couldn't it have happened five years from now? And what am I supposed to say? No, my career and being near you is more important than what is probably a once-in-a-lifetime chance for my husband?"

Helen inhaled silently and quietly released her breath, not responding immediately. Oh dear, what a dilemma! Of course she didn't want Tricia to pack up and go, not so soon, not after they barely arrived—not after Helen thanked her lucky stars to have her daughter and son both near, both in good marriages, good careers, and with grandchildren probably soon to be on the way. She knew not to say any of this that was flashing through her mind. "Oh my, that must have come as quite a surprise," she said instead. "This would be very quick, wouldn't it? The move, I mean."

Tricia nodded as she took another sip. She reached out and stroked one of the yellow tulips with the tip of her finger. "We didn't really have a chance to get to that, although I'm sure we would be talking a matter of weeks."

"Did Justin give an answer already?" Helen couldn't see him doing that.

"Oh no, no, he said that it needed to be a joint decision."

Helen caught the sound of exasperation in her daughter's voice as she pulled her hand back. "There's no reason to pretend that this isn't terribly important to Justin," she said evenly. "This isn't the sort of chance he'll get again if he turns it down, is it?"

Tricia's shoulders slumped momentarily; then she straightened in the chair, her voice firmer. "That's a possibility, I suppose, but not a very good one," she said. "The reason he's being given the opportunity is because of his former boss, and if he stays as the chief of homicide, then he could probably bring Justin in whenever he wanted." She seemed to be struggling to speak objectively. "Except, of course, he wants him now and if Justin turns him down, why would he ask again? We both know that the only reason Justin will say no is if I ask him to."

Helen heard the question in Tricia's voice. "What do you honestly want?"

"For the call never to have come," she said quickly and allowed a small smile. "When I left the workshop today I was in such a good mood—I actually learned a few things from this one. I'm prepared for the end of the school year, and we have a nice summer planned. The house is in good shape and while I'm not trying to make light of Gabe Thatcher's murder, it is nice to know that the sheriff thinks enough of Justin to trust him with this." She looked as if a favorite toy had broken. "Things never stay perfect for long, do they?"

Helen smiled sympathetically. "Not usually. You haven't answered my question yet. Do you want advice or a shoulder?"

Tricia drank some tea before she shifted her chair to fully face her. The conflict in her expression was clear to see. "For all the world I want to tell Justin that no, we shouldn't go to Baltimore. I have a job that I love and it's wonderful being here with you. Despite the adjustments that I know Justin's made, he's getting used to the town and he admires Sheriff McFarlane. We aren't living in our dream house, but that will come." She shrugged, her hands wrapped around the mug. "And none of that matters if I tell Justin to turn this down." She blinked rapidly again, although tears weren't pooled in her eyes. "He'll do it and tell me it's okay, and maybe it will be. And maybe it won't be and we won't have any way to know that unless it eats away at him and erupts someday."

"That can happen," Helen said and watched Tricia's mouth twitch at the corner. Typically, that was a sign she was holding something back. "Is there anything else?"

Tricia drained her mug and set it down on the saucer with enough force to make a clinking sound. "Look, I never told Justin, never told you, hardly wanted to admit it to myself, but I used to worry about him on the streets on patrol. Do you know that two officers were killed in the line of duty and three were wounded from the time we were formally engaged until we moved here?"

Ah. Helen had wondered how Tricia felt about being a police officer's wife. She hadn't raised the subject, thinking it wasn't her place to do so. "I know it's not an easy thing to cope with," she said simply, letting Tricia pick the words she wanted to use.

"There are wives' groups," Tricia said. "I guess I didn't want to join because I kept thinking I could do this on my own. And then when Daddy..." her voice faltered, "when Daddy died the way he did with virtually no warning, no real chance to say good-bye, I thought, my Lord, what if I lost Justin, too?" This time she couldn't stop the tears from welling and Helen passed her the paper napkin from the tray. Tricia dabbed and sniffled. "I know it was much harder on you than on us..."

Helen touched her daughter's arm. "Come here, honey," she said and moved her chair so Tricia could lean into the hug, place her head on Helen's shoulder, and give into a silent sob as Helen stroked her hair. "It was terrible for all of us and with everything that happened. It didn't occur to me that you would be even more worried about Justin because of your daddy. Of course it makes sense, though, and it doesn't for one minute make you a weakling. Human, yes, but if you didn't love Justin the way you do, it wouldn't have affected you so strongly."

Tricia nodded without speaking and Helen held her lightly for a few minutes until she pulled back and grabbed at the napkin from her tray. She blew her nose and straightened, exhaling a deep breath. "Wow, I didn't know that was inside."

"Now it's out where it belongs," Helen said, giving Tricia the I'll-kiss-it-and-make-it-better smile from childhood days when that worked. "I wish you'd told me before instead of trying to keep it all bottled up."

The tension seemed to have left Tricia and she laughed self-consciously. "You're right, as usual. Okay, that's the rest of it then. With us moving here, that worry was behind me. On top of every other reason why I want Justin to say no, if we go back I'm going to have to tell him the truth, to maybe check out the wives' group. I have to learn how to deal with this in a better way."

Helen reached out and patted her cheek, finding it still a bit damp. "Honey, you know that I love having y'all in town and I would give anything in the world for you not to go. However, you didn't fall in love with a local boy and it wasn't as if you didn't have the chance. Justin is a good man, a man your daddy was glad to see you marry. I will absolutely support whatever decision you make. I want you to be happy, and yes, I agree that if y'all do pack up for Baltimore so Justin can be a rising star in homicide, then you need to get whatever support is available on that end. We'll have the summers like we did before."

Tricia held up the wet napkins, her eyes clear. "Waterworks are over," she said in her familiar voice. "I'll tell him the truth, but I do love him too much to force him to turn this down for my sake. Even though Principal Taylor will be disappointed and I'll miss him, the school, and the students, there are other teachers he can bring in and I'm pretty sure I can get on with my old school. I was happy there as well."

Helen offered her saucer for the napkins and looked at the quilt. "Here's what I suggest. This has been draining and, as therapeutic as quilting is, the last thing you need to worry with is dinner tonight. I have a pork tenderloin in the refrigerator. Why don't we cut it into medallions, braise them in herbed gravy, do scalloped potatoes from scratch, and green beans? We can make blackberry cobbler, too. We'll spend time in the kitchen and the house will be full of all those delicious smells. You can text Justin and tell him to come for an early dinner if he can. If he can't, we'll eat and you can take leftovers to him. If we have time after we get everything done, we'll start on the quilt again. Fair enough?"

A teasing glint appeared in Tricia's eyes. "Wasn't there something about a bottle of wine in that mix?"

"Naturally," Helen laughed and they stood, Tricia's anxiety apparently gone. "Thanks, Mamma. I wish this hadn't come up..."

"And, 'if wishes were horses even beggars would ride,' so don't you give that another thought," Helen said, masking her own desire to reach across the miles and thump this Louis Becker on the head. How dare he dangle a carrot like that in front of Justin? All she could say was that he had certainly better stick to whatever promise he made to Justin because if he didn't, he would be answering to her.

CHAPTER NINETEEN

A s he and the sheriff waited, Justin resisted the temptation to call Tricia. He didn't think their pending decision was something to be discussed on the telephone, although a quick text to tell her he would be home as soon as he could might be a correct gesture. They weren't a texting couple, using it only as an infrequent means of communication. His phone buzzed a message as he contemplated what to do. *Am at Mamma's. Dinner here tonite. Call when you can. T.*

OK. Love U. J, seemed to be the appropriate response. He had expected her to go directly to Helen's, hadn't he? There was no way Tricia wouldn't seek her mother's advice and if he were to give Lou an answer in three days or less, Helen was going to find out today or tomorrow anyway. He truly regretted the timing of Lou's offer. Despite his excitement, he couldn't deny that it was disruptive and Tricia was immensely happy being near her mother and in her job. Taking her away was a sacrifice, as had been his leaving Baltimore. In fact, when Tricia had first tentatively raised the subject after Principal Taylor called, they hadn't made an immediate decision either, understanding the magnitude of what she was asking of him.

By coincidence or fortuitous timing, his cousin, who was a career Army officer, had been visiting prior to his new assignment at Fort Lee, Virginia. His family had returned to Baltimore from North Carolina to wait out his second tour to Afghanistan, and when he and Justin were down at The Skipjack Tavern he'd given a hint of the frustration of frequent moves. "There are good parts to it," he'd said, ordering another round of beer. "The kids have skied in the Alps and have been to London. On the other hand, Katie, like a lot of wives, doesn't even look for work anymore. You barely get started at a job and you have to leave, and the kids haven't been in the same school for more than two years in a row."

"Katie's okay with that, though?" Justin had batted Denny's hand away from paying for the drinks. Two tours in Afghanistan, and the man's money was no good in a neighborhood tavern.

Denny tipped his mug against Justin's. "It's about family, man. Army wives, well, all military wives, really, they have this toughness that comes through. They pack up and go for our sake and find something good wherever the new place is." He'd taken a swig. "At least this time we're closer to home. For a while I thought we'd be headed all the way across the country to Washington state. Nothing wrong with that, but it will be nice for all the grandparents to keep the grandkids within driving distance."

The next morning Justin told Tricia that he would call the sheriff in Wallington about the job that Helen had said was open.

Interrupting his thoughts, Kelly opened the door wide enough to poke her head through the double doors, wiping out further thoughts concerning his own situation. It was two seventeen. "Mrs. Newton, Virgil, and Melissa are here," she said.

No mention of Paul. Well, that had probably been too much to hope for. He glanced at the sheriff's office and saw him rising from his desk. "Thanks, Kelly," he said and followed her out to where a stern-faced Martha, a stricken-looking Melissa, and an uncomfortable-looking Virgil waited, standing at the edge of the reception counter.

Sheila asked if anyone would care for a beverage.

"Thank you kindly, Miz Tipton, but we aren't here for social doings," Mrs. Newton said calmly.

"Thank you for coming. I'm Officer Kendall," Justin said, having propped the door to the bay open. Mrs. Newton nodded, Melissa cast her eyes down, and Virgil extended his hand as the women preceded them through the door.

"Martha, Melissa, Virgil," Sheriff McFarlane said in greeting, standing halfway across the wide room indicating they were to file into the large room. Justin noticed that the sheriff had modified the seating; five chairs were in an arc instead of at the table. Three were set closer together, and two allowed him and to sit with their backs to the table, creating a more informal arrangement than an interrogation-style setup. He also noticed that a box of tissues was on the corner of the table. That was different—although judging by the redness around Melissa's eyes, it was a good call. It only took a few minutes to get everyone seated with Martha between her children.

The sheriff passed the box of tissues to Martha before he spoke. "Thank you for being here, Martha. Y'all know that Officer Kendall is in charge of the investigation."

"Better you be here, too, Sheriff," Martha said with a nod to Justin. "No offense meant by that."

"None taken, Mrs. Newton," Justin said politely since that seemed to be the tone that the sheriff wanted to set. "Are you planning to have a lawyer join us?"

The look she shot him bordered on derision although her response was not combative. "We don't have one and there's no sense us beating around the bush." Martha Newton's thin face was set hard against the trials of scratching for a living, but there was an unmistakable pride to her posture as well. "Melissa swears Mr. Gabe has never touched her, but she's got some talking to do."

If Melissa was more than a faint image of what her mother had been, life had indeed been unkind to Martha. Justin was beginning to see why the sheriff was being so solicitous. Melissa's face, splotched though it was, nose slightly swollen from crying, was pretty enough to make a man look twice and allow his gaze to linger. Her wavy, light brown hair with blondish streaks fell like silk to her shoulders and, under other circumstances, it would be easy to imagine laughter in her blue eyes.

"I'm eighteen now," she blurted, taking a fresh tissue from the box her mother held out. "And Gabriel hadn't done anything wrong. He was being a total gentleman about everything, talking about things to me—lots of things that had nothing to do with dishonorable intentions. We hadn't even had a date yet."

Yet. Well, there was a word to raise a red flag.

"Never mind with excuses, girl," her mother snapped and nodded at Virgil. "You tell them."

Justin started to object and saw the sheriff's warning glance. Virgil, at nearly six feet, had a scarecrow build, rough hands with enlarged knuckles, and crooked tobacco-stained teeth. He was uncomfortable in the straight chair and cleared his throat twice before speaking. "Paul saw Missy and Gabe out at her car four, maybe five days ago. He didn't like how it was looking between them and, soon as Gabe left, he went over to see what was going on. Missy started talking about how it wasn't his business, and that she could make up her own mind about who she'd see. That made him real mad because everybody knows what kind of man Gabe is. He chewed on it for a while and came over to my place that night. We went through half a bottle of whiskey and that didn't help none. Fact is, Paul got madder the more he drank. Said he would take care of this."

He pointed his chin toward his sister. "Missy's first one in the family to be going to college, always been good in school, and she's got a chance to really make something of herself. We all been saving to help her out and she knows that. Paul didn't want a man like Gabe getting her all confused about what she ought to be doing."

Melissa was leaking tears again, and her mother shoved a wad of tissues at her. "Paul might have got up a head of steam, but he's not a killer, Sheriff. You know that," she said, her voice somehow mixing firmness and a plea. "He hasn't ever seen the inside of this place, now has he?"

"He wasn't talking about killing Gabe, just making sure he left Missy alone," Virgil interjected quickly. "Fact is, though, I wasn't with him after that and I don't know exactly when Paul took off. He might have gone into the woods before Gabe got beat on. Paul gets mad like that, sometimes he heads on out to work it out of his system—takes to the woods, hunts and fishes, out of sight of everybody. He always keeps camping stuff in his truck in case he gets a notion to go off. He was gone for a week after Nancy left him. He's got one of them pay-as-you-go cell phones, but there's no reception once you get off the main road. Not being able to reach him isn't unusual."

"Does that mean you've been out looking for him?" Justin wanted to steer the interview in a productive way.

Martha nodded first. "I went over to see Helen, to ask her advice. She told me how if we could find Paul, it'd be better to get this over with. I sent Virgil on his way."

Justin hid his exasperation. For crying out loud, why would the woman go to his mother-in-law for exactly the same advice that the sheriff had given her—or that he would have given her, had he been allowed to talk to her.

"There's nearly half a dozen spots Paul favors," Virgil explained, unconsciously popping the knuckles of his left hand, "most of them hard to get to. I've been to all 'cept one now, so I reckon that's where he is. Problem is that with the bad rain last week, the road's washed out in one section. Need a four-wheel drive to get in there and my truck won't make it." He shifted in the chair. "I saw couple of the Wildlife Fishery guys while I was out and they hadn't seen Paul either, so I figure he's at Crazy Dan's old shack. You know they posted it for sale for back taxes last year? Guess the family inherited it, but they didn't want to pay the taxes from what we heard. Going for practically nothing and Paul is looking to buy it. Makes sense that he'd go there. He's been sort of working around the place, see. No harm in that since he's only making improvements."

The sheriff turned to Justin. "Dan Gabler, an uncle in the family, always was on the strange side." Mrs. Newton snorted as he continued. "Several years ago he started running around town saying as how Wallington was being taken over by federal agents, or maybe it was aliens disguised as federal agents. He wasn't very clear about it. They were building the new post office and he said it was a cover story for what was really going on. That was the high point in what had been a long life of warning about the town being targeted. No one ever figured out why Wallington would be of such interest, but that didn't matter to Dan. He was harmless other than he'd get a snoot full of liquor in him and he was prone to taking up the defense of the square with his rifle."

"Now he never shot nobody," Virgil said firmly.

"No, he didn't, except it was getting way too frequent," the sheriff said. "So the last time I told him I'd take his guns. And that's when he said we were a disgrace to the town and if we were too bamboozled to see the danger, then he'd go where it was safe and we could all go to the devil. Sorry, Martha."

"That's why his place is off Turner Lane, no more than an old logging road that you can't get over unless you got four-wheel drive," Virgil said. "There's three acres, I think, and a nice creek runs close to the shack. Crazy Dan dug himself a well, but got no power or phone, of course. He didn't mind Paul coming around. He trusted him and I think Paul used to haul provisions out to him sometimes."

Justin really didn't care about the story and he wanted to bring it to an end. "I gather Mr. Gabler is deceased?"

Virgil grinned unexpectedly as both the sheriff and Mrs. Newton looked as if they were suppressing a chuckle. "He came into town, it was what, Sheriff, two years ago?"

"About that," Sheriff McFarlane said.

"Crazy Dan rolled into town one morning at sunup. The clock tower was being repainted and they had scaffolding in place. He climbed right on up, a jar of moonshine in one hand and an American flag in the other, like the kind you wave around at Fourth of July," Virgil said. "He commenced to hollering about giving the town one last chance to understand what was happening in our midst, I believe was the way he put it."

"He'd shoved the scaffolding away from the building when he climbed up, and before we could get it back up, he came tumbling right down," the sheriff finished. "Lucky for us it was on the grassy side, so it wasn't as much a mess as it would have been had he hit the sidewalk out front."

"Crazy old coot that he was, the family did do up a nice funeral for him," Mrs. Newton said, her voice a little warmer. She looked to see that Melissa had stopped crying and moved her gaze between the sheriff and Justin. "I think Virgil's right— Crazy Dan's place is most likely where Paul is."

The sheriff looked directly into Virgil's brown eyes. "You want to give us directions?"

"I figure it'd be better if I go with you," he said slowly. "We don't know for sure what happened and depending on what he did, Paul might not even know Gabe is dead."

Justin replayed the scene of the crime as he watched everyone in the room. Murder fueled by anger was an ugly thing. He'd seen his share of bodies with entire magazines emptied into them, multiple stab wounds, and knew what a tire iron could do to a man. He knew the difference between a beating meant to kill and what had been done to Thatcher. "Mrs. Newton, would you like us to have a car take you and Melissa home while Virgil goes with us? That way, when we get back, Virgil will have his truck here."

"I'd be grateful," Martha said, standing and motioning for the others to stand also. "Virgil, Paul will have at least one gun being as he's gone that far into the woods. Sheriff, Officer Kendall, I'd ask you to let Virgil talk with him first. We got enough trouble as it is with this."

"Yes ma'am," Sheriff McFarlane said solemnly. "And we appreciate you coming in," he repeated.

Justin asked Sheila to call for one of the patrols to swing by as Mrs. Newton and Melissa asked for the ladies' room. There was a brief discussion about who to take and the sheriff said that, under the circumstances, he thought Justin and Lenny would be enough with Virgil along. Ordinary procedure would call for an extra vehicle, but the department only had two Explorers and one of them was in the shop getting a service. While half the men owned four-wheel drive vehicles, the sheriff was convinced that Paul wouldn't cause them problems. "If he is the one that beat on Gabe, it was because of Missy, and no other reason," Virgil said flatly. "He won't be taking a shot at one of you, long as he knows who you are."

Justin wasn't as comfortable with that decision as everyone else seemed to be, although there were obviously dynamics at play here to which he was unfamiliar. He'd seen similar situations in Baltimore, though, where a friend or family member could take an explosive standoff and persuade an individual to come out peacefully. In each of those cases, however, there was normally a significant police presence prompting the intervention. Ah well, he supposed they could always call for backup if a standoff did happen, and this way he wouldn't look like he didn't trust the sheriff's judgment.

Lenny was on patrol in the Explorer and he arrived at the station minutes ahead of Dave, who volunteered to drive Mrs. Newton and Melissa home. Virgil climbed into the back seat. Lenny knew how to get to Turner Lane with no problem, but beyond that he would need Virgil's directions.

"Nobody's logged these woods since the paper mill shut down better than ten years ago," Lenny said as they cleared the main part of town. "The roads weren't very good roads even then, and the county had no call to keep them up. Not more than two or three are passable these days, and then it might be only part of the road. Lots of brush has grown up, too," he said, easing around a truck loaded full of chicken crates approaching the Happy Cackling Poultry Farm.

Virgil spoke up for the first time. "You know where the burnt store is on Turner?"

Lenny nodded and swiveled his head to Justin. "There's only about four or five houses left on Turner. Back when the loggers were coming through, the original Mr. Turner, that would be Joe Turner's granddaddy, put in a store with a BBQ pit, an extra big cooler for beer, and might have been peddling a little moonshine, too. Did a good business until they quit logging. Rumor had it that since no one wanted to buy the store, the fire might not have been an accident." Lenny slowed to make the turn. "It was pretty old, though, and it wasn't a clear case of arson, so the fire chief didn't think it was worth making a fuss over."

Justin wondered, as he often did, at the habit of everyone in town feeling compelled to tell a story no matter what topic came up. Was it this way in all small towns or was it some uniquely Southern trait?

It was obvious that the county wasn't putting a great deal of money into the upkeep of Turner Lane either, and the only way Justin could tell there were houses were the gravel drives marked by mailboxes, all of which had some sort of decoration. They were mostly stone-clad columns with the mailbox on top, although one was a wooden carving of a raccoon on his hind legs with his paws holding the box. Every house was set far enough into the trees so as to be screened from sight. Long lines of barbed wire or split railing fences lined both sides of the lane, although no livestock was visible. Justin almost reached out to grab the dashboard when Lenny bounced across a series of different size potholes as they approached a blackened area to the left. Small green growth was scattered among the burned remains that featured a concrete foundation with rotting remnants of a roof and walls lying on or around it.

"Road ends 'bout a half mile down," Virgil said, leaning forward. "You'll see a break in the trees to the right. That's the entrance. What's left of the road goes in another half mile or so. Can't see the shack from the road, but it's 'bout a hundred yards in."

Justin keyed the radio to report their location and landmark. He hoped again that everyone was right about the reception they would get from Paul Newton. They couldn't sneak in with the sound of the Explorer sloughing across the rough terrain. In this kind of an environment, Newton could be lining up a shot at them and they wouldn't know until it was too late.

CHAPTER TWENTY

Justin supposed that the faint indentation of ruts they were navigating could have once been a road, and he was grateful it was no longer a distance to drive than it was. No wonder Virgil hadn't attempted it in a regular truck. They broke into the slight clearing of a structure that was actually a fairly respectable cabin, even though they had referred to it as a shack. A stone chimney rose on the side, and what were obviously newly installed steps led from the short graveled walkway to a porch with four brand new posts and new boards two thirds of the way across. The newness was jarring against the grayed exterior of the rest of the cabin. An old brown Bronco was parked under the wide branches of an oak tree to the right of the porch.

As they cautiously climbed out of the Explorer, pistols still holstered but safeties off, a man stepped from the cabin, a tool belt around his waist. In the strictest sense of the word, perhaps the hammer in his hand could be declared a weapon. If this was Paul Newton, he didn't look as if he was on the run from the law.

Virgil was two paces in front of them, his hands raised high. "Paul, this here's Deputy Kendall and you know Lenny. You got a gun in there?"

"Of course I've got a gun, you idiot. Got two as a matter of fact. You here about Gabe? He take out a complaint, did he?" Paul leaned against one of the posts, arms folded across his chest. "How come you doing their job for them?" He wasn't as tall as Virgil or as lean; he was closer in build to Justin, his short hair lighter in color. His upper chest and arms were clearly defined from a life of working carpentry and other handyman tasks if what Justin had been told was correct. He had the same shape face as Virgil, and if you heard his voice on a telephone, you might not know which brother was speaking.

"Virgil is trying to look out for you, Mr. Newton," Justin said carefully, reluctant to pull his pistol with no overt threat coming from Newton. "What do you mean about Mr. Thatcher?"

Paul glowered, not moving. "I mean I gave him exactly what he deserved and I thought he was at least enough of a man to take it like man. I reckon he's a mamma's boy after all to go whining to the police."

Nothing like a confession with a witness present.

"Gabe's dead. You done killed him," Virgil blurted to Justin's irritation.

Oh great, Justin thought. He had wanted to get Paul Newton on record.

"You don't know what you're talking about," Paul said with a frown. "He was sitting on the floor holding his nose when I left him."

Justin noticed that Lenny had positioned to Virgil's right, the three of them creating a barrier between Paul and his truck, although his surprise at the news about Thatcher seemed genuine. "Your brother is correct," Justin said. "Mr. Thatcher is dead, apparently from a blow to the back of his head."

Paul released his arms and hooked his thumbs into the tool belt. "That don't make sense. I didn't hit him on the back of his head. I smacked him in that pretty-boy face and a couple of times in the belly to make my point. It's what the man deserved."

Justin was at the bottom step now, still sensing no discernible threat from Paul. "Well, we need to take you in," Justin said, ready to leap up the steps. "That's the only way we're going to get this cleared up."

"Take me in. You mean arrest me?" He glared at Virgil, then at Lenny. "Like some crook? That's what you think?"

Lenny's voice was steady. "Paul, if what you're telling us is true, then you've got a story the lawyer will be interested in."

"Lawyer, what lawyer?" Paul was in a defensive stance now, legs slightly apart, hands by his side.

Justin stood his ground and locked his eyes onto Paul's, despite the fact the man was looking down on him. "Mr. Newton, by your own admission, you assaulted Mr. Thatcher, and Mr. Thatcher appears to have died as a result of that assault. I am going to place you under arrest and read you your rights, one of which is the right to a lawyer that will be provided for you if you cannot afford one. I would prefer to do this without anyone getting hurt."

Paul turned his head, slipped the hammer into the tool belt, and spat on the ground. The look on his face was undisguised disgust. "Who are you again?"

"Deputy Kendall—the Yankee boy that Tricia Crowder married," Virgil interrupted. "Mamma sent me along to make sure you didn't cause trouble. Now come on and let's get this figured out."

Paul took a deep breath, spat again, and broke eye contact. "I got to go with y'all or can I drive my own truck?"

"I'm going to need to put the cuffs on," Justin said, holding them aloft. "It's standard procedure."

"It's standard BS," Paul snapped. "You may not be from around here, but he sure is," he said pointing at Lenny. "Not a man in town don't know that Gabe Thatcher is up to no good when he starts paying attention to a woman."

"Paul, we hear you," Lenny said, "but we didn't make this mess, so you come on and cooperate and let us get it sorted out."

"Fine, if that's what it takes to straighten this crap out, and that's what this is," he said and jerked his thumb over his shoulder. "Virgil, I got some provisions inside and I don't want my tools getting stole. Can he pack up and drive the Bronco in for me?"

"As long as we take possession of the guns," Justin said. "You coming down or shall I come up?"

Paul slowly moved his hands to unbuckle his tool belt and he dangled it over the edge for Virgil to take. "Don't get in a snit, Deputy. You think you got to cuff me, go ahead on and do it." He held his hands out front and grimaced as Justin motioned for him to turn around.

Justin fastened the cuffs and recited the Miranda warning while Virgil looked pained. They were on their way with no further delay, leaving Virgil to tend to his tasks. Justin radioed in to the station and the sheriff said they would telephone Mrs. Newton on Paul's behalf.

The chairs had been rearranged into an interrogation setting, and the sheriff asked Justin to remove the cuffs. Sheila brought coffee in for them all.

Paul had said he didn't care if a lawyer was present or not, but the sheriff didn't want to take any chances and Jesse Shipley, the senior public defender, arrived as they were going through the preliminaries of a statement. There was no need for introductions and Sheila brought another cup of coffee. Jesse stressed to Paul that he wasn't required to say anything, especially since they hadn't had a chance to confer privately. Paul swore he had nothing to say other than the truth. Sheriff McFarlane nodded to Justin to turn the video camera on again.

Paul was stubbornly insistent that there was some kind of mistake. "I tell you what I think happened," he said. "Gabe was drunk or well on his way to it when I got there, and at first he just sat at his desk and laughed, telling me there wasn't nothing other than flirting and that it was good for Missy. I grabbed the cell phone off his desk and looked to see that he had three calls from Missy on it, plain as day," he protested. "She's eighteen years old and Gabe ought to have known she'd get a crush on him like every other fool woman in town does. I told him to stand up and yeah, he came around the desk and I knocked on him a couple of times and left him moaning on the floor. He didn't so much as try to block a punch. That ought to tell you that he was either so drunk he couldn't or he knew he had it coming. And yeah, I think I probably told him I'd do worse by him if he didn't leave her alone, but if I'd wanted him dead, I would have shot him to begin with. How is it that he couldn't have gotten up and slipped on the rug or something like that and hit his head after I was gone?"

"So you're saying that you didn't hit him on the head," Justin repeated carefully.

Paul smacked his fist into his palm. "I gave him a bloody nose and doubled him over with no more than two or three punches. He was on the floor, curled up like a baby," he said. "I didn't even kick him when he was down like I could have. He pulled up into a sort of sitting position. By that I mean he had his back to the desk and I left him like that."

No one challenged his version. "Why did you leave town without telling anyone?"

Paul shrugged. "I'm not going to say that I wasn't drinking some before I went over and I was still mad when I left him. The more I thought about it, the better idea it seemed for me to head out and be by myself for a few days. Didn't have TV, radio, or phone. How was I to know Gabe was dead? I'm telling you that what I did to the man shouldn't have killed him."

Jesse looked at Justin and the sheriff. "Could I have a few minutes with y'all?"

The sheriff opened the door and called for Lenny. He came in and the sheriff nodded to Paul. "You probably need a break. Lenny will escort you to the bathroom, then get you another coffee if you want."

Justin almost groaned with the thought of having an uncuffed murder suspect, well, okay, maybe it had been manslaughter, wandering the station in the custody of a single deputy. On the other hand, Paul had been surly and snappish, not violent.

As soon as the door was closed, Jesse spread his hands. If he was the senior public defender, the other two must have been fresh out of law school. Justin didn't think he was much over thirty. His brown hair was just long enough to have some curl to it but barely touching his ears, and his brown eyes looked both men over carefully.

"Sheriff, Justin, you have that autopsy report yet? If Paul's right and Gabe was legally drunk, him falling and hitting his head is plausible."

"I'll check on the status, but they were backlogged," Justin said. "I don't think we have it."

"Well, you've got to take into consideration that Paul said he'd been drinking, too. His remembering could be more the way he wants to remember it than what really happened," the sheriff pointed out.

"True," Jesse said and fingered the knot in his red paisley tie.

He'd hung his suit jacket on the back of the chair when he'd come in. "You know what the D.A. is looking at for charges?"

Both men shook their heads. "That's something you can try and work out with the D.A.," Sheriff McFarlane said with a half smile. "Our job was to find out who did it, and no matter what else I'd say we have the right man."

Jesse tapped the outside of a very thin file with his forefinger. "I wouldn't have minded Paul keeping his mouth shut until I could talk privately with him, but I'll have a go at Wayne this afternoon if I can find him, and for sure by in the morning." He sighed and stood as Lenny escorted Paul in. "You want me to see about bail?"

Paul set a fresh cup of coffee down on the table. "I don't want Mamma or anyone spending money on that. You think you can talk to the judge about letting me go on...what's that they say on TV? The one about taking my word for me not running off?"

"On your own recognizance," all four said together. Jesse looked at his watch. "I won't be able to get the judge this late unless it's an emergency."

"Don't be interrupting the man at supper or having a drink after work. That'll put him in a bad mood," Paul said. "I guess I can do a day or two with the sheriff 'til y'all come to your senses and find out that the couple of whacks I gave Gabe didn't kill him." He waved toward the video camera that Justin had shut off. "Let's get this over with and maybe you can talk to the judge tomorrow."

The remainder of the interview, a written statement, and processing Newton were accomplished with no delay and Justin was startled to see that they wrapped up before six o'clock. He sent a quick text to Tricia telling her he could be on his way within thirty minutes. He took her return text of, OK, cobbler in the oven, as a good sign. If she was really upset with him, wouldn't she want to be alone so they could talk about it? Although he supposed that she and Helen could be planning to double-team him, he didn't think that was their style.

Jesse departed to pay a courtesy visit to Martha Newton, and Sheriff McFarlane asked Justin to come into his office as the evening shift swap was underway.

"You have any problem getting Paul in?" he asked, leaning on the corner of the desk rather than taking his seat.

Justin stood behind the chair in front of the desk, grasping the back of it with both hands. This was obviously not intended to be a long conversation. "Nothing different from what you heard in there. I think he honestly believes he didn't kill Thatcher, but that would be a lawyer point to sort out. Intent versus outcome, that kind of defense. Sorry about the autopsy report. I should have followed up on it yesterday."

The sheriff shrugged. "They said it was on the way; we had no reason to not take their word. It'll be in tomorrow's delivery. According to Irma, Howard comes in later tonight. Jesse can talk to him from a medical point of view and for all I know, there's a good case to be made for Paul." He paused and looked at Justin carefully. "You've handled this well. How are you feeling about digging around in some of the town's dirt?"

"It's been eye opening, that's for sure," Justin said, hesitating for a fraction of a second longer than he intended.

Sheriff McFarlane cocked his head. "Something else you wanted to tell me?"

This was definitely not the right time. It had been a tumultuous day and the issue of Baltimore was far from settled with Tricia. He shouldn't bring it up to the sheriff yet. He shook his head. "Naw. It's been quite a day, though, hasn't it?"

The sheriff eased from his position, now moving around to his chair. "Yep, and I'd say it's coming up on time for a cold beer. See you in the morning."

Justin lifted his hand in acknowledgment and hurried to his car, wanting to swing by the liquor store for wine. It wasn't that Helen didn't keep a stock on hand, it was more that he liked making the gesture. She was a woman who constantly gave to others and small expressions of thoughtfulness seemed to suit her. A flash of regret registered as he thought of her generosity of spirit and, quite frankly, the enjoyable nature of his mother-in-law. He would miss the frequent visits with her and the instant sensation of warmth when you crossed the threshold of her home.

The truth was that when he agreed to leave Baltimore—his Orioles, his Ravens, the familiar hangouts, family, and friends— he'd done so because he loved his wife. There was no other reason, and he had braced himself for living in a town stalled in time. After all, who in Baltimore even knew where Wallington, Georgia was? Sure, his family thought Tricia and her parents had charming accents, and when they'd come for the wedding weekend they all had a good time, but that was hardly the same as giving up the hum of a major metropolitan east coast city.

Virgil's description of him earlier—Deputy Kendall, the Yankee boy that Tricia Crowder married—summed it up. Aside from the fact that Maryland was well below the geographic Mason-Dixon Line and that you could get great fried chicken, he was considered a big city Yankee who had only been accepted because of the esteem that most people felt for Helen and Mitch Crowder. There had been more curiosity than skepticism, and even though he found the story-telling inclination of virtually everyone in town to be a bit odd, he had paid attention. The profusion of guns among the citizenry of Wallington had initially taken him aback, as had advertising in the local paper encouraging customers to be sure and check out the gun stores' holiday offerings for children's and ladies' models of guns before they all sold out. He had to admit that the preponderance of firearms had not led to a single shooting since he'd been on the force.

Adapting to the slower pace of life, remembering that you had to stock up on liquor on Saturday because you couldn't buy booze on Sunday, and going to an actual covered dish dinner on the grounds at the church had come more easily to him than he imagined. There was a comforting familiarity to a place that still had a town square dominated by a 1920s red brick city hall with a white clapboard clock tower.

Despite the inconvenience of no mega hardware store and a town lake that couldn't begin to compare to the Chesapeake, he didn't miss hearing a sobbing mother on the television news describe her ten-year-old who had been caught in the crossfire of rival gangs or whatever the particular violence was. And yet, in the space of the conversation with Lou, he'd seen himself returning to that very environment—the gritty reality of life on the streets and daily tragedies served up by careless or career criminals. There were the successes, too, of police who made a difference for people of the inner city. They helped kids to turn from the seething emotions that could erupt into deadly encounters with a wrong word, kids who viewed jail time as solidifying their street credentials.

He didn't know how to explain that to Tricia, and probably never would be able to articulate it in the right way. The very fact that he was being offered an opportunity he had never expected was important to them as a family, wasn't it? How could he turn it down?

He pulled into the parking lot of Mike's Liquors and sent a text to let Tricia know he was on the way. If he was lucky, she and Helen had talked through their dilemma and all would be calm in the Kendall household. Was that really too much to hope for?

CHAPTER TWENTY-ONE

The aromas from the kitchen permeated the house. The tenderloin medallions and pot of green beans were simmering on the stove. Hot, sweetened blackberry juice peeked through the golden lattice of the cobbler crust as it sat cooling on the counter. The casserole of scalloped potatoes was bubbling to completion and a mixed green salad sat in the refrigerator with plastic wrap over the top. The table was set and glasses of red wine had replaced mugs of tea on the trays in the quilting room. Tricia was relaxed now, her fingers making smooth, small stitches as she quilted the tulip square.

They both tilted their heads to the sound of a car pulling into the drive and Tricia rose to walk to the front door and open it for Justin.

"Wow, it smells great in here," he said predictably, holding a wine bag in his left hand, slipping his right around Tricia's waist, and turning his cheek to accept a kiss from Helen.

"I'll take this while you kiss your wife," she said, tugging the bag from his grasp and discreetly leaving them alone for a few minutes. Their murmured exchange was too low for her to hear, not that she would have wanted to eavesdrop. She was glad she had been there for Tricia today and, as much as it pained her to think of them leaving, she meant it when she said she would support whatever their decision was.

She carried a third glass of wine into the quilting room, happy to see the couple still in an embrace. "Into the kitchen while we finish up and I want as much a report as you can give us," she said briskly, handing the glass to Justin. "Did you find Paul?"

Justin lifted his glass to her in a toast. "I would ordinarily ask how you would know that, but Mrs. Newton explained that she sought your advice yesterday."

She waved her glass in the direction of the kitchen and spoke over her shoulder as they moved through the dining room. "I didn't know for certain what Martha might do. My only part was to urge her to locate Paul and convince him to come in."

"Quit stalling," Tricia said, reaching into the refrigerator. "What's going on? If Sheila was at the station everyone in town will know by breakfast anyway. I would hate to be the only one at school tomorrow who isn't in on it."

"What can I help with?" Justin asked instead with a hint of a grin.

"Sit, stay out of the way, and talk," Tricia said, pointing to a stool at the island.

He held up both hands in surrender, being careful not to slosh the wine. "Mrs. Newton, Virgil, and Melissa did come in to give us some information. Virgil then went with us out in the woods off Turner Lane and Paul was there. We took him back to the station and Mr. Shipley is representing him."

Tricia whisked the plastic wrap from the salad bowl. "Did

he confess?"

Justin hesitated. "I can't give you much detail, but he did admit to assaulting Mr. Thatcher."

Helen sighed, removing the lids from the pans on the stove. This was exactly what she was expecting and what she had hoped wouldn't happen. "Poor Martha, I'll call her in the morning. I know she's devastated."

Tricia pursed her lips and scanned the table as if checking to see if they'd overlooked anything. "Jesse is a good lawyer. I mean, you are talking manslaughter instead of murder, right? I can see Paul losing his temper, but not plotting to kill Gabe."

Helen could tell Justin was struggling as to how much he should say. She appreciated his desire to maintain confidence, but really, Tricia was correct. Anything Sheila overheard would have already started making the rounds.

"How the prosecutor wants to handle this is up to him," was what Justin tried to settle on.

"Oh, piddle," Tricia responded, returning to the refrigerator for salad dressing—ranch and Italian, both light varieties. "Paul is not a cold-blooded killer. He didn't give you a problem bringing him in, did he?"

Helen couldn't help feeling sorry for Justin, no matter that he was in the process of once again carrying her only daughter almost 1,000 miles away from her. "Tricia, honey, don't badger your poor husband. He was put in charge of the investigation and it looks as if he has done what needed to be done. Whatever happens next is not up to him."

Tricia gave a semi-scowl. "Well, I would have preferred it to have been Tommy Hillman. He's a man who's due a comeuppance. Well, that whole family is when you get right down to it."

Helen switched the burners off and took pity on the look of confusion on Justin's face at the sudden tangent. "Tricia, the Hillmans' lack of true compassion and their other unpleasant traits are not what are at stake here," she said and opened the oven door to take the potatoes out. "Justin, we'll be needing another bottle of wine opened. I'm fine with sticking with red unless either of you want white."

"I'm on it," he said, slipping from the stool and passing his glass to Tricia who blew him a kiss with her free hand.

Tricia started again as soon as they sat. "Paul wasn't really hiding out was he? I mean, not like some survivalist?" Tricia asked, passing her plate to be filled. It was easier for Helen to serve than send the hot bowls around.

"Let me explain about Paul and Tricia's relationship," Helen said, thinking it might help Justin. "Martha has been cleaning for me for a long time, and Tricia could do no wrong in her eyes," she said. Tricia adopted a "who, me?" look. "Paul was a couple of years younger than Tricia, but he would come along sometimes and play with her as long as it didn't involve dolls. He was also mechanically inclined and could fix toys that had maybe been handled a bit roughly. When she was older, Tricia rode her bicycle to school and had a habit of running over things with her tires or managing to slip a chain and Paul would come to her rescue."

"Like my big brother should have, but Mr. I-Don't-Have-Time-For-My-Baby-Sister couldn't be bothered," Tricia said with a teasing look thrown Helen's way, then speared a tomato chunk with her fork. "So, what was Paul up to?"

Justin tore a piece from a roll and buttered it. "He was at some place they called Crazy Dan's that you couldn't get to without a four-wheel drive. He didn't give us any trouble."

"Poor Dan, I know people couldn't resist calling him that, but it truly was a shame," Helen said, remembering the shock of the community at the news of his bizarre death. "He'd always been an odd duck, but nobody thought he would go off like he did."

Tricia swirled potatoes in the gravy. "Didn't the circle do that beautiful quilt for the Esther House fundraiser after that?"

"We did," Helen said. "As a matter of fact, one of the Savannah Wallingtons was visiting. She attended the luncheon, was set on having that quilt, and bought a fistful of tickets to win it." She gestured for Justin's plate for seconds and he held up his thumb and forefinger to indicate a small portion. "Esther House works with the hospital's mental health people, not that Dan ever got any proper help. Oh, he was the oldest of the four Gabler brothers. Clancy married an Alabama girl and moved away right after high school, Randy has the business, Mike works at the factory, and poor Dan never did fit anywhere. Hard to know if he could have been helped, even if they had tried. Truth is that everyone considered him to be harmless, which, really he was, except to himself as it turned out. Y'all want coffee with the cobbler?"

"I'm fine," Justin said and Tricia shook her head. Helen didn't want to brew a whole pot for only one or two cups. She'd stay with wine and maybe have hot tea after the kids left. She wasn't trying to prolong their visit, although they didn't seem to be in a hurry. Perhaps they needed a little more time before they had their next serious conversation. She heard her name and realized she'd missed part of what Justin was saying.

"Oh, it has to be a dozen or maybe two, if not more," Tricia said, looking at her as though for an answer.

"I'm sorry, what was that?"

Justin's plate was almost as clean as if he'd licked it. "I was asking about how many quilts you do for charity each year?"

Helen reached for the dirty dishes and Tricia hopped up. "You stay put. I'll clear the table and get the cobbler," she said. "Impress Justin with the volume of quilts you and the circle turn out."

"Oh well, that's not as easy to answer as it should be," Helen said moving her hands as Tricia grabbed her plate, salad bowl and silverware. "We do have a dozen or so that we routinely provide for annual fundraisers, then people come to us for different ones, and that doesn't count what I and some of the others do for our individual causes. Quilts are really popular at the hospital, the assisted living facilities, the nursing homes, places like that."

"The Red Cross office keeps a stack on hand, don't they?" Tricia set cobbler in front of them and that reminded Helen that she needed to add vanilla ice cream to the grocery list.

"Oh my, yes," she said, noticing a questioning look on Justin's face.

He poised a forkful of cobbler almost to his mouth. "And you do all these by hand? How can you do that many?"

Helen exchanged a smile with Tricia before she answered. "Hand and machine quilting. Now that can get a discussion going. No, there are a few women in town who do only quilting by hand. Most of us mix the two because you are correct in the amount of time it takes. Especially with most women working now, using a sewing machine for part of the work is essential." She waved a hand in the direction of the quilting room. "The weekly circle meeting is only by hand because that's the way we wanted to do it. Most everyone has multiple projects going at one time, though. Each of the women in the circle brings whatever she happens to be working on unless it's a specific project that we're doing together."

Justin had one bite of cobbler left and he glanced at the quilted placemat under his dessert plate. "Uh, I hope this doesn't come out wrong, but quilting sure seems to be a big thing here."

Tricia gave him one of those sidelong looks that are the equivalent to kicking a husband under the table, and Helen laughed softly. "Oh it is, and has been for as many generations as

I can recall." She motioned with her hand to see if Justin wanted more cobbler and he shook his head. "Mitch, God rest his soul, was the same way when we married. He couldn't believe the number of quilts and amount of quilting stuff I had." She allowed a fond smile at the memory and raised a finger. "He, however, had this car that he dearly loved and was restoring."

As Helen expected, Justin's eyes registered interest. "Oh yeah, what was it?"

Helen smiled. "See, I mention old cars and it's like flipping on a light switch. Anyway, Mitch's was a Duster in this yellow color with a black stripe."

"Oh yeah, that might have been a Duster 340. Bright yellow, black stripes was a popular choice," he said quickly and looked chagrined. "Sorry, didn't mean to interrupt."

Helen laughed. "That's what I'm talking about, though. I say Duster and you know right away what it was. Lord, the time and money Mitch spent on that car and all the tools. Heavens, we never parked in the garage, well, carport, because there was no room with the car in pieces, all the parts, extra tires, and what have you around. Even after he finished with it, there was always something that he was messing with on it. He gave it to Ethan as a college graduation present. You could have knocked me over with a feather when he did that, but then he told me he was on the lookout for a Barracuda. I think it was so he could start all over again."

"Your Uncle Joe has some classic car, doesn't he?" Tricia collected the dishes and carried them to the counter.

The admiration on Justin's face was immediate. "Oh man, yeah, he has a 1968 Ford Mustang GT Fastback Bullitt, the one from the movie. I mean, it's like the one in the movie. Got it on a great deal because the guy who had it let it get in terrible shape and his widow wanted it gone. Man, he spent almost two years restoring it and what a beauty it is now. He took it completely apart and went all over the place locating the right parts. He was really careful about who he let touch it, but I would go over and hang out with my cousin and he'd let us help a little bit on some of the stuff where he really needed an extra pair of hands." He stopped. "Oh, you mean quilting is sort of like cars?"

Helen smiled. "Exactly. That passion for something, the connection you feel—for us, instead of metal parts, it's fabric. Instead of a certain make or model, it's a pattern or technique. There's incredible history when it comes to quilts, much of it personal family history." She lifted one finger. "And the history of quilting goes back thousands of years."

"Look at all the websites, magazines, books, car clubs, rallies, and so forth that you have devoted to cars," Tricia said, coming behind Justin and giving him a quick shoulder rub. "Quilters have that same kind of personal and group exchanges without the noise, grease, rust, and all."

He nodded once and moved his right hand up to squeeze Tricia's as he looked at Helen. "Okay, sure, I can see that now that you explain it like that. Makes a lot more sense to me."

Helen stood, sending what she hoped was as warm a smile as she felt, holding back the pang at the idea that there might not be many more impromptu dinners like this. "I must say that it has been a very long day for everyone, so why don't you two run along?"

She dismissed their offer to stay and clean up and Tricia told Justin to go, that she would be right behind him. Her eyes were wet and the hug was prolonged. "Thank you so much, Mamma. No matter what we do, you know I love you. We love you."

Helen held back a sniffle, wanting to send Tricia off with the assurance that the decision was theirs to make. "Honey, there is not one thing that can change that no matter where you live. You head on home and y'all get this situation worked out in whatever way is best for both of you, not for what you think is good for me. Promise?"

Tricia bobbed her head rapidly and slipped from the door. Helen stood there, her arm raised in good-bye until Tricia's taillights disappeared down the street. It wasn't very late and Helen put the kettle on to boil as she puttered with the dishes. What a lot of emotion the day had brought—everything from Martha helping the police locate her son, to Justin's out of the blue news, to bringing up the memory of poor Dan Gabler.

Helen carried her tea into the den, stretching her legs onto the footstool, holding the mug of tea on her lap instead of using the end table. She was content to sit and sip, reflecting on all that had happened rather than bothering with the television, not even a music station. Gabriel's handsome face with his charming smile came to mind, the face that had been pretty no matter that he was a boy, the laughter and freedom of spirit that was like none of his contemporaries. Actually, Helen couldn't think of a man of her generation who was like Gabe. Despite the turmoil he constantly stirred up and behavior that she truly shouldn't excuse, she did excuse it, as did most people when they stepped back and put it into perspective.

The problem came during that space of time before perspective kicked in—that heat of anger that Paul had evidently not been able to let go of. But, and as Tricia said, Paul was not a killer. She was certain that he would never have confronted Gabe with the intent of doing more than teaching him a lesson. Although she did not for one moment approve of him confronting Gabe the way he did, Paul was by no means the only man who had done so. She was glad that Jesse was his lawyer, meaning no offense to Dale McKenzie or Lorie Smith, the other two public defenders that usually drew cases in Wallington.

Jesse was the senior of the three, had grown up in the town, and he had been a freshman on the basketball team the year that Wayne Dickinson was a junior. Not that Wayne would be unduly influenced in his prosecutor duties, but Jesse would have a better chance of talking a deal with him than if he were trying to negotiate with a stranger. Of course, with the way Gabe's death had been uncovering his escapades, for all she knew Stacey Dickinson might have once been involved with Gabe. If so, Wayne would happily charge Paul with the lightest crime that he could. She immediately chided herself for being flippant with such a serious subject.

The tea was still warm, a soothing beverage as she let her thoughts drift to Tricia and Justin. That, too, was a matter to put into perspective. It wasn't that difficult to get to the airport in Atlanta and not only were there multiple daily flights to Baltimore, there were bargains to be had when you weren't obligated to fly at peak season. In addition to the summer weeks when Tricia could come stay for extended periods, she was fully capable of taking off for a few days pretty much whenever she wanted. Yes, it was wonderful to have Tricia and Justin a ten-minute drive from the house, but they had spoken almost daily before they moved to Wallington and they could do so again. In fact, while she didn't spend a lot of time on the computer, Katie Nelson's sister lived in Arizona and they had that video camera thing that they used. Katie swore it was as easy as pie to do and it was practically like being right there with the person. She could ask Katie to come a little early to next week's circle and talk to her about it.

Helen yawned, a wave of fatigue rising through her, which was hardly unexpected. She swung her feet from the stool, walking slowly into the kitchen. It was time for bed and tomorrow was likely to be another very busy day.

CHAPTER TWENTY-TWO

Justin thought about waiting at the end of the street for Tricia, but he had learned from experience that her saying she would be right behind him wasn't necessarily the same as if he said that. Even though he didn't grasp how saying good-bye to her mother could stretch into another twenty-minute conversation, it often turned out that way. He accepted this habit as one more thing that he didn't need to understand, somewhat like why a woman would buy a pair of black shoes when she had six other pairs of black shoes sitting in the closet, or why beige and taupe were different colors.

He considered a beer when he entered in through the kitchen and opted for a soda instead. If Tricia wanted to talk, he would probably need the beer afterwards, or possibly a stiff shot of something stronger. Being over at Helen's and watching the two women together, he genuinely did appreciate the strength of the bond between them and what he was asking Tricia to give up.

His gaze fell onto the table with the quilted placemats and

he sat and took a close look at them. They were rectangular; each had a dark green background with a light blue fleck and a navy blue cloth border. A wide stripe of the same light blue as the flecks ran horizontally across, about two inches from the bottom, and three stripes were in a vertical position beginning approximately two inches from the right edge. A narrow stripe of the dark blue like the border was between two wider stripes of the lighter blue. The napkins were of the same fabric, with the only variation of the pattern being a single horizontal and vertical stripe that used the color scheme of one dark blue and one dark green. He had no idea how often Tricia put those placemats out and he turned it over looking for a tag that said "Made in China." The back was blank, and in fact it was the reverse pattern of the other side, blue background with green flecks and two different shades of green for the four stripes. Hmm, he'd never noticed that. Maybe these were handmade by either Tricia or Helen.

His mother-in-law's comparison of quilting to cars was interesting, and it did help explain why the women never seemed to tire of talking about quilts. He had to admit that he enjoyed the Speed Channel on TV and regularly watched shows where they restored classic cars. When he and Tricia talked about the eventual dream house, his version always included a three-car garage so he could devote one bay of it to tools, equipment, and a rebuild project. He wasn't focused on any particular car since there were a dozen different ones he would be happy with. The real bargains usually came not from seeking out something specific, but rather in keeping an eye out for situations like when his uncle found the Mustang.

"It has been quite a day, hasn't it?" He hadn't heard Tricia drive up. She came in and sat next to him at the table, her eyes going from the placemat to his face. "Do you know when I made those?" Her voice was tender.

"No, but they're nice. After the discussion tonight I was wondering if you had done these or maybe your mom."

Tricia touched the fabric with her fingertips. "These are much too basic for Mamma. I was fourteen and it was my first significant quilting attempt. Mamaw Pierce said I was old enough to be serious about it, and it was really more her than Mamma who helped me with them. Mamma worked full-time, plus it was sort of an informal family tradition that it was the grandmother who initiated the granddaughter. I can show you the flaws, but they aren't that important. There are six placemats and napkins in the set, and when I was done Mamma thought we should use them. Mamaw said no, I should put them in my hope chest."

Tricia leaned onto the table, her palms flat, and her shoulder close to his. He leaned so their arms were touching. "You had a hope chest?"

Her smile was gentle. "Yes, silly, it's the hickory wood chest that we have at the foot of the bed. It was made by my grandfather, or maybe great-grandfather, I forget. Anyway, you know what else about my hope chest?"

His voice was nearly a whisper now, sensing that she was trying to tell him about more than placemats and hope chests. "No, what?"

"The quilt on the bed is the first full-size one I made. That went in the chest too, and each time I thought something was special enough to go into the chest, I kept imagining the kind of man that I would marry. What I didn't know was that I would find him as soon as I did."

"Well," he said, "I was planning on a few more years as a swinging bachelor. I had no idea when I walked into the party that night that my single days were numbered. What I did know was that I wanted to take you right out of that room and have you all to myself. I went outside to get a beer to try and clear my head, to tell myself that I was being ridiculous. It didn't work because there was no question in my mind that you were why they have the expression love at first sight."

She reached for his hand and squeezed it. "That's what counts, isn't it? Us, together, wherever that is?"

"I like to think so," he said, hoping that he wouldn't accidentally say the wrong thing. "You're okay then about Baltimore? Going back?"

She lifted his hand to her mouth. "I won't pretend that I wish the call hadn't come this soon, or that I'm not going to worry about you being in homicide, but sweetheart, if this is what you want, then I'm okay with the move. Mamma and I talked for a long time about different things and she helped me get my head around it."

Relief coursed through him and he slowly disentangled his hand so he could pull her close to him. "I love you," he said into her hair. "I love you more than I know how to say." As she lifted her mouth for a kiss, he fleetingly wondered if he was making the right decision.

CHAPTER TWENTY-THREE

The next morning was routine in the Kendall house as Justin and Tricia moved through their well-established schedules. It was a quick breakfast of coffee and juice, the main variation during the week being whether the bread was biscuits, toast, English muffins, or bagels. Leisurely breakfasts were strictly for weekends and holidays. It was normally a toss up as to who left first. While it was usually Tricia out the door so she could enjoy a peaceful half hour in her classroom before students arrived, this morning it was Justin. He wanted to put in an early call to find out why they hadn't received the Thatcher autopsy report.

He drove to the station, their good-bye kiss fresh on his lips, conversation between them carefully avoiding the subject of what he was going to say when he spoke to Lou Becker. Technically, he had told Lou that it might be three days before he gave his decision, but why wait? He and Tricia had quietly discussed the logistics of a sudden move before they turned the lights out for sleep and curled against each other.

As much as he hated to be separated from her for a long period, it did make sense for her to remain in Wallington for at least several weeks. There was a decent market for rental properties and that would be both faster than trying to sell and make the departure seem less permanent. Justin could go ahead, get reinstated into the Baltimore Police Department, assigned to whatever this special task force was, and see if there were any houses available to rent in the neighborhood they'd lived in before. Justin promised that, wherever they lived, if they had to choose commutes they would make it closer to where Tricia would be teaching. She would make a discreet call to the principal of the school she'd left to see if there were vacancies. If not, then she would ask for recommendations as to other schools. They had also briefly touched on the idea of her signing up as a substitute instead and beginning work on her master's degree. Justin had pretended not to notice the catch in Tricia's voice as they'd discussed practical matters of leaving.

"Good morning and I have two things for you," Sheila said when he arrived at the station. "That cousin of Gabe's, Fletcher Brown, finally called us. He's been off in Thailand or Japan or somewhere in Asia and didn't get back until late yesterday afternoon. Like I thought, he hasn't seen Gabe since Virginia's funeral. Anyway, he'll be coming in tomorrow or the next day. I gave him Father Singletary's and Sterling Lawson's numbers. I imagine he'll come by here first."

Justin didn't think the sheriff had left a very detailed message on voice mail for Mr. Brown. "Does he know what happened?"

Sheila sniffed. "He didn't seem to want a lot of information. I mean he was polite and all, but not nearly as curious as you'd think he would be. As for item number two, Lisa is trying out two new muffin recipes—a variation on her carrot cake and a marbled chocolate and pecan. She also dropped off two dozen donuts in case we didn't like the muffins."

Lisa Forsythe's habit of bringing pastries at least once a week was one of the first things that Justin had learned when he joined the department. Sheila might not be as circumspect as he thought she should be about telling stories of the local populous, but she was at least usually accurate. According to her, Lisa's first husband had been a major mistake, a man who was long on ideas and very short on willingness to work to make them happen. Maybe it was that he wasn't capable. Justin hadn't been paying attention that closely.

The bakery across and down from the police station had been vacant for years, slowly deteriorating after the original owner died, leaving two squabbling heirs who hadn't lived in Wallington since graduating from college. Lisa, who was not classically trained as a pastry chef, had been baking since she was old enough to hold a sifter; she waited until the legal tangle was cleared and took on the task of reopening the business. Her husband, whatever his name was, had been oh-so-supportive, except what she didn't know was that practically as soon as she had the place going successfully, he'd taken out a second mortgage. The main point of the rambling tale was that for some reason or the other, the husband determined that burning the bakery down for the insurance money was a way out of the mess he'd gotten into.

Dave Mabry had been on patrol in the early morning hours, noticed something that had seemed out of place, whatever that had been, and caught the fire before it was totally out of control. He discovered evidence carelessly left by what's-his-name. During the time that the bakery was out of commission for repairs and Lisa was struggling with a husband who had deserted her after draining their joint checking and savings accounts (which is how she discovered the second mortgage), Sheriff McFarlane had quietly come to her financial rescue. A few words in the right places about Lisa's true plight were all it took. The four main restaurants in town suddenly decided they wanted to try outsourcing their pastry needs, and the Lions Club offered up the kitchen in their facility for her temporary use. Dozens of women in town found reasons to host dessert parties, and many Easter baskets that year featured packets of cute bunny cookies.

Justin needed coffee more than muffins, although with only eight left, he snagged a marbled chocolate and pecan to save for later. An apologetic woman at County assured him that the autopsy report was being hand carried. He replaced the receiver, wondering if her promise was genuine or if the "being hand carried" was more like, "I'll see about having it hand carried when I get around to it." No, that was what he could expect from a big city bureaucracy, not the genuinely friendly type of help he was becoming accustomed to. On the other hand, he didn't think it ordinarily took anywhere near this long to get an autopsy report. The sheriff strolled in waving a packet and stopped at Justin's desk.

"Rory Neely came by the Calico on his way to Augusta. Said it wasn't that far out of his way and he hadn't found anyone yet could make a better biscuit than Dorthea. Neely was the guy you replaced."

The sheriff often joined the Calico Café Codgers, as they referred to themselves. If Justin understood correctly, there were two former mayors, the founder of one of the banks in town, a retired judge, a semi-retired doctor, and the founder of the hardware store as the regulars and a few others who occasionally appeared. The sheriff, more by virtue of his personality than position, was a welcome visitor and he claimed that if you wanted to know where any potential problems might bubble to the surface, these were the men who could tell you.

"It's addressed to you," Justin said, looking at the label.

Sheriff McFarlane smiled and pointed to the coffeepot. "Yeah well, you've done fine with the investigation, so it seems only fair for you to take a look at it first. Let me get coffee and then come on in."

Justin didn't want to appear too eager opening it, but considering how fervently Shipley, Tricia, Helen, and even the sheriff were hoping for a solid defense for Paul Newton, he wanted to see what Thatcher's blood alcohol level had been. Maybe Newton was correct in his assertion. He read through the report, whistling at the high blood alcohol level, and then almost dropped his mouth open at the preliminary finding of cause of death. What? He read it again more slowly, and nearly trod on the sheriff's heels as he went into his office.

"Something wrong?" The sheriff took his seat and reached for the report with his free hand, holding the coffee mug at a safe angle. He read quickly; then he looked at Justin over the rim of the mug. After a moment, he used hand motions to tell Justin to close the door and have a seat. "Well, this doesn't appear to be what we were looking for," he said nonchalantly.

"What do we do next?" Justin knew what his response would be, but didn't want to act without agreement.

The sheriff swapped his mug to his left hand and punched in a telephone number. Two rings and he said, "Morning, Howard. Hate to bother you at this hour with you just getting back and all, but I'm going to put you on speaker if you don't mind."

The doctor, whom Justin assumed was Dr. Cotton, obviously agreed since the sheriff hit the speaker button. The sheriff then said, "Got Justin Kendall in here with me."

"You're Helen's son-in-law, right?" the voice said.

"Yep, that's him. You know about Gabe Thatcher, I suppose," the sheriff said before Justin had a chance to answer.

"I saw the paper last night when I got in and Irma passed on a fair amount of gossip. Said somebody caved his head in and you were looking at a number of suspects. Must have been several on the list considering that it was Gabe."

"Well, we do have Paul Newton in a cell. Seems Gabe had been paying a lot of attention to Melissa and Paul decided he should discourage Gabe."

Justin wondered why the sheriff didn't get right to the point.

"Melissa? That's a surprise," the doctor said after a pause. "I'd better give Martha a call, hard as this will be on her."

"That's why I'm calling, Howard," the sheriff said. "The autopsy report had been delayed and we didn't receive it until a few minutes ago. Now, seeing as how neither of us are medical experts, I'd sure appreciate it if you would come take a look at it."

There was another, shorter pause and the sheriff sipped his coffee.

"You mean right now, I gather?"

"I'll have one of the patrols swing by if you'd like," the sheriff offered.

"No need, I've been up since six. I'll be there in fifteen minutes, give or take a few. You want to give me an idea of what's going on?"

McFarlane shot a wink at Justin. "Nope. See you when you get here." He disconnected the call, stood, and grinned. "Didn't want him dawdling. Why don't we walk back and have Paul tell us again about what happened?"

Justin allowed the sheriff to exit first. "Should we notify Shipley?"

"I don't think Paul will mind talking without him here, but we'll let him decide," he said and led the way to the cells.

Twelve minutes later with essentially the same story as the previous day, they saw Dr. Cotton as Sheila was pouring him a mug of coffee, probably pumping him as to why he was present. But pumping wasn't Sheila's style—she would have asked him outright.

"Thanks, Howard, and come on in," the sheriff said, giving Shelia an innocent smile as he steered the doctor away from her.

Justin brought a second chair in, watching the doctor as he read. He had one of those strong faces that might be referred to as "horsey," with deep-set green eyes. The little brown color left in his receding hair was losing the battle with silver. He was dressed casually in a pair of gray pants and a short-sleeve cotton shirt with gray and white stripes, no tie, and gray slip-on shoes with charcoal gray socks. He was in better shape than a number of his contemporaries with no sign of a paunch. At age sixty-three, he'd given most of his practice to a younger doctor whose name Justin couldn't immediately recall. Dr. Cotton retained a few elderly, longtime patients who were said to find humor in being treated by the man who now spent most of his time as a medical examiner. He idly spoke of completely retiring when he reached seventy, although no one knew if that was his real intent. He removed his black frame reader glasses and held them in his hand.

"I see they sent for a full toxicology report and that won't come in for another two to three days, but they're correct in the preliminary cause of death. It was not due to the acute subdural hematoma. Who was the ME on scene?"

The sheriff scratched his chin. "John Miller."

Dr. Cotton snorted. "This doesn't surprise me then. The man should have retired ten years ago. If he'd bothered to look close enough, he'd have realized the blow wasn't fatal." He shook his head and sipped his coffee. "It was Gabe being a fool, I'll bet. I warned him about mixing booze with those meds."

"So you're saying..." Justin trailed off.

The older man sighed. "Look, patient confidentiality isn't the main issue here, but for the sake of everyone, I'd like to keep the details that I'm about to tell y'all quiet. Can we agree to that?"

He passed the report back to the sheriff, and slipped his glasses into his shirt pocket. "People who thought Gabe Thatcher led a charmed life didn't know about his family's medical history—bad genes on both sides of the family. Weak hearts. Killed his daddy at only fifty-four, and Virginia was barely sixty-six. They had different problems, but Gabe had the hereditary odds stacked against him and it's one of those things that you can't change." He drank more coffee and lifted his mug in a semblance of a toast. "I advised Gabe, of course, that he was in a high risk category and a moderate lifestyle would be in his best interest."

"Guess we all know how well that advice was taken," the sheriff said drily.

Dr. Cotton lifted his free hand and let it drop to his lap silently. "We all make our choices. For some, live fast, die young, and leave a good-looking corpse is a viable option. Anyway, Gabe started having the first sign of problems maybe four months ago. Didn't want to have the tests done in town, so I sent him to a friend of mine in Atlanta. It wasn't as bad as it might have been, but there was no question that if he was going to see many more birthdays, he was going to have to make some major lifestyle adjustments."

Dr. Cotton paused, finished his coffee, and gave them a pointed look. "Even if he had, though, the simple truth was that you can't fight genetics. The odds were that, in all likelihood, Gabe was headed to an early grave like what happened with his parents."

Justin fought to keep his mouth from falling open and shot a glance at the sheriff, who looked as surprised as he had ever seen him.

"Seriously? You'd never know it by looking at Gabe."

Dr. Cotton nodded. "It's not the sort of thing that shows on the outside. It starts with little things like slight dizziness, but family history is a big part of it. That's what caused Gabe to come see me in the first place. He knew something wasn't right. Anyway, the medications he was on were for his heart and asking for valium wasn't unusual either. Facing your own mortality is not something that most people handle well."

"Huh," the sheriff said without inflection. "Give us your take on what could have happened from a medical point of view."

Dr. Cotton glanced at the report on the desk. "Did you bring back the medications from his place? If so, I can tell how many he might have taken from when the prescriptions were filled."

"I saw several bottles of pills in his medicine cabinet and didn't think anything of it. Didn't seem relevant considering what we thought we had," the sheriff said.

Something tugged at Justin's memory and he couldn't bring it into focus.

The ME shrugged. "I'll need to see the actual tox report to see the specific drug interaction, but I know what he was supposed to be taking and the preliminary findings support that as well as the presence of valium. Based on the time of death, stomach contents, alcohol level, and what you told me, I'd vote for accidental. I suspect he took his regular meds, didn't have a whole lot to eat, went up to his studio, and started in with the bourbon. He's sitting at his computer or whatever, and Paul shows up about the time the drug and alcohol interaction is taking effect."

"He said Gabe acted drunk—and as you saw in the report, it doesn't look like he put up a fight."

"I doubt he could have," Dr. Cotton said. "Paul assaulted him, and even though that head injury would have needed attention, it wasn't what killed him."

Justin wanted to verify one point. "Could Gabe have been

groggy enough to have stood up after Paul left and fallen onto the desk before he passed out?"

Dr. Cotton nodded. "Sure, and although that's speculation, it's within a plausible scenario, though. I'm not sure where that puts you legally with Paul. All I'm telling you is what the medical evidence shows." He held up one hand. "Like I said, they'll have to get the full tox report in to make the official final determination, but unless Paul, or someone later, sat on Gabe's chest and forced pills down his throat followed by whiskey, this was an accidental overdose." His wide brow furrowed. "That can be done, but there's no physical evidence of that, by the way."

"Suicide?" The sheriff's question hovered in the air.

The ME looked into the sheriff's eyes first, then Justin's. "Neither one of you found any sort of a note, did you? Any indication in whatever else you looked at?"

Justin thought to the fragment of poignant poetry on Thatcher's computer.

"No," the sheriff said, "Never crossed my mind to look."

Dr. Cotton shifted to the edge of the chair, his voice steady. "Then there is no way to differentiate between accidental and deliberate. Gabe might have been a fool about more than one thing, but I'd say he didn't do this on purpose. The man was a writer after all. You think he made a conscious decision to kill himself and he wouldn't leave a letter or at least a note?"

Sheriff McFarlane scratched his chin again. "Well, I guess we'll have to call the DA to let him know about this. I appreciate you coming in like you did. Want to take a coffee for the road?"

Dr. Cotton pushed up from the chair, shook hands, and left without the coffee. Justin didn't know what to say.

Once they were alone, Sheriff McFarlane looked at Justin carefully. "If that's not one for the books. I guess Gabe was just having a harmless flirtation with Melissa and she misunderstood. It was such a part of his nature he probably didn't give it a second thought."

Justin glanced over his shoulder to make sure there was no one within hearing distance. "What do we do now?"

The sheriff slid the report into the center drawer of his desk. "I'd like you to go out, gather all the pill bottles you can find— prescription, over-the-counter, whatever—and bag them. I'll call the DA while you're doing that and see how he wants to handle this. Paul did admit to assault, and I suppose there could be a trespassing charge, too. Without the assault being the cause of death, though, and Gabe not able to fill out a complaint, it wouldn't seem to be something to waste taxpayer money on." He let his hand rest on the telephone. "That's not our department, but I'm betting we have Paul on his way before lunch."

Justin grasped the back of the chair to carry it out of the office. "What are we going to tell people?"

The sheriff's smile was bittersweet. "More or less the truth. Although there was an altercation between Mr. Newton and Mr. Thatcher, there was an error made as to cause of death. The injuries Mr. Thatcher sustained were not as severe as initially supposed, and he died from accidentally mixing prescription medication and alcohol. It happens all the time and that'll be enough gossip to last for a while. Stanley's and Virginia's early deaths are known by most folks. I figure they can draw their own conclusions without us discussing the family's personal medical business. You okay with this?"

"Fine by me," he said and thought back briefly to the snippet about the heart's betrayal that he'd seen on Thatcher's computer. Maybe that hadn't been about love after all.

CHAPTER TWENTY-FOUR

Justin hadn't paid close attention to the property itself the last time he'd been at Thatcher's. He'd been focused on it only as a crime scene. He took a moment to look at it as a place instead, standing in the driveway. There were a number of older houses in town that had a detached garage with space above, in this case a studio. Justin presumed that was because the garages were either once old carriage houses or were added after the main house was built. This was a nice arrangement if you wanted a separate workspace, guestroom, or even to rent it out. The wooded section of the property lines that more or less formed a sideways "L" to the back and right of the area screened the two buildings from the neighbors. In the quiet with no cars on the road, Justin could hear a variety of bird songs. Deer, rabbit, squirrels, raccoons, possums, and maybe foxes no doubt flourished within the trees and shrubs. The coons and possums would venture out after dark, the others in early morning, and squirrels would dart about any time of the day they chose. It would be a good setting for a writer. There was room for a stable, too, if you wanted a horse, and plenty of space for a big dog if you were an animal lover. It was the kind of place that would be great for raising kids if that happened to be part of your plan.

Justin wasn't sure what made him think of that as he entered the still house, a faint mustiness taking hold with no one having been in since the murder. He collected every pill bottle he could find, put them in an evidence bag, and carefully locked the house, vaguely curious as to what the unknown cousin would choose to do with the place—sell it, he supposed, maybe rent it.

On the drive out, he remembered what it was that Dr. Cotton's comment about taking medication with booze had triggered: he'd found that one medicine bottle cap in the wastebasket in the studio, and no medicine bottle. He had bagged the cap for no reason other than it seemed odd at the time, then forgot about it with all the other drama that unfolded.

He climbed the stairs to the studio and stopped on the landing that was really more like a balcony. Whoever built the stairs and landing probably made them wider than normal in order to facilitate moving items in and out of the space. The railing of the landing was wide, too, wide enough to comfortably lean on and rest a cup or glass without danger of it tumbling to the ground. Yes indeed, this was a spot where you could lean against the sturdy railing, drink in hand, and gaze out for a breath of fresh air, contemplate the next line you were going to write, and do a little nature watching. Ah, there in fact was a rabbit, tentatively hopping from the protection of the trees onto an expanse of grass. Justin wasn't sure what its destination was as it rose to sniff the air, mindful of potential predators. Satisfied it was safe, it angled slightly and hopped toward the small back porch of the house. Justin watched until it disappeared around the corner.

He stood that way, closed his eyes, and breathed in and out deeply, slowly, until the vision clarified in his mind. If Gabe—in a moment of self-pity, maybe frustration, or maybe just because— had only one or two pills left in a bottle, he might have popped the cap off the bottle, tossed the cap into the wastebasket and brought the bottle outside. Why would he have done that? Well, maybe he hadn't wanted to take the pill or pills with water from the bathroom. For whatever reason, he stepped outside instead, washed the pill or pills down with a drink, and hurled the bottle from the landing. Justin could see that and the question became, where would it have gone?

Justin lifted his hand, certain it would have been a hurl rather than a drop, and mimicked the motion. A lightweight plastic bottle couldn't go far, and he mentally mapped out a three-to-six-foot arc from the landing. He zipped down the stairs, moving slowly along the imaginary arc, his eyes carefully studying the grass. The empty bottle was resting on its side, which caused it to be blocked from casual view. He turned it to look at the label and didn't recognize what it was, but there was a No Refill among the other information. He added it to the evidence bag and decided to take one more look around the studio, although he was positive he hadn't previously missed anything. He didn't really count the empty bottle as a miss, since, as the sheriff said, Thatcher's medications hadn't seemed relevant at the time.

Funny, though, that was what they often told witnesses when they interviewed them. "Tell us everything you can remember, no matter how small. You never know what might be important."

The studio had also taken on a musty air, but nothing that a few hours of open windows and a fan couldn't remedy. After he made a thorough last sweep through the bathroom, cabinets, and drawers, he stopped in front of the quilt hanging on the wall.

He noticed it the first day without paying close attention. The colors were beautiful with a total of seventeen images—four on each side and a center one of pale gold with the outline of a book laid open, an old-fashioned fountain pen across it. The pages of the book were a creamy color, the edges faintly gold, and the pen black with a silver nub. He took in the other images, starting at the top and reading left to right as if it were a book. The more he looked, the more he thought that might be what it represented. The first one was a white house with green shutters, a gray-shingled roof, and a front porch with three steps leading up from a short, brick walk. There were flowers in beds spanning the width sporting red roses, purple irises, and some yellow variety he didn't recognize. Next was an antique cradle near the profile of a woman in a rocking chair holding a baby. There was a decorated Christmas tree with a tricycle underneath, a small boy flying a kite, a baseball glove superimposed on a bat, an old manual typewriter, a graduation cap, a historic looking brick building that could be maybe on a college campus, a skyline of a city, the Eiffel Tower, and unless he was mistaken, the final one was of the Wallington town square. He'd seen that on other quilts around, although this image seemed to be a smaller size.

He found himself inexplicably drawn to the quilt and gently touched each image with his forefinger, tracing the puffy part that he guessed was the actual quilting. There was an intricacy to it that he grasped as something that had required a great deal of thought. He couldn't imagine how much patience and skill had gone into making it and he didn't know how to tell if a quilt was handmade or machine stitched. Knowing what he had learned about Gabriel Thatcher, he could guess that his mother must have made this, maybe as a housewarming present for him when he returned for good. He wondered if Helen was familiar with it.

Thinking of Helen, he owed her the courtesy of what would soon be public knowledge, or at least most of it. He would call and see if she happened to be available for lunch. That would give him time to check in at the station and see if the sheriff had spoken with the DA about Newton.

It was actually closer to one than noon when he walked into Helen's kitchen. She threw him a kiss and pointed to the pitcher of iced tea and glasses filled with ice on the counter. She had mitts over her hands and was about to open the oven door.

He caught the kiss and tossed it back as he filled the glasses and carried them to the table. Two leaves of romaine lettuce with thick slices of tomato and some kind of garnish on top were already on the plates. A green quilted hot pad decorated with a rooster was in the center of the table. "Oh man, what's that smell?" It didn't matter that he almost always asked that question when he arrived. Helen's cooking deserved that kind of homage.

"Plain old chicken potpie, fresh tomatoes on the side, and I do have cobbler left," she said, placing the casserole dish on the pad. "I appreciate your offering to bring lunch, but something like this is very simple to whip up. It is hot, though, so you might want to eat salad before you dig in." She snapped her fingers for his plate and covered the center of it with golden crust, chunks of chicken, potatoes, and vegetables in a white sauce that made it difficult to take her advice about waiting. Curls of steam were still rising, the aroma tickling his nose.

Her eyes were expectant and she salted and peppered the tomato. "You said Paul had been released and you had news."

He gave her a little more information than would be in the statement to the paper, and in reality he agreed that Thatcher had probably been careless rather than suicidal. People who wanted to believe otherwise would do so no matter what the official report said.

Helen smiled sadly. "My Lord, what a tempest in a teapot this turned out to be."

Justin waited to savor a few bites of the potpie before he responded. How could something that was admittedly a simple dish taste this good? It had to be the crust. No, the filling was terrific, too. Maybe it was the balance. "It did stir up a lot of stuff and I admit that I learned some interesting things about the town."

He stopped before his next bite. "Oh, Sheila said that Mr. Brown, the cousin, was coming in either tomorrow or the next day."

Helen nodded. "If he doesn't have it, please give him my number. The circle will help him with whatever he needs."

Justin must have looked as puzzled as he felt.

Helen's smile was gentle this time. "Well, honey, the man can't just waltz into town, stick Gabe in the ground, and leave. I imagine he'll have Sterling Lawson handle the funeral as they did for Virginia and Stan, for that matter. There will be the house to get cleaned up, what to do with the estate, what to do with the items of Virginia's that Gabe had in storage—just a lot of details to be dealt with. He'll need help or at least he'll need to be introduced to the right sources."

Justin hadn't thought about it; but yeah, it probably would be sort of overwhelming. "Oh, you know him?"

Helen shook her head. "I can't say that anyone here really does. He came in for Virginia's funeral, but I think he was only here for a day on either side and stayed at Gabe's." She put a slightly smaller portion of potpie on his plate for seconds. "Someone has to do for him and it's appropriate that it's the circle. Almost everyone in it knew Virginia, and there was a special connection with Gabe."

He thought he heard a bittersweet note in her voice at that, but she didn't elaborate.

"We won't intrude, of course, but we'll make sure he knows

that we're available for as much or as little help as he wants."

"That's very nice of you," Justin said, and thought of how different it would be if a distant relative came into Baltimore to cope with a similar situation. Would a group of ladies be set to help like this? He supposed it would depend on the situation. Then he remembered the quilt.

"Helen, when I was in Mr. Thatcher's studio today, I noticed a quilt that was on the wall..."

"A Celebration of Gabriel," she said immediately.

"It has a name?" Helen's laugh reminded him of Tricia's, although technically he guessed it was the other way around.

"Quilts usually have names, particularly when you're doing a special one for a person or event. You can always use a standard pattern, but part of the beauty of quilting is that you can easily create your own design. You begin with a theme to convey a message. Many times, all or part of the fabric strengthens that message. The quilt you're talking about was for Gabriel's thirtieth birthday. Virginia took fabric from some of his old clothes. She cut a swatch from Stan's high school graduation robe that she had stuck back in a closet. Every stitch was by hand and a lot of the work was done here when Virginia would come over. I mean she did the squares here. She used her own frame when it came time to put it all together, and I helped her with that part over at her place. It was a lovely piece, no question about that."

There was a softness to her tone that stirred a sensation in his chest, the recognition of the depth of Gabe's mother's affection. "It must have taken her a long time."

"Oh, my yes, that type of quilt does, but that's one of the reasons that you create a special quilt for a specific person. It's an expression of love and caring. Each of the squares represents something important, even if you and the person you give it to are the only two who know the significance of the design."

Helen reached for his empty plate and when she moved it, he noticed the placemat for the first time. They were the same pattern as those that Tricia had told him about. He lifted one corner. "Did Tricia make these by any chance? She was telling me last night about learning to make these."

An unmistakable look of pride and humor passed across Helen's face. "She did indeed. Bless her, placemats and napkins were all she felt confident in doing for a while. That was the summer she was thirteen, no, maybe it was fourteen, and I was so very busy. My mother worked with her, letting her select the pattern, and showing her the little tips to make them look more professional. I think everyone in the family got placemats and napkins for Christmas that year. It didn't take too much longer after that for her to move up to other projects. She let her quilting lapse when she went to college and we were talking about her seriously starting again. I do hope she does."

The scene came to Justin's mind unbidden: three generations of women sitting together quilting, a companionship that had been repeated for no telling how many generations. It must have made Helen so happy to have Tricia coming home, to know that they could repeat that mother and daughter scene as often as they liked. Now, it was something that he was going to take away from them. Well, not completely take away. They would have summers when Tricia visited. Visits where he and Tricia would be separated.

"Cobbler?" Helen asked it in a way that made him wonder if she'd asked once already.

"Uh no, that was great, but I think I'll pass. Lisa Forsythe was testing new muffin recipes on us today."

"The carrot cake one she changed up a little and the marbled chocolate pecan one she was tinkering with?"

Justin pushed his chair back. "Is there anything in this town that you don't know about?"

Helen's laugh was merry. "Oh there's plenty that's kept secret, even after everything that's come out about Gabe. Lisa is such a dear that we all try to use her as much as we can; Phyllis and I were in last week to order a cake for Phyllis's bridge night. She was working on the recipes and naturally we talked about it."

Justin made his usual offer to help with the dishes, and Helen sent him on his way with a peck to the cheek. He backed from the drive idling the patrol car up the street, a neighborhood of older homes, porch swings, and trees meant for shade and climbing. It was a snapshot that if you didn't see a car and the angle didn't include satellite dishes on the roofs, you probably wouldn't be able to tell what decade it was. It wasn't that it stood still in time. Rather, they had seemed to move more slower through time, choosing to not jettison the concept of neighbors helping each other even as they embraced other cultural shifts. Wallington couldn't and never would be able to offer so many of the things that an urban area did, and there was the matter of having the Chesapeake Bay at hand. Still…

Justin bumped his fist against the steering wheel to clear his thoughts. Lou Becker was giving him a shot at homicide in Baltimore, for crying out loud; what he had in Wallington was the first murder case in two decades that turned out to be something other than a real murder. The homicide rate in Baltimore topped 200 this past year, and when Justin turned toward the station he took a moment to reflect on why he thought that was better than having zero.

CHAPTER TWENTY-FIVE

Helen had barely hung the telephone up from speaking with Martha when it rang again. It was Phyllis, then Sarah; the story had remained fairly intact as it rippled throughout town. In the course of talking with most of the circle members, Helen also made certain they had a plan in place for Fletcher when he arrived.

She had summoned up her memory from the limited time she'd spoken with him at Virginia's funeral and the reception that followed. As always, Gabriel's sense of style had shown through. Not that it had been an ostentatious display—that was definitely not Gabe's style. It had been a lovely graveside ceremony instead of a church service because, like Phyllis, gardening was Virginia's other passion in addition to quilting. The profusion of sprays, baskets, and mounted wreaths had been arranged into a room-like enclosure around the gravesite. Mixed floral scents hung in the air that day as friends and the few remaining family members bid their farewells. Their sorrow in her parting was offset with the relief that her suffering was over. She was laid to rest in the

Thatcher family section of the cemetery and Helen couldn't recall if there was a plot for Gabe. Hadn't Virginia mentioned that he had talked about being cremated? That seemed to be an option preferred by many of his generation. Well, those were all things that were Fletcher's to decide. She remembered him as polite and comfortable speaking with people whom he either didn't know or hadn't seen since he was a teenager. He was about the same height as Gabe, although he had brown hair and eyes, she thought. She remembered him as a nice-looking man, but no distinguishing features came immediately to mind.

Helen was drawn into the den thinking of Justin's question about the quilt A Celebration of Gabriel. She vividly remembered Virginia discussing the different squares she was planning, fabric she could find, and appliqués she might make. She also remembered thinking that what Virginia ought to include was a square featuring Botticelli's Venus emerging from the sea if she truly wanted to display what was important in Gabe's life. That, however, was not the sort of thing one said to a friend, unless the friend was like Phyllis.

The thought of Phyllis triggered the last quilting circle night that would no doubt come to be known as Confessions About Gabriel, or maybe Small Town Lies Revealed. Now that would be a doozy of a quilt if they chose to put words to fabric!

Rita had been the last telephone call, a hurried one from the parking lot during a break so that she wouldn't be overheard. Mrs. Jackson had apparently been in for a checkup of that obnoxious Pomeranian of hers and broadcast the news about Gabe to the waiting room. She rightfully doubted Mrs. Jackson's version, although it had been fairly accurate for a change. She took the time to thank Helen again for the "night of her rescue" as she phrased it. She said that Steve had surprised her with a brochure describing a romantic getaway to Saint Simons Island that he had booked for them at the end of the month.

The memory of Virginia's quilt for Gabriel had drawn Helen to stand in front of the Family Love quilt that her grandmother had made. It was the first time Helen had been invited to put needle to fabric for a genuine quilting square. She'd been ten; no, it was actually a few months before her tenth birthday. Prior to that, she'd been allowed to watch as her grandmother and mother sewed and she always helped keep supplies sorted. There were needles, threads, pins, remnants of fabrics, rolls of ribbon, and binding. She closed her eyes to travel back to her grandmother's parlor, as it was called, not a living room.

That house had been a rambling structure, vestiges of the farm still evident with the barn that was both garage and workshop. With no sons to help on the farm and neither daughter interested in it, most of the acreage had been leased out. A massive garden became her grandfather's agricultural domain, yielding beans, peas, potatoes, corn, tomatoes, cucumbers, collards, and cantaloupes. There was a small pecan orchard, too, that he tended. The livestock dwindled to only chicken and rabbits, providing an endless supply of fresh eggs and adorable bunnies that Helen and her sister eventually learned did not all magically grow up and ascend to "bunny heaven" as they thought. Well, perhaps in one sense they did while making a stop on a dinner platter. Fortunately, her grandfather had taken their wails seriously instead of teasing them, explaining that it was the nature of the business. Perhaps their understanding was why her grandmother suggested that her first square be of two bunnies, nose to nose, one brown, one gray. Helen didn't know where the fabric had come from.

In thinking of the old house, Helen could vaguely remember the excitement of getting running water, the wood burning stove remaining the primary source of heat with no more than a small kerosene heater for each of the three bedrooms. Limited heat in the bedrooms was probably why there were mounds of quilts to cover the feather beds. Christmas Eve at the farm was a tradition. Helen and Louise snuggled under the covers wondering if Santa really would pass them by if they didn't go to sleep. She traced the outline of that house on the quilt.

Her grandmother insisted on creating circles around each image within each of the squares. "All families are circles," she said when explaining the design. "Whether we stay or go, we begin our lives in the embrace of our families. It is not until later that we are able to make choices about staying within the circle or moving beyond it."

Helen could not fully appreciate the intricacy of the concept, much less the artistry that was involved. She'd been allowed to complete the square with bunnies that her grandmother later encircled with a ring of red rosebuds like the ones that grew on a trellis on one side of the house. Then her grandmother set her to making a stack of crib quilts while she and her mother continued with the Family Love quilt.

Eight circles in all, there was a tree in the center with roots spreading out, the tree surrounded by leaves of fall colors. It represented not only the family roots, but also the magnificent oak that endured on the property until a lightning bolt struck it, branches splintering, with no choice but to bring it down. The church was a given element, encircled with musical notes to show her great-grandmother's love of hymns and spirituals. There was a plow in the center of a circle of peas in pods. One had a silhouette of a girl in a dress and pigtails and a boy in a straw hat, that circle consisting of kites and spinning tops that you could only find now in antique stores. The old cast iron cooking stove was there, too, with a skillet on top, and miniature burlap sacks like they used at the general store as elements of the circle. The final part was another silhouette. This one was of an older man and woman in rocking chairs inside a daisy chain. Knowing what she did now, Helen couldn't imagine how many times her grandmother must have moved the placement of the squares to get the exact look that she wanted. Most of the appliqués had been made separately by hand and stacked up in a dedicated wicker basket until it was time to integrate them into the design.

It was a quilt that was never intended for a bed, but to hang like this as a piece of family art, passed from generation to generation. Granted it came to Helen sooner than it should, but that had been her grandmother's wish, and one her mother respected. After her grandfather died at age eighty-one of a massive heart attack in the midst of feeding chickens, her grandmother, whose hands were slowed by advancing arthritis, saw the merit of selling the farm and moving into town. The young man and woman who bought the property were a hardworking couple from church with plans to slowly recover the acreage as the leases expired. Their long-term view was a farm that could serve as a produce and cheese market for the public and provide fresh ingredients to local restaurants. Their vision had so far been quite successful.

The single drawback to her grandmother's move was that it occurred in the time before the independent and assisted-living facilities in town were built. No one felt she should be placed in "an old folks home," as she called it. The ideal solution was to convert Helen's parents' garage into a small apartment, a feat accomplished in record time. The Family Love quilt was among the limited possessions she kept after insisting they have a multi-day yard sale to "trim the load," as she said. During the not quite two years Grandmother lived as a widow, the three women quilted together for an hour or so after early dinner or on languid weekend afternoons, family stories unfolding as surely as did a bolt of cloth. As with her grandfather's sudden death, they were spared the heartbreak of slow decline. When a stroke felled her grandmother, she remained in a coma for less than three days. One of the few provisions of the simple will was that Helen was to get the Family Love quilt. Her mother knew of the intent and, in truth, as often as her mother was in Helen's house, it wasn't as if she were deprived of seeing it.

The sound of the telephone startled Helen from her memories. She didn't realize how long she'd been standing in the same spot, reminiscing about her grandmother. On the other hand, it was definitely a day for reflections.

CHAPTER TWENTY-SIX

D on't you two look like the proverbial cat that ate the canary," Helen said, accepting a kiss on the cheek from Justin and what bordered on a bear hug from Tricia. She stepped back and eyed the bag in Justin's hand that appeared for all the world to be a bottle of champagne. She supposed celebrating was in order, but at 8:00 a.m.? "Come on in and tell me what's going on."

"Sorry for calling so early, especially on a Saturday," he said and held the bottle slightly aloft before he set it on the counter, still concealed in the bag. "This is for later. I have time for one cup of coffee, and then I'm meeting Mr. Brown at the station. He took an early flight into Atlanta and is driving over."

Helen waved her hand to the table. "I've been up since six as usual, and I've got apple cinnamon muffins," she said in case they somehow missed the aroma.

"I can do a muffin, too," Justin said, taking his spot at the table, Tricia going directly to the coffeepot.

"Let's sit and we'll explain why we wanted to come so early," she said, a smile on her face that looked as if she were about to burst to tell more.

"I think that's a good idea," Helen said, trying to restrain her own curiosity. What on earth could have them both in this kind of mood, considering how things had been the day before?

"Thank you, sweetheart," Justin said, taking the coffee when Tricia sat next to him. He had consumed a third of the muffin and looked at Tricia as if deciding who would speak first.

"You're the one who brought it up. You tell," Tricia said, teasing in her voice.

Justin swigged his coffee and Helen sipped, not waiting to spoil whatever this was. She could wait them out.

"I know the offer for me in Baltimore came as a surprise," he said, a flash of solemnity replacing the grin. "It was a shock to me for all sorts of reasons and I called Lou late yesterday to thank him for giving me the chance."

Helen wondered if a tiny frown was creasing her forehead. Why would their going back to Baltimore generate this kind of glee? Not only had Tricia been reluctant, they couldn't think that Helen would be happy about it—supportive, yes, in a mood to celebrate, no. Maybe she'd played her role of don't make a decision for my sake more expertly than she'd realized.

"Tell her the rest," Tricia chided affectionately, bumping his shoulder with hers. "Well, the rest about Baltimore."

Justin's grin was strangely mischievous. "And as much as I was tempted and as much as you two were willing to support me, I told him that it just wasn't the right thing for me to do."

"What?" Helen tried not to shout with delight. "You turned him down? Y'all aren't moving?" Had she heard him correctly?

Tricia shot out her hand to grasp Helen's. "Yes he did, and no we're not," she said, laughter behind her words.

Helen fought back the welling of tears that she didn't want to give in to and looked at Justin. "But it was such a good opportunity for you. One that you might never be offered again."

He nodded and extended his hand to briefly pat both of theirs. "Yes, and there are three or four other guys Lou knows who, quite frankly, will do as well for him as I could." His voice took on a serious note, his eyes moving between her and Tricia. "I appreciate that you would have let Tricia go without a harsh word to me, but the more I thought about what she, well, what we would be giving up, I realized that it wasn't worth it. It might be different if Lou honestly didn't have some others to choose from or if all I cared about was my career." He detached Tricia's hand from Helen's, raised it to his lips, and kissed it before returning his gaze to Helen. "I don't want that kind of life," he said. "I want the balance between family and career, and if that means hauling guys off from bar fights and tracking down teenaged bicycle thieves as the major crimes, then that's okay."

Helen exhaled a long breath to forestall the tears of gratitude. "Well, you know that I'm happy to hear this."

Justin glanced at his watch. "I've got to run and the two of you have things to talk about."

Helen half rose and offered, "Do you want to take some muffins with you?"

He waved her into the chair and put his hand on Tricia's shoulder. "I'm good, thanks. Both of you stay where you are and I'll take off." He pushed his mug and plate aside, dabbed at his mouth with the napkin, and grabbed a quick kiss from Tricia. "I'll see you back at the house."

Neither Helen nor Tricia spoke until they heard his footsteps fade and then Tricia stretched out both hands. "I am so happy, Mamma." Her eyes were bright, tears probably not far behind.

"Did he say what made him change his mind?"

Tricia slowly withdrew her hands and wrapped them around the mug. Her voice was soft, filled with a warmth that comes from a deep love that isn't always expressed in words. "He came home last evening with a roasted chicken, a loaf of fresh bread, and a bag of salad and said he didn't want us to have to cook dinner, that we should talk instead."

"Did that make you nervous?" Helen was finished with her coffee, but didn't want to break the flow of the conversation by getting up for a refill.

Tricia nodded once. "A little. I thought to myself that here it was, him telling me that we were leaving. Then we sat at the table and he said with everything that had happened this week, he came to see how important family was—how there were times when it needed to take priority over a career, especially since staying here was good for my career."

"What did you say to that?"

Tricia sighed contentedly. "I was so relieved that I wanted to make sure he was okay with it and basically asked him if he was sure, that he wasn't doing it only for my sake. I had to know that he wasn't going to resent it later."

There was an inflection in Tricia's voice, as if there was something else that she wasn't saying. "And," a wide smile brightened her face, "he gave the Boy Scout pledge sign and promised that yes, he really was comfortable with this decision." She paused, reaching out her hands again. "So then I told him that he couldn't possibly have made me happier, except for one thing." She lightly squeezed Helen's fingertips. "And that was that we would be here for the baby to be born."

Helen gasped. "No! Yes?"

Tricia laughed. "Yes, well, I'm ninety-plus percent sure. I have a doctor's appointment Monday afternoon." She tilted her head to the bottle on the counter. "That's sparkling apple cider."

Helen and Tricia pushed their chairs away from the table, meeting for a hug, tears trickling until they pulled back, swiping their tears with a finger. "I'll get the glasses, you get the tissues," Helen said after a moment.

Tricia popped the cork and had the box of tissues on the counter by the time Helen returned with champagne glasses. They topped off and clinked a toast. "You did the at-home pregnancy test?"

"Yes," Tricia said, leading the way back to the table, the box of tissues in hand just in case. "I actually picked it up on the way home and was planning to use it the next morning. That was the day Justin hit me up with this Baltimore business."

"So you waited to do the test?"

Tricia ran her finger around the base of the glass. "Yes. I was sure it would be positive and even though I hoped Justin would decide against moving, I didn't want to add in something as monumental as me being pregnant to confuse the issue." She sighed happily again. "When he told me what his choice was, I didn't care about waiting until this morning for the test and neither did he. I literally jumped up and went and took it right then. You should have seen the look on his face when I told him the results. I repeated it this morning, too."

Helen ran a hand through her hair. "You'll be using Dr. Fraiser?"

Tricia laughed. "Of course. He swears he's not retiring until he's at least seventy, and how can you not want to have him deliver a second generation?" She did a rapid count on her fingers. "I should be only about six weeks along."

"Oh my, it might be a December baby," Helen said. "That should make for a lively Christmas."

Tricia held her glass up before she took another sip. "Then we'll make three crib quilts, one blue, one pink, and one with Santa, elves, and reindeer. Whichever color I don't need we'll contribute to the hospital nursery."

Helen reached for her daughter's hand again, designs for the quilts already forming in her mind.

About the Author

Charlotte "Charlie" Hudson, born in Pine Bluff, Ark. and reared in Louisiana, is a 22-year career military veteran as well as a wife, author, and speaker.

After graduating from Northwestern State University in 1974, she entered the Army. During her extensive military career, Hudson was deployed to Saudi Arabia for Operation Desert Shield and Desert Storm as well as to Haiti in support of Operation Uphold Democracy. She retired from the Army in 1995 as a lieutenant colonel.

Hudson has a master's of science degree in organizational development from East Texas State University and is a graduate of the U.S. Army War College in Carlisle Barracks, PA.

After retiring from active duty, she began to write and publish both fiction and non-fiction books. *Small Town Lies* is the first in a series of Hudson's novels to be published by the American Quilter's Society.

She and her husband reside in South Florida, where they enjoy their love of scuba diving.

Discussion Questions

Was it right for the sheriff to put Justin in
charge of the investigation into Gabe's death?

Have you ever known a man who was a
romantic and didn't mind showing it?

Who in the quilting circle is your favorite? Why?

What do you think Tricia should have
decided about returning to Baltimore?

Should Gabe have modified his behavior to try
and stop some of the town gossip about him?

What's coming up in
Small Town Haven,
the next title in the Helen Crowder
Adventure series?

More Books from AQS

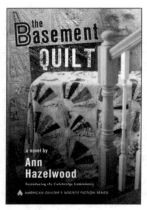

#8853 $14.00

#1256 $14.95

Coming Soon!

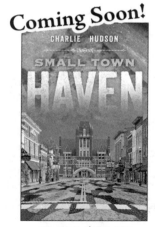

#1424 $14.95

Coming Soon!

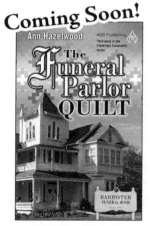

#1257 $14.95